L. BALLEW

His Wild Rose

Love on Tap Series

First published by L. Ballew Writes 2025

First edition

ISBN (paperback): 979-8-9928281-4-6
ISBN (hardcover): 979-8-9928281-5-3

Editing by Nova Nox

This book was professionally typeset on Reedsy.
Find out more at reedsy.com

To my street team, who always has the answers I'm looking for. This book is yours.

To women everywhere.
You are not property. You are not livestock. You are not solely meant to fulfill a man's pleasure and be a breeding machine. You're Queens and worthy of everything life has to offer and so much more.
We will not go back.

Contents

Foreword

Irish Lingo & Phrases

Jacks - bathroom

Runners - tennis shoes

Chancers -dubious person

Uppers - drugs

Dosser - someone that is doing anything other than what they should be

Wans - kids

Arse - ass

Shite - shit

Clinker - prison

Wanker - an insult that means "someone who masturbates"

Mot - girlfriend

Boot - trunk of car

How's she cuttin'? - another way of asking "what's the story?"

Black stuff - Guinness

Having the craic - having fun

Taking the piss - teasing

Slagging - teasing/joking

Jammers - busy

Dryshite - someone who is boring, no fun

Aul fella - old man often used as term of endearment

Chancer - someone who behaves in a dubious manner

A chéadsearc - first love

Mo stóirín - my little darling

Eat the head off - scold

Wagon - woman one dislikes

The messages - groceries
Cute hoor - crafty, manipulative person
Minerals - soda
Bloke - man or guy
Stall the ball - hang on
Bloody/Bleeding - a way to add emphasis to other words (that bleedin' dosser)
Acushla - darling
Thick - stupid
Pox - annoying person
Hallion - troublemaker
Gob - mouth
Eejit - idiot
Gobdaw - someone who is foolish
Courting - dating
Ructions - fight/argument
In ribbons - hungover
Gobshite - someone who is foolish

Preface

Welcome to the final installment of the Love On Tap Series! If you've hung around long enough, you know that I'm more of a rom-com writer, keeping things light with a little bit of heart-wrenching sorrow, but the dark is always short-lived.

Rowan and Alicia were supposed to have a similar story, but like my characters tend to do, they re-wrote what I had planned.

Friends, these two go on a journey, and it's going to hurt. Please be advised that this book will address topics including drug and alcohol addiction, domestic abuse, child abandonment, depression, thoughts of suicide, and other difficult themes.

Oh, and lots of open door sexual acts.

Your mental health matters, so if these topics will trigger or cause you any sort of distress, please do not read this book.

That being said, you will always get a HEA from me, so don't fret.

The Love On Tap Series

His Ringsend Rose

His Spanish Rose

His Wild Rose

Chapter One

Alicia - November

"I'd love to see the tattoos *under* your clothes."

Wow...that's original.

I roll my eyes even though this idiot can't see me, toss back a shot of whiskey, and then whirl to face my nasal-voiced admirer with the intention of telling him exactly what he can do with his lame pickup line.

Only, it's not a stranger.

"Goddammit, Ro! You just about got throat punched!"

"So the accent worked?"

The fact that Rowan Gallagher—a six-foot-five, ginger-haired, Irish soccer player, *and* royal pain in my ass—was able to hide his thick Irish brogue is pretty impressive.

"Are you saying your goal was to be throat punched?" I quirk an eyebrow at him. I know what he's asking, but I like to give him as much shit as he gives me.

"No! 'Course not! I've been working on my American accent so I can better blend in," he says, smiling proudly.

I snort a laugh. "You wouldn't blend in if you were wrapped up in an American flag. Everything about you screams *Irish.*"

He leans in slightly, bringing his face inches from mine. "Are you stereotyping me, darlin'? Because I take offense to that."

Ignoring him—and the way my body reacts not only to his proximity, but to the way he calls me *darlin'*—I turn back to signal the bartender for another shot. The irony of a bartender spending her only night off at the receiving end of familiar bottles isn't lost on me, but it's been a shit day. The check engine light came on in my car—again—and my little sister was suspended—again. At least I'm not mixing business with pleasure and drinking at O'Nelly's.

Two muscled and tattooed forearms cage me in on both sides as Rowan presses his chest to my back; whispers of his ginger and clove cologne enveloping me. My skin prickles with goosebumps. It's not unusual for Rowan to invade my personal space, and it's not unusual for me to lash out when he does.

"Gallagher," I grind out.

"Petersen," he purrs into my ear, beard tickling the sensitive skin there.

The way my name rolls off his tongue has me pressing my thighs together, but I disguise it by crossing one leg over the other.

"Move your fucking arms before I remove them from your body."

"Ach, no need to get violent, love." He lifts his arms and takes a seat on the bar stool to my right. "What are you drinking tonight?"

I arch an eyebrow at him. "Why do you want to know?"

"So I know what to tell the bartender when I buy your next one," he states, like it's obvious.

"You're not buying me a drink."

"I am, actually. And," he cuts me off when I open my mouth to protest, "as it's not your money, you can't tell me what to do with it."

Damn.

"Fine," I relent with a heavy sigh. "Buy me the damn drink."

* * *

He bought me that drink. Then another. And yet another. When I drink too much I become flirty and horny, so once the alcohol starts working its magic, I pull him to the dance floor and spin with my back to his chest, grinding my ass against his quickly stiffening cock. He's not shy, so his hands immediately grab my hips roughly to keep me flush against him. One song turns to two, and by the third? We've locked ourselves in the bathroom, making out like a couple of teenagers. The moment we fall through the door, he slams me against the wall and shoves his hand down the front of my leather pants.

"Fuck me, you're soaked," he growls, licking up the column of my neck. The feel of his tongue on my skin has me panting and riding the heel of his hand harder.

"If you tell anyone about this, I'll kill you."

"For someone so ashamed, you don't seem to be too upset about what I'm doing with my finger at the moment." Rowan chuckles darkly against my clavicle as he curls that finger, massaging my G-spot.

"Fuck..." I hiss, then bite down on his neck.

The groan he releases as my teeth sink into his skin is so animalistic, I almost come on the spot just from the sound.

"Christ, woman. You're not just all bark, are you?"

"Shut up, Gallagher." I grip his hair with one hand and pull his head back, silencing him with my tongue down his throat.

The hand that was digging into his shoulder snakes down to his belt buckle. Once it's loosened, I reach in to wrap my hand around his cock and gasp against his mouth.

He. Is. Huge. What do they feed them in Ireland?

"Like what you feel, love?" His words land softly against my mouth.

I'll stroke his dick, but I won't stroke his already swollen ego.

"Just surprised I found it and wondering if it can do what your fingers can do. *Oh...God,*" I choke out as Rowan curls his fingers deeply. "Don't stop doing that."

"I'm going to give that smart mouth of yours a new job, hen, if you keep talking. Now shut up and come on my hand like the good girl I know you can be."

And I do.

"Rowan!" I scream as my body shatters.

"Fucking perfect," he whispers against my ear in a tone I'm not familiar with. Especially coming from him. It's too intense, too expectant, and I can't handle it.

I pull his hand out of my pants and make sure he's watching before closing my mouth around his fingers, sucking them hard. His warm, caramel eyes blaze with the spark of challenge I'm used to seeing and it riles me up all over again. It may not be the cleanest place, but I'm pretty certain I'm going to let Rowan Gallagher fuck me in this bathroom.

He's your typical player. All charm and sex appeal, making you feel like you're the only one he sees. But as soon as he's nailed you? He ghosts. I'm fully aware of this. I don't expect —or want—a relationship or declaration of love. I just want to have this one night of pure, sexual bliss. And after what I felt in my hand, I know Rowan will deliver.

"Do you have a condom?" I ask hurriedly, my hands moving to his zipper.

Long, freckled fingers grasp my wrist, stopping my progress. "No."

"It's fine. I'm on the pill, and I'm clean," I mutter, trying to pull free of his grip. "I get checked regularly."

"Alicia, stop."

The finality in his voice stops me in my tracks, and my eyes whip to his. "What's wrong?"

His normally smirking and roguish face looks pained. "We can't do this."

I pause a beat trying to discern why he hit the brakes on a sure thing.

"Gallagher, I was kidding about the size of your dick. I'm confident I won't be unsatisfied."

He scrubs a free hand over his eyes and down, stroking his beard. "It's not that. I just…I don't want you…"

A cold rage fills my veins. He doesn't want me?

"Wow. If that," I gesture towards his still hard cock, "is what you look like when you don't want me, I can't even imagine what you'd look like if you did want me."

"No…fuck," he groans, pinching the bridge of his nose. "That's not what I was saying. You didn't let me—"

"Oh, I think I let you do enough." I dart around him to leave the bathroom, but he steps in front of me, blocking the way.

"Alicia, would you stop for one fucking minute and listen to me?"

I glare at him and cross my arms over my chest.

"We're drunk. And in the jacks. It's a recipe for regret, yeah? I don't want you waking up tomorrow wishing you'd never met the likes of me."

At this point, I'm completely mortified and want nothing more than to slink away and lick my wounded pride.

"Whatever, Gallagher. You and your excuses can fuck right off. Now," I seethe, "get out of my way and let me leave."

"Li," he starts.

"Don't. Just move."

He sighs heavily and steps aside. I shoulder-check him as I storm out of the bathroom and head for the exit, vowing to never let my guard down with Rowan Gallagher again.

Chapter Two

Alicia - One Year Later

It's buzzing at Paddy's tonight. I haven't had a moment to catch my breath, let alone pee. Paddy is off mingling with the patrons, which leaves me manning the bar by myself, as usual. God love Pat O'Nelly, but sometimes it feels like he thinks I'm Wonder Woman. I probably brought that upon myself though since I insist on working six days a week. Most of the time it's not a big deal, but I'm in a piss-poor mood tonight. Not even the sound of the Irish Trio playing pub songs can bring me out of it.

Bridget stayed out past curfew and came home high as a kite. Whatever higher power thought that placing me as the sole provider and caretaker of a younger sibling was a good idea has overestimated me. Our father went to prison when I was eighteen and my sister was six, and our mother just up and left without a word. We haven't seen or heard from her since. As I was a legal adult, and had basically raised Bridget anyway, the State of North Carolina made me her guardian. That was nine years ago. I tip my hat to all young, single moms out there. This gig is not for the weak.

My thoughts are interrupted when Norah Kennedy sits across the bar from me. Norah and I have been friends for a handful of years, but she only recently learned about my sister. I'm not ashamed of Bridget at all, but I tend to be a pretty private person.

"Hey, Alicia!" The redhead beams at me.

"Hello, Mrs. Kennedy!" Norah married Eamon, one of the Irish trio, a couple of months ago in Ireland, and that newlywed glow is radiating off of her. I don't normally put much stock in love at first sight, but I got to witness their meet-cute and knew right away they were perfect for each other.

Norah giggles, her grin impossibly wider. "I haven't grown tired of being called that yet."

"No? Couldn't tell," I tease her. "Need another pint?"

"Nah. Just getting some space from the horde surrounding the guys."

"They're on fire tonight. Pat knew what he was doing when he begged them to play every month."

I was against the idea at first. The trio consists of Eamon Kennedy, Teagan O'Brien, and none other than Rowan Gallagher. They've been playing here since they transferred to UNCW from Ireland and found their way into the pub. All of them sing but each play a different instrument. Eamon on guitar, Teagan with a harmonica, and Ro usually plays the fiddle. He is Irish, through and through.

Our conversation pauses when Norah turns back to the stage. As the door to the pub is pulled open, the little bell Pat recently installed tinkles, alerting us of incoming guests. Setting down the glass I just finished drying, I make my way to the register to greet them. The closer they get, the more I realize how strikingly gorgeous the two of them are. Especially together.

"What'll it be, guys?"

The guy - tall, bearded, and ruggedly handsome - eyes the bottles shelved behind me and replies in a deep voice, "Whiskey, neat," then nods to the curvy goddess with lilac-streaked chocolate tresses next to him, "And she'll do a glass of your finest red."

I rarely take a man's word for it when he orders for his date who is right beside him. Women can make their own decisions. So, I look to her for confirmation.

"Red?"

She nods. "Please. But the house is fine."

Content with that, I fill their order and set the glasses down in front of them. The guy opens a tab and I begin drying glasses again, listening to the low murmur of conversation between them. I smile to myself when she says, "They're really good, Rhodes."

Rhodes. I like that. It suits him somehow.

"Don't let them hear you say that," Norah answers, making me snort in amusement. "The dark-haired one, that's my husband. I'm Norah."

"Ames," the girl replies. "This is Rhodes, my husband."

A twinge of jealousy hits me. Everyone is married or getting married. I wouldn't be surprised if Teagan O'Brien proposes to his girlfriend, Layla, soon. They're just as in love as Norah and Eamon are.

"Ah. Well, you'll have to have a pint before you leave, yeah? Maybe a bowl of Irish stew?" Norah tells the couple before yelling out, "Alicia!"

Oh lord. Here we go.

Eamon saunters toward the bar, eyes locked on Norah. "Aye, love. Who is this?"

"This is Ames and Rhodes. They're in for a visit, and I was just getting ready to have Alicia pour them a pint." She smiles mischievously at him.

He stretches a hand out to Rhodes. "I'm Eamon, this spitfire's husband. Hopefully, she hasn't asked Alicia to line them up yet."

Rhodes doesn't budge, keeping his grip firmly on his wife, but says humorously, "She was about to, I think."

I lean my elbows on the bar and grin at Eamon. He tosses me a wink. "Do not line up a single glass, Alicia. All they need is a pint or two, yes?"

The night Eamon and Norah met, he accused her of not being able to hold her Guinness, so she challenged the Irishman to a drinking contest.

They were pretty evenly matched until Pat came and broke it up. The rest is history.

Smirking, I grab a couple of glasses and turn to the Guinness tap, where I wait the allotted time between pulls. When Pat hired me, the first thing he taught me was how to properly pour a Guinness. Hold the glass at a forty-five-degree angle, aiming the nozzle of the tap towards the golden harp logo. Fill the glass only to the top of the harp, then set it down and wait sixty to eighty seconds before filling it the rest of the way up. It's important to let it rest between pulls. While it's resting, I dart into the kitchen to ladle up a bowl of stew, as requested by my red-headed friend.

When I come back out, Eamon and Norah are bantering back and forth, while Ames and Rhodes watch on with amusement in their eyes. The two couples are vastly different in demeanor, but it's as plain as the noses on their faces that they're deeply in love. The twinge from earlier comes back. I look away, my eyes instinctively finding Rowan across the pub, talking with Pat. I could easily blame it on his red hair and beard because they are eye-catching, but who am I kidding? The guy is right up my alley. He has nearly as many tattoos as I do, has a great sense of humor, and the memory of his mouth and hands on my body will linger until the day I die.

As if my staring calls to him, his eyes snap to mine. The amusement in them turns questioning and his lips part like he wants to say something. I glance down immediately, telling myself it's time to get back to pouring pints. I don't let myself look at him again for the rest of the night.

Chapter Three

Rowan - Three Months Later

This is the moment I've been waiting for from the time I kicked my first football. Racing along the state-of-the-art pitch with a ball at my feet while listening to the fans cheering in the stands is a dream come true. I've wanted to play professionally since day one. When the side of my tattered, second-hand runner connected with the leather, sending it flying, a new part of me was born.

My da and two younger brothers didn't understand my need to kick a ball around everywhere I went, but I imagine they would have groused about it less had they realized the energy I spent honing my skills kept me from throwing punches at their ugly mugs. Nobody gets me more riled than the other three Gallagher men I shared space with. Nothing but a bunch of useless chancers, that lot.

Da's been on the uppers for the majority of his miserable life, but it got worse when our mam walked out on us after Barry, my youngest brother, was born. I can't say that she was a great mammy, but it was a right shock when we realized she'd gone off without us. Leaving our da I could understand, but three lads ages six, four, and newborn? Nah, mate. If not for me and my gran, Barry wouldn't have survived.

My middle brother, Cian, was always a proper little dosser, getting out of doing chores and the like. He could win an award for the stories he tells to get himself out of any type of work. He learned it from our da, to be sure. Several years of taking care of those two plus wee Barry made me realize just why she left. Fuck, I wanted to leave too. And I did the moment an offer was presented. Did that make me as bad as Mam for abandoning my brothers when a better opportunity came along? Probably, yeah, but they weren't young wans when I finally escaped. Barry was eighteen and Cian twenty-two when I got the call from UNCW. I didn't spare them a second thought as I packed up the few belongings I owned and headed for the airport.

Five years later and here I am, a starting forward for the Charlotte Football Club. I worked my arse off to get here, earning a business degree with a minor in foreign languages, just to have as a fallback. Realistically, I know I can't play forever. By the time footballers hit their mid-thirties, it's about time to retire…no matter how fit they are. When that day comes, I'll work my way toward coaching. Football is the only passion I have and the one consistent thing in my life. When I'm having a shite day or get a message from my gran about my brothers being thrown in the clinker again, I head to the nearest pitch with a couple of balls and pretend that I'm kicking their worthless arses. They have no idea what I've done for them since I left Galway. I'm happy to never hear from or see them again, but the small bit of caretaker left in me can't seem to leave them to rot completely.

The money I wire to the only mate I have back home gets deposited into an account that only Gran can access. There's no chance of any of them getting a hold of it to stock up on their uppers or drown their sorrows at the pub. The money I send keeps a roof over their heads and the lights on. What they do from there I haven't a clue, and I don't give two shites. Fine. Maybe I give a single, solitary shite, but it's the same kind of shite I'd give to the homeless man sitting on the corner of the street. The idea of anyone without someplace to shelter will always tug at my heartstrings. Basic human decency is what that is. Despite what my mates here say, I do actually care about someone other than myself.

Eamon and Teagan are the only ones who know about my family, and only information they got was that I have a worthless da, two worthless brothers, and Gran. She's not worthless, but she's also not the sweet, nurturing type most envision when they think of a grandmother. She smokes like a chimney and swears more than a sailor in a hurricane. I learned all my best curse words from her. She helped keep Barry alive as an infant, but once he could talk and piss on his own, she made herself scarce. The only reason I trust her to handle the money I send is because I told her she could have whatever was left after paying their bills. I always send more than they need, keeping Gran happy and so that everything runs smoothly.

I'm not wealthy by any means, but I have very few expenses outside of the standard costs of living. No fancy clothes or fuel-guzzling car, and all of my electronic devices are secondhand. Growing up poor teaches you how to stretch things and the finance classes I've taken at university taught me the importance of investing. Because of that, it's easier to be generous with others. Under the radar of course. I may preen in the spotlight when I'm running the pitch, but never when I'm helping someone else. If I'm giving something, I'd rather it be private so no one feels indebted to me. We survived on handouts in Galway, but they always came with a cost. I'll be damned if I make someone else feel that way.

* * *

"Gallagher, good work tonight," Coach Myers commends me, thumping my back with the palm of his hand on our way through the tunnel to the locker room. "Keep that up and you'll be starting more than sitting on the bench."

Our first game of the season was a shutout, with an end score of four to zero. One of those goals was mine. I can be an arrogant bastard, but some early hazing for the new teammates at the beginning of the preseason taught me to keep my mouth shut until I can gain some seniority. I came to play, so whatever I have to do to stay off the bench, I will.

"Thanks a million, Coach. I'd like that," I tell him sincerely.

"What are your plans before the game next week?"

"Nothing major," I assure him. "Headed to Wilmington to see some of my mates and do a small set with them at the pub."

"I heard you were a musician too. Impressive. Don't get into too much trouble, but go celebrate your win. You've earned it."

Coach Myers is the most encouraging coach I've ever had. He's firm, yeah, but he rarely loses his temper, which is a new experience for me. Our Coach at UNCW was strict and brutal, which ended up being exactly what the team needed. Especially with that wanker, Mac. Decent player he may be, but he wouldn't have been drafted by St. Louis on talent alone. Guess having a rich family really does open doors for a person.

By the time I reach the locker room, the guys are all singing Imagine Dragons' "On Top of the World" at the top of their lungs, snapping rolled-up towels at any bare arse that comes into view. I laugh as I rummage through my bag in search of my body wash. It's a three-and-a-half-hour drive from the stadium to Wilmington, and the last thing I want is to show up at Paddy's smelling like the inside of my gym bag. I could skip tonight and go out with the fellas or hit up a club with my team and roommate, Marcos Diaz, but for some reason, the only thing I can think about is getting to Wilmington.

* * *

"Yo! Gallagher, wait up!"

I'm almost to my car when Marcos' voice rings out across the parking lot. I stop, turning to wait for him to catch up.

"Hey, man. Good game! That goal was sick."

"Thanks, mate. You played a good game yourself, yeah?"

He did, too. His footwork is next level. I might even have him teach me a thing or two.

"*Gracias,*" he responds with a grin. "Hey, Coach said you're going to Wilmington. Can I ride with you? I promised my sister I'd come see her."

Marcos is also the brother of Layla, the mot my mate, Teagan, is dating. Oh, and at one point he was the fella sleeping with Teagan's cheating ex-girlfriend. Small world!

"Yeah, 'course you can. You ready to go now?" I hit the button on the fob to open the boot of my Subaru so we can toss our bags in.

"Yeah, amigo. You hitting up that pub of yours tonight?" He asks as he rounds the car to the passenger side.

"Paddy's? Aye. Promised I'd join the boyos for a song and a pint or two when I got in. Should be a good time."

Once we're settled, I send a quick text to Eamon and Teagan letting them know I'm heading their way then hand the phone to Marcos with permission to pick the music. We make small talk for the first hour of the trip before he pulls the brim of his hat over his eyes and nods off. Bad Bunny plays as my mind wanders back to the first time the guys and I played together.

* * *

"What are you young bucks up to this evenin'?" Paddy O'Nelly greets us warmly as we saunter into the pub.

We've been in Wilmington for a month now and have come in at least three times every week. It feels like home with the mahogany wood bar and tabletops, Paddy's lilting accent, and the smell of stew coming from the kitchen. We all have our reasons for leaving Ireland, but there's something about it that will always call to us—that we'll always miss.

"Hiya, Pat. How's she cuttin'?" Leaning on the bar, I extend a hand in the elderly man's direction.

Gripping my palm in a firm handshake, he grins. "Grand, grand. Hired a new barkeep and I think she might run this ship better than me-self. She certainly can pour the black stuff better than me."

"Get outta here with that nonsense," I say in disbelief. "Nobody pours better

than an Irishman. You'll not convince me otherwise."

I jump clear out of my skin when a low and warm voice says, "Is it because I'm a woman or because I'm not Irish?"

Glancing over my shoulder, my eyes widen at the dark sprite of a lass balancing a tray on one hand and glowering at me. She's sneaky, this one. I didn't see or hear her behind me. The first thought that crosses my mind is how much she reminds me of a black cat, bristling at an unwelcome visitor. She's all angles and sharp edges, complimented by the way her eyeliner swoops upward at the outer corners of the biggest and brightest blue eyes I've ever seen. My immediate instinct when I see a cat is to stretch my hand out for them to sniff, but I have a feeling this lass will bite my hand clean off if I get too close. Doesn't mean I won't try though. I've always loved cats.

"Sorry?" I ask, feigning ignorance. I don't miss how her eyes track my movement as I turn to face her fully.

"You don't think I'm capable of pouring a better Guinness than Pat here. Is it because I have tits or because I'm not a leprechaun?"

Two things happen. Eamon and Teagan choke on their beers, spewing it across the bar top and my eyes immediately drop to the tits in question. And of course, she notices.

"Hey, asshole," she snaps her fingers in my face. "My eyes are up here, and yours should be too."

My gaze flies to hers, a corner of my mouth tipping up in a smirk. Kitty has some seriously sharp claws.

"My apologies, love. Didn't mean to offend."

"Answer my question." If looks could kill, I'd be in a wooden box.

"No." I shrug and start to turn back to the bar.

"No? What do you mean, 'no'"?

Glancing at Pat, he raises his bushy eyebrows at me in warning. I do love a challenge, so I slowly spin around, leaning my elbows back on the bar and letting my eyes travel from her black hair down to her black combat boots. The tight tank top and ripped jeans are also black. The only color gracing her features are her sapphire eyes, ruby red lips, and the tapestry of tattoos covering nearly every exposed inch of her arms.

Fuck me, she's bleedin' gorgeous. I'm not usually too picky when it comes to the lasses I hook up with as far as looks are concerned, but this wan here? If not for the murder in her eyes, I'd say she was handpicked straight from my dreams. Hell, maybe even with the murder in her eyes.

"I mean," I start slowly. "No, I won't be answerin' your question."

She narrows her eyes at me. "Why not?"

Shrugging, I glance to where one of her fists is balled at her side. "You're itchin' for a brawl, lass, and I can think of others ways to expend some energy, if you catch my meanin'."

Her ivory skin reddens, not in embarrassment, but rage. Ah, a hellcat.

"Christ," Eamon mutters to my right. I can see his head shaking in my peripheral vision.

"Alicia, love," Paddy soothes. "Don't mind Rowan here. He's just having the craic, is all. He meant no offense, did ya, Gallagher?"

Craning my neck to peek over my shoulder, I give him a wink before directing my attention back to the sprite. Extending a hand in her direction, I offer a truce.

"Aye, just takin' the piss. Pleasure to meet you, Alicia. Like this aul fella said, I'm Rowan. But you can call me Ro."

She sneers at my outstretched hand. "I think I'll stick with asshole." With a flick of her hair, she spins and marches through the swinging doors that lead to the kitchen.

I can feel my lips stretch into a grin as I watch her walk away. For such a petite thing, she has an arse that is just begging for my handprint. My cock stirs at the mental image of bending Alicia over the bar and giving her a good spanking while I'm driving into her. Bet she'd fight it the entire time but secretly love it. Girls like her spend their lives being in control, but what they need is someone to take the reins and make the decisions for them.

"Alright," Patty barks out. "Quit harassing the staff, you dosser, and get on that stage. The three of you promised live music, and I'll see that you do it."

He's right. We did say we'd give open mic night a try. I doubt we'll do it ever again, but it won't hurt to entertain him this one time.

* * *

And here we are a handful of years later—Alicia still thinks I'm an arsehole, and we're still playing for Paddy any chance he can get us on that stage. To be honest, we all enjoy it, and we play well together. Bringing an extra bit of Irish culture to O'Nelly's takes the patrons on a temporary journey to the place we all called home.

Chapter Four

Rowan

By the time we arrive, O'Nelly's is jammers. Everyone is packed in tight like sardines, but spirits are high. Marcos and I are stalled just inside the door, scanning the pub for a pathway through the crowds, when we spot Teagan and Layla in our usual corner. My mate's got an arm draped over the Hispanic beauty's shoulders, whispering something in her ear that makes her blush.

"Fucking gross," Marcos mutters.

"Ah, c'mon now, Diaz." I jab him in the side with my elbow. "Don't be a dryshite. Your sister's gorgeous. Teag's alright, I s'pose."

Glaring at me, my teammate keeps his voice firm. "Bro, that's my sister you're talking about."

I just laugh and raise a hand in greeting when Eamon and I make eye contact. As I start in his direction, my eyes sweep surreptitiously around the pub, telling myself it's just to see who all is here and *not* searching for a certain dark-haired stunner with cerulean eyes.

Before making it even halfway across the space, a jolly Irish voice calls out. "Ach, there's trouble if I ever saw it. Mr. Gallagher, did you think I'd let ya in me pub without even a proper greeting?"

That voice belongs to the older gent standing behind the bar, drying pint glasses. He's a cheeky codger, Paddy O'Nelly is, but I love the aul fella something fierce. Even when he's busting my bollocks. *Especially* then. He hasn't aged a bit in the four years I've known him. Still portly with grey hair, a neatly trimmed beard, and rectangular, wire glasses covering mischievous eyes. He's normally sporting a flat cap, but tonight his head is bare of any covering, hair combed back. His usual cable knit sweater is replaced with a hunter green button-up, maroon bow tie, and matching suspenders. I've never once seen him dressed up, so I'm immediately curious. Veering off my original course, I saunter in his direction, Marcos close behind.

"Paddy," I greet him cheerfully. "You're looking mighty fine tonight. Am I correct in thinking you've got someone to impress this evenin'?"

"Ach," He says. "Go on ya, chancer! Can't a man look his best just because he wants to?"

Paddy is properly flustered, his round cheeks turning scarlet. I'll be fecked! I was just codding him, but looks like I struck gold. He doesn't give me a chance to comment further as he glances behind me.

"Now, who's this young fella here? I'll forgive yer cheek, Gallagher, for bringing in a new patron as long as he behaves himself." His threat is lifeless as he winks at Marcos.

"Aye, this here is Marcos Diaz." I step aside for the man in question to approach the bar. "He's my teammate, roommate, and oddly enough, Layla's brother."

"Is that right? Small world we live in, aye? Pleasure to meet ya, Mr. Diaz. I'm Paddy O'Nelly, owner of this fine establishment. Yer first drink is on me tonight. What'll you be drinking?"

Marcos grins and extends a hand to Pat. "Nice to meet you, Paddy.

Appreciate the warm welcome. I'll have whatever Ro's having, thanks!"

Paddy darts his eyes to me expectantly. He doesn't know this, but after the night I met her, I only order a pint of Guinness when Alicia is behind the bar, because she actually does pour the best I've ever had outside of Ireland. When it's Paddy behind the bar, I order whiskey. Glancing around, I casually scan to see if she's out in the crowd serving drinks.

"She's in the back, lad," Paddy informs me, peering over the rim of his glasses. "We're down a hand, so she's bussin' and washin' tonight."

"Who?" I ask, trying to play stupid.

"Ah, Rowan, my boy. I may be up there in years, but my eyes work just fine, they do."

My spine straightens at the implication, but I'm not about to admit it. Especially not with Marcos listening.

"I was gettin' ready to have her take over anyway so I can announce you young buskers," Paddy adds nonchalantly before turning toward the swinging doors that lead to the kitchen. He pushes one open and calls out, "Alicia, leave those dishes, lass. I've got to take the stage and need ya tending bar."

"Gladly," I hear her say sharply. Her voice grows louder as she comes through the doors. "I fucking hate..." She freezes when she sees me. "Rowan."

I nearly groan out when I finally lay eyes on her. Fucking stunning, as always. Maybe it's because it's been so long since I've seen her, but right now I want to fall to my knees and worship her. The knot on top of her head is messy, but the sexy kind of messy. Loose wisps of her onyx hair frame her angular face and those eyes. Those bright blue eyes that seemed dull at first, spark to life when they lock on my face. The giant hoops in her earlobes sway back and forth, and her nose ring glints in the lights. She's wearing a faded Flogging Molly t-shirt tied into a knot at the hem, showing off a sliver of skin just above the waistband of her black jeans. The combat boots are standard for her when she's working. She's so effortlessly beautiful.

She won't meet my eyes directly, but she's taking in every inch of me just like I'm doing to her, and I don't mind it a bit. I know there's a spark between us. No, not a spark. A fecking line of electricity that burns and crackles the closer we are to each other. It's been there since day one. Part of the reason I constantly say and do things to rile her is because I want to be the one who fuels her fire, and there's nothing sexier than Alicia when she's ready to explode, in and out of the bedroom.

The first time I made her come was a religious experience. I'm Irish, so that means I was born Catholic, but my family never practiced it. I've only ever stepped foot in a church one time and that was for my Granddad's funeral. But watching Alicia's face as she fell apart on my hand made me want to lay my sins at her feet, while simultaneously avoiding the confessional booth, because if giving her orgasms is an iniquity, then I don't ever want to repent. On the other hand, if it's the key to heaven, then consider me a converted man. I'll attend Mass multiple times a day for the rest of my life.

The only problem is that she turned me away and locked the doors. Now, no other house of worship will do. I haven't even gone looking.

Chapter Five

Alicia

I knew he was coming tonight, but seeing him still sends a shock through my system. It's been three months since Rowan has been in O'Nelly's. God, he looks good. All those hours of training took his already toned body and turned it into a powerhouse. The navy blue Seahawks t-shirt he's wearing is one I am familiar with. It fit him well last year, but now it's stretched tight over his chest, the sleeves almost busting around his biceps. He runs a tattooed hand through his hair, and I notice it's gotten a little longer on top. In the span of five seconds, I've studied every inch I can see from my spot…except his eyes. I can't bring myself to meet his gaze, even though I can feel it burning into me. Suddenly, I'm feeling self-conscious and desperately want to bring my hands to my hair. This just pisses me off because I don't get nervous around men, and I *certainly* don't primp for them.

Apparently, this is all I needed to fuel my fire. My eyes narrow as I let a bit of snark loose. "How nice of you to grace us with your presence, Gallagher."

Finally making eye contact, I watch his own widen before crinkling at the corners as that smug smile of his spreads across his face. He takes a second to peruse me from the messy bun on top of my head, down to the black combat boots I always wear to work. His appraisal makes my body heat in response. Damn him.

"I always aim to please. Lookin' good, Alicia."

Ignoring the compliment, and the way it sends a pang of longing through me, I step to the rack of pint glasses, grabbing one, then another, when I notice the guy next to him. He's handsome and looks vaguely familiar. Something about his dark hair, deep brown eyes, and tawny skin niggles at my brain.

"Who's your friend?" I ask while I begin pouring the Guinness I know Ro's going to order.

He looks disappointed that I'm not engaging in our usual verbal sparring, but I just don't have it in me tonight. My day job was a nightmare today and tips were abysmal.

"This is Marcos, Layla's brother. We play together and are roomies in Charlotte."

Ah, that explains it. He and Layla have similar features.

"Oof, that's rough, Marcos. Sorry you're stuck with this one," I nod toward Ro. "But it's nice to meet you. What are you drinking?"

"Whatever you're pouring for Gallagher. And he's not a bad roomie," Marcos states, tossing an arm over Ro's shoulders. "He cleans up after himself, cooks his fair share, and pretty much sticks to the apartment when we aren't on the road. He's never even brought a girl back to the place!"

My eyes dart to Rowan, only to find him watching me intently; scanning my face for what, I don't know. I'm honestly shocked by this revelation.

It must show because he cocks his head to the side. "Were you expecting something different, darlin'?"

My breath hitches at the nickname, summoning a slew of memories from a night not that long ago that I've been doing my best to forget. With a shake of my head, I shrug as I let his Guinness rest for the required amount of time before topping it off.

"I don't expect anything as far as you're concerned."

His auburn brows furrow in frustration and he sighs heavily through his nose. He opens his mouth to speak, but Marcos interrupts.

"What's the deal with the Guinness pour? I've heard it's a slow process, but why?"

I'm about to answer when Pat steps up. "Good question, lad! Come down here and I'll tell ya all about it." He motions for Marcos to follow him to the end of the bar, though if he was going to give a lesson, sticking close to the tap would probably be the better option. Rowan and I watch as Pat leans close and whispers something in Marcos' ear, causing his eyes to widen and immediately zero in on us.

Great.

I hand Ro his beer without looking at him, but before I release it, he covers my hand with his. Startled by the contact, I look up, ready to tell him off, but words rush from his mouth.

"Li, can we talk? Please?" His eyes are pleading with me, and my resolve starts to waiver. I vowed to never speak to him again more than what's necessary to do my job.

"We don't have anything to talk about, Rowan," I tell him firmly, trying to pull my hand away.

I can't go down this path. I can't get caught up in those amber eyes and the lilt of his voice. I can't let myself remember the feel of his calloused hands on my skin or the way he tastes.

"We bleedin' well do and you know it," he seethes, his hand tightening over mine. "That night was more than—" His jaw clenches, and he looks away for a second before aiming his stare at me again. "You fuckin' left, Alicia. No explanation, no goodbye, nothin'. And now, if you bother to speak to me at all, it's nothin' but ice and venom. I deserve somethin'. Just tell me a reason, and I won't ask again. I swear it."

I feel the heat of tears beginning to form. He's right. He deserves an explanation for why I disappeared like a thief in the night. He deserves a lot more than that, but I can't give him any of it.

"Ro," I whisper, warring with myself over how to respond. "I can't—"

"Gallagher!"

A hand slams down onto his shoulder and I release a shaky breath in relief. Eamon Kennedy to the rescue.

"Oy! It's time to go on stage, mate! Can't ya hear Paddy up there?"

Ro holds my gaze a moment longer before turning to Eamon. "Yeah, mate, sorry. I'm ready."

I watch as the two weave through the crowd and climb the single step to the stage. Teagan is ready and waiting, harmonica in hand. Eamon takes the stool in the center, pulling a guitar strap over his head and tuning the instrument. Ro picks up a fiddle and bow, inspecting it closely before placing it into position between his chin and shoulder. Once settled, Pat announces them.

"Now that they're all up here," he remarks, aiming a look at Rowan. "Let me introduce you to three lads that have been gracin' this stage since they arrived from Ireland over four years ago. On harmonica, we have Teagan O'Brien from Thomastown. Here on the guitar is Eamon Kennedy from Kilkenny."

A loud whistle sounds from the corner table closest to the stage. Norah, Eamon's wife, is grinning broadly, cheeks flushing when he winks at her.

"Yes," Pat says with a chuckle. "We all know how you feel about Eamon, Ms. Grady."

"Ahem." Eamon coughs into the microphone, giving Pat a meaningful look.

"Ah, *Mrs. Kennedy,* I mean. Sorry, friends. They're both spoken for."

Eamon nods curtly. "Aye, you bet your arse we are."

Laughter titters through the crowd before Pat continues. "And this handsome lad on the fiddle is none other than Rowan Gallagher, the starting forward for North Carolina's very own Charlotte Football Club!"

Cheers ring through the space, and Ro beams as he raises the hand holding the bow into the air. His shirt sleeve shifts with the movement revealing a tattoo on the inner part of his bicep. He's too far for me to identify it, but it didn't use to be there. I don't know why I'm even curious about it. It's not like it matters.

Paddy makes a few more comments before turning the mic over to Eamon, who doesn't waste time talking. He immediately begins playing Galway Girl, much to everyone's delight but my own. The amount of times Ro has sung this song to me over the years is countless. He must be thinking the same thing, because he catches my eye and winks. As hard as I try, I can't fight the small smile that plays on my lips as I recall the first time.

* * *

Another busy night but not a bad one. The customers have been happy, and Pat's been more helpful than normal. He'd even cleaned the booths and tables before opening. But he gets that way when the anniversary of his wife's death comes around. It is almost like he needs to keep himself busy so he doesn't sink into despair. I've never met someone that loved their spouse more than Paddy loved his Ellie. I don't make a big deal out of it,—just give him a quiet hug and the space to remember her however he needs to.

It's open-mic night. These are a crowd favorite, especially when Pat can rope the Irish trio into performing. Eamon is usually the lead singer, but tonight, I'm surprised to find Rowan in the hot seat, with the mic in his hand.

"How's it cuttin', gang?" He asks jovially. "Havin' a good night?"

The crowd cheers their answer with loud whistles and a few cat calls that have Ro grinning ear to ear.

"Right. So for those that don't know, I'm an Irish bloke from Galway." The patrons laughter travels around the pub. "If you ever hear anyone insulting Galway, it's all true."

Another round of laughter that gets louder when Teagan calls out, "Aye, and he's the perfect example."

"Oy, haul yer whisht, O'Brien! I'm not a cannabis smoking, Buckfast drinking Weshterner!" He mocks indignation, then grins again. "But my da sure as feck is."

Even I laugh at that one while pulling a beer. We got off to a rocky start, and I still act like he's the bane of my existence, but the ginger is growing on me. He's charismatic and sexy, with a knack for getting under my skin like no one I've ever known. When I glance up, he's looking in my direction. I look to my left and right, not seeing anyone near me, then give him a questioning look.

He winks. "I'm going to sing a song for ya, if that's alright? But this isn't just any song. This one is dedicated to our favorite bartender—."

Pat yells out from the table he's been harassing, "Yer too kind, Mr. Gallagher!"

Rowan scratches the back of his neck sheepishly. "Well, Paddy, this is embarrassing. I was talking about Alicia."

I gape, and the audience hoots and hollers with laughter. Pat huffs good-naturedly then concedes, "Aye, fair enough!"

"Anyway, like I was sayin'. This one goes out to our favorite bartender, Alicia. Make sure you tip her well tonight!"

The majority of the customers swivel their heads my way, calling out their thanks and clapping. I've never been so thankful for the low lighting in the pub than this moment as embarrassment shades my skin pink. To be honest, I'm flattered, but he doesn't need to know that. I smile cheerfully and give him the finger.

Rowan roars with laughter. "And that, mates, is why we love her, yeah?"

More cheering has me shaking my head while I ready a shot of whiskey for myself just in case I need it to get through whatever he has planned.

"Enough gabbin'. This song is called Galway Girl." Without another word, Eamon starts strumming his guitar with an upbeat tune.

"Well I took a stroll on the old long walk
Of a day -I-ay-I-ay
I met a little girl and we stopped to talk
Of a fine soft day -I-ay-I-ay
And I ask you friend, what's a fella to do
'Cause her hair was black and her eyes were blue
And I knew right then I'd be takin' a whirl
'Round the Salthill Prom with a Galway girl
We were halfway there when the rain came down
Of a day -I-ay-I-ay
And she asked me up to her flat downtown

Of a fine soft day -I-ay
And I ask you friend, what's a fella to do
'Cause her hair was black and her eyes were blue
So I took her hand and I gave her a twirl
Oh and I lost my heart to a Galway girl."

I know he's just singing this to mess with me, but a small part of my heart warms against my will. No one has ever dedicated a song to me, and it's nice to be recognized. As the song comes to a close, I grab a glass and begin pulling another pint of Guinness for him. He doesn't think I've noticed how he never orders one from Pat.

As he approaches the bar, I slide the pint toward him, careful to keep my expression hard. I don't want him thinking one song has me all gooey now.

Before he can utter a word, I state, "This one's on me, but don't go thinking I'm giving you a free drink every time you dedicate a song to me, Gallagher."

He grins as he brings the glass to his lips. "Wouldn't dream of it, love."

Chapter Six

Rowan

Our set was some craic tonight. The crowd was lively and eager to have another pint or two while singing along to a surprising amount of songs. Eamon ended the set by performing 'Ringsend Rose' for Norah. The sap has been head over heels for her since the moment he met her, but now that they're married? He's a lovesick fool. I gave him a fair amount of shite for it too, even though, if I'm being honest, I'm green with envy.

After that little interaction with Alicia, I'm feeling right sorry for myself. She thinks the walls she's built up around her are solid steel, but I've seen them up close and they're bricks and mortar, just like the rest of us. She thinks that I don't notice the way her eyes track me when my head's turned, or how the pupils of her gorgeous blue eyes dilate when we touch, but I see it all. I know that night in Ireland meant just as much to her as it did to me.

I've given her plenty of space and time, but I'm done waiting. We will have it out—one way or another.

"How long are you in town for?" Teagan asks while we pack up our instruments.

Latching the case of my fiddle, I shrug. "Not sure yet. Tonight for certain, but it depends on how long Marcos wants to hang around. We don't have training until Monday, so my weekend's free."

"Grand. You still leasing the flat here?" Teagan asks.

"Aye," I confirm. "I knew I'd be back enough times that it just made sense to keep up with it."

He begins talking, but I tune him out when I see Alicia looking down at her phone with a frustrated look on her face. Could be anything, but when she slams it down on the bar before pinching the bridge of her nose, I'm already moving.

"Ro!" Teagan barks, confused by my sudden departure.

Skirting the crowd, I slide up to the end of the bar and stand there, watching her for a moment. Her phone is back in her hand, fingers flying over the screen as she curses under her breath.

"Alright, darlin'?" I keep my voice low enough to not draw attention, but loud enough for her to hear over the ruckus.

Alicia tenses, closing her eyes and inhaling deeply through her pierced nose. "Fine, Gallagher."

"Sure about that? You seem like you're ready to rage."

"I said I'm fine, Rowan," she snarls, slamming the phone back on the bar top before grabbing a towel to wipe a perfectly clean and dry spot.

"I know what ya said, but what I'm seein' is something completely different." I normally let her have her moments, but if she won't even have a civil conversation with me, I'm left with no choice but to pick a fight with her.

"Yeah. Well, it doesn't concern you, so just leave it." Alicia turns her back to me, yanking spotless bottles from the shelves to wipe them down.

"And I'm tellin' *you* that I won't leave it until ya talk to me. I can do this all night, love." I shouldn't say it, but I know it will be the spark to light the fire. "Wouldn't be the first time I've stayed up all night with ya."

In a move quicker than I can track, she's spun around. Her hand slaps over my mouth, her face close to mine.

"Would you shut the fuck up?" Her question is hissed between us.

Because I can't help myself, and because it's been too long since I've tasted any part of her, I flick my tongue against her palm just like I'd do if I had her spread wide before me. This would earn me a cry of disgust from anyone else, but not Alicia. *Oh no, not my Galway girl.* Her pupils dilate, and she gasps softly. I love watching the blush stain her porcelain skin. Taking advantage of her stunned state, I gently wrap my fingers around her hand, pulling it away from my mouth just enough to place a kiss to her inner wrist. It is a spot I learned is quite sensitive on her.

"Now," I murmur, holding her gaze. "Will you please talk to me? I just want to help."

Alicia takes a deep breath through her nose, and as she exhales, whiskey laced breath fans my face. She doesn't normally drink on the job, so I'm more than a little surprised.

"It's family stuff," she mutters, looking down at her boots. "And it's been a really long day."

I'm still holding her wrist because I'm afraid she'll bolt the moment I release her, but she's not resisting.

"What happened?" I ask softly.

Her shoulders drop as she heaves a sigh. She sounds exhausted when she finally spills.

"Bridget got written up again so I told her she couldn't go out tonight. She was just caught by our neighbor drinking with her piece of shit friends in the park by our apartment."

Ah, that will do it. Bridget is Alicia's fifteen year old little sister that is rarely spoken of, especially in a positive light. From what I've gathered, she's a troublemaker. I don't know their backstory, but I do know that Alicia has been the sole provider for the two of them for quite some time. It can't be easy.

"Is the neighbor going to report her to the police?"

"Fuck, I hope not. That's the last thing I need right now." She moves her arm like she's going to rub at her forehead only to realize that I still have a hold of her. The look she gives me would freeze a man's bollocks, so I loosen my grip and give her an apologetic smile that she doesn't return.

"How can I help?" I ask earnestly, eyes still locked on her face.

Now that I'm up close, I can see how tired she is. The dark circles under her eyes are still visible beneath her makeup.

She scoffs and looks away. "Unless you can become my clone, there's nothing. I can't afford to lose the hours, so she'll just have to wait until I get off work. Who knows what kind of trouble she'll get up to during that time though."

This is the part where I want to offer her every red cent in my bank account if it will alleviate her from even one of her burdens, but she's too proud to accept a handout. I wouldn't disrespect her like that.

"Do you want me to go get her?"

Alicia raises a brow at me like I've gone absolutely mental. "Let's play this out, shall we? A strange man my sister has never met approaches her and says, 'Hey, your sister sent me. Get in my car.' She may be a pain in the ass, but she knows better than to take rides from strangers."

I purse my lips and nod. "Yep, right you are. That wouldn't look a bit suspicious at all, yeah?"

A faint smile graces her face for just a second. "Look, Ro, I appreciate you wanting to help, but I've got this. I've made it this far in life without any help, and I'll just keep on trucking. Don't worry about me."

"Li," I start, but she sets her palm against my chest and looks at me fully, pleadingly.

"Please. Just let it go. This isn't the first time Bridget has put me in this position, and it won't be the last. Now, go back to the group and let me do my job."

My jaw clenches, teeth grinding together to keep me from opening my mouth to make things worse. The frustrating part is that she doesn't have to do any of this alone. Anyone of us would drop everything to help her. An idea starts to take form, so I nod once then walk away from the bar.

Chapter Seven

Alicia

"Alicia, love. Why don't you go ahead and take off for the night," Paddy says from behind me.

I glance over my shoulder at him and raise my brows. "Why would I do that? We're swamped and still have two hours left before close."

My employer sticks his thumbs through the suspenders he's wearing, pulling them from his chest before letting them snap back into place. He winces, and I snort a laugh.

"Ach," he growls. "I can handle it from here. You've been working yourself to the bone all week. I was thinking of roping Mr. and Mrs. Kennedy into dish duty, for old time's sake."

For the first time tonight, a genuine smile forms as I remember the way Paddy arranged for Norah and Eamon to not only spend time together, but to make amends for the drinking contest they engaged in the night they met.

"It's fine, Paddy. I don't mind staying. I need the money anyway."

Turning, I grab the tray of dishes, intending to take them back to the kitchen, but he stops me.

"How about this? Check your tips, and if they're enough to make up for the last two hours of work, you go. If they're not, you stay."

The twinkle in his eye is a dead giveaway that he's up to something.

"What's the catch?"

"No catch, my dear. Just think you deserve a break, is all." He shrugs with one shoulder while swiping his hand over his trimmed, grey beard.

"Alright," I agree hesitantly. "I'll play along, but I'm telling you there's no way my tips will be enough to cover what I need for the week."

Patty's shoulder lifts. "We'll see. I pulled the jars to the office for you to count. Go on. I'll finish up here."

I'm incredibly confused as I skirt my way around him and move toward the kitchen. The office sits off to the left by a short hallway that has a storage closet and small bathroom. When I enter the room, I jerk to a stop and my jaw hits the floor. There, on the desk, are the two tip jars we keep on the bar. They're nearly overflowing. Two industrial pickle jars almost full of generosity. On a good night, combining both tip jars fills one halfway. This has to be a mistake.

I march back through the swinging doors, calling Paddy's name as I go. He's standing at the bar, talking to Norah and Eamon, who are laughing at whatever he's just said.

"Pat," I say sternly.

"Alicia?" He answers back.

"What the hell is that?" I point behind me toward the office.

He looks past my shoulder then back to me like I'm slowly losing it. "Ah, that my dear happens to be a set of swinging doors that lead to the kitchen. I thought we went over this the day I hired you."

I narrow my eyes at him. "That's not what I mean and you know it. The tip jars. They weren't that full an hour ago, and I've only served a few patrons.

Who put that money in there?"

Eamon and Norah swap glances as Pat folds his arms over his chest. "I'm sure I don't know, love. You must have made some customers very happy or made their drinks extra stiff."

"But..." I start.

"Alicia, lass, don't look a gift horse in the mouth. Go on—count your tips, then get out of here." He says kindly, making my eyes burn.

I'm thick-skinned and do a pretty good job of locking up my emotions, but every now and then, Paddy gives me a grandfatherly look that makes me feel like a little girl who never had to provide for her family.

This is one of those looks.

Inhaling deeply through my nose, I slowly release the breath from my mouth. "Okay. Thanks, Pat."

He winks at me before turning to Eamon and Norah. "Alright, you two. You promised me dish washing, and I mean to see that you keep that promise."

* * *

Three hundred dollars.

That's how much money was stuffed in the tip jars. It's nearly what I make in three or four shifts. I left work completely flabbergasted and completely suspicious. I don't know what, but *something* was definitely going on.

There isn't time to explore what happened as I pull up to the park, finding my sister waiting on a bench next to the single mom who lives in the apartment next to us. Bridget is laughing at something she said, and it hits me like a punch to the stomach. I haven't seen her laugh like that since she was little. Her whole face lit up, and she looks so different with that smile. Her hair, black like mine, is french braided down her back, highlighting her high cheek bones. She got our father's green eyes, while I got mom's blue. She did get mom's freckles though. Genetics are so weird.

Killing the engine, I step out of my RAV4 and round the front. As soon as Bridget sees me, the smile disappears, disdain in its place. *Ah, there's the sister I'm familiar with.* She averts her eyes, so I don't utter a word to her.

"Hey, Kat," I greet our neighbor. "Thanks so much for calling me and staying with her. I'm sorry that your night was interrupted."

She smiles at me knowingly, tucking her blonde hair behind her ears. "It's all good. The boys are with their dad this week anyway."

Kat and her husband split up a couple of years ago and share custody of their sons, ages thirteen and sixteen.

"Bridge," I say quietly. "Please go wait in the car."

She sighs loudly, heaving herself from the bench and stalking toward the car. Kat and I watch her until the door shuts.

I turn back to my neighbor. "Does this shit ever stop?"

"I wouldn't know," she shrugs. "I'm still in the thick of it. Mason isn't that bad yet, but Nick? I feel like it's a weekly thing, being called into the principal's office. A couple of weeks ago, he was getting high in the bathroom when he should have been in geometry. And God, the attitude. It takes every ounce of energy to not pop him upside the head some days."

I huff a laugh and nod in agreement. "Girl, it's unreal. I can't do anything right with Bridget. I'd give anything to just be her sister again, you know?"

Kat places a hand on my elbow and gives it a gentle squeeze. "You're doing great, Alicia. Teens are rough. Life is tougher. I took this weekend off, so if you need any help, just let me know. Bridget and I get along well enough that I think I could find something to keep her busy without it feeling too much like a chore."

"I appreciate that, but I don't want to infringe on your kid-free weekend. You need it just as much as I do."

"It takes a village, babe."

I know she's right, but accepting help from anyone just feels so foreign to me. And the guilt of adding another kid to her plate just doesn't sit right, but I'm starting to feel desperate.

"I'll let you know," I tell her noncommittally. "Thanks again for everything."

"Anytime. I'm good for a vent session anytime you need it, too."

"I just might take you up on that one night soon." God knows I could use it.

With a tight smile, I turn towards my car. I'm actually surprised Bridget listened to me. Since our apartment is just on the other side of the building, she could have easily stomped off in that direction and locked herself in her room. She's slunk down low in the seat, scrolling through her phone. My first instinct is to swipe it out of her hands and toss it in the garbage, but that will only escalate the situation.

Once I'm in and buckled, I start the car, ignoring the weird ticking noise coming from the motor in hopes that if I don't acknowledge it, it will go away. I steel myself for the conversation I have to have with my sister. No matter how I approach it, it's going to be ugly.

"Do you want to talk about what happened tonight?"

"No." Bridget turns her face toward the window.

"Bridge," I counter. "I can't just ignore this. I specifically told you that you couldn't go out."

An irritated sigh leaves her mouth. "I said I didn't want to talk about it. What's the point of even asking me, if you're just going to do what you want anyway?"

"Oh, that's rich." I scoff as I pull into the designated parking spot for our unit. "Kind of like how you do whatever you want, even though I've told you otherwise?"

She throws open the door and slips out the car, giving me a mocking smile as she nails me right where I stand."Must be where I learned it, then."

The door slams as she stomps away. My vision turns red, but I stay rooted to my seat, watching as she lets herself into our bottom floor apartment, slamming that door closed as well. The moment it shuts, I grip the steering wheel as hard as I can and scream my frustrations. I'm so angry, that the urge to put my fist through something almost overpowers me. The thought of it is enough for me to stop short. I'm not a violent person. A hard ass with a sailor's mouth? Yes. But never violent. My father was an abusive man. Mostly to my mother, but occasionally he'd bust my ass for the dumbest shit. I vowed that I'd never be like him, working hard to manage my anger in healthy ways.

For years I did kickboxing to let off steam, followed by yoga to center myself. I had to stop when the gym membership went up significantly. This reminds me of the huge amount of cash I have in my purse that I don't want stolen. Our complex is in a nicer area, and crime has been at a minimum, but growing up in the rough neighborhoods teaches you early on to not linger too long beyond your front door. Tucking my purse tightly under my arm, I quickly exit the vehicle and jog to our door. Thankfully, Bridget left it unlocked, so I don't have to fumble for my keys. Once I'm inside, I close and deadbolt the door, kick my shoes off, and head to my room.

I have a small safe tucked into the corner of my closet. It's underneath a pile of clothes, and it is where I keep important documents and a stash of cash in. When there's a good week, after all of the bills are paid and tips are better than normal, I take half of my tips and stick them in the box within the safe. If anyone asked, I'd tell them it was an emergency fund for when my car inevitably dies, but the truth is that I'm saving up a down payment to buy a house. I want a place that's wholly ours— one where we can feel safe and not have neighbors just on the other side of the wall.

I want a home.

Counting out one hundred fifty dollars, I place it in the box then lock up the safe. Remaining on the floor, my arms resting on bent knees, I hang my head before taking a few deep breaths.

Meow.

Lou's soft, grey head rubs against my arm. He chirps again, this time rubbing the length of his body against my side before burrowing his head under my bicep to bump my nose with his.

"Hey, buddy," I murmur. "How was your day?"

Meow.

Raising my head, I crisscross my legs and he immediately climbs into the open space, extending a paw to my cheek. I love everything about this cat, but this is my favorite quirk. Whenever I have a particularly hard day, he senses it and comes to comfort me. I get a good nuzzle in before he gently taps my cheek.

"Thanks, handsome. You're my favorite guy, you know that?"

He begins to purr loudly as he curls up between my legs, winding his body so that he's on his back. I stroke his belly a few times—only a few because he'll bite the shit out of me if I do it more than that—then let my mind wander back to tonight.

Rowan wanted to talk about what happened that night in Ireland. Deep down, I know this conversation has to happen eventually, because he's right.

It did mean more.

And that's what scared me away.

Chapter Eight

Five Months Earlier - Norah and Eamon's Wedding

Alicia

We just watched our friends get married, and are now celebrating with drinking and dancing in the same room of the Butler House as their ceremony. I've been sipping on a single drink the entire evening, just so I can remember this night. Eamon and Norah are wed, and the love pouring out of them is palpable. The sight of them lifts my spirits so much that I don't scowl at Rowan when he stretches his hand in my direction.

"C'mon, darlin'. Just give me one."

His eyes are begging me to dance with him, and I cannot deny him.

I've been watching him all night. He looks sinful in his grey suit, but when he removed the jacket and rolled the sleeves of the white button up to his elbows, I was entranced. Much like the previous November, one dance leads to more. He pulls me close as the music slows, pressing a hand to my lower back. Calloused fingers scrape across the exposed skin courtesy of my backless dress and clasp my free hand. We sway like this for a moment before he places my hand onto his shoulder, wrappings both arms tight around my waist. I don't resist but settle into his embrace as we dance, my temple against his bearded jaw.

"I'm sorry," he whispers into my hair.

I start to pull back to look at him, but he tightens his hold, "For what, Ro?"

His fingers absently trace my spine, causing goosebumps to bloom along my arms.

"For that night in November. At the club," he murmurs.

Stilling, I manage to meet his eyes. "Which part are you sorry for, exactly? What almost happened? Or stopping?"

He looses a whiskey-laced huff of a laugh. "Neither and both, all at the same time."

"Gallagher," I warn, arching a brow.

Pressing his forehead to mine, he inhales deeply before the levee breaks. "I'm sorry for kissing you for the first time at some fecking club, but I'll never regret kissing you. I'm sorry and *not* sorry that I stopped. Sorry because I wanted you—*still want you*—so badly." His growled words cause me to suck in a sharp breath. "But I'm not sorry that I realized the first time with you deserves more than a quick fuck in the jacks. I am sorry that I made that decision for you and for making you feel like I didn't want to be with you. It's all I want, even if you deserve so much better than what I could give you."

Uninvited tears well in my eyes at his admission, and it overwhelms me—it *scares* me. I don't do tender moments, so rather than say anything, I tilt my head up and bring his mouth to mine. Just a simple press of my lips to his before moving my mouth to his ear.

"Let's try again."

A slight shudder rolls through him, but Ro says nothing as he takes my hand and slowly leads me from the reception to the elevators. We don't speak until we reach his room on the second floor. I'm nervous as he opens the door for me, and I step inside. The space is green with a single queen sized bed near an elevated alcove that leads to the French doors of a small veranda. Two dark green, velvet covered chairs take up the far wall by bow windows overlooking the garden.

The sound of the door snicking shut doesn't startle me, but a knuckle trailing down my back does. I sense Rowan stepping closer then feel the heat of his breath on my neck. I hold absolutely still, allowing him to make the first move.

"This tattoo is stunning." His voice is soft, reverent. "When did you get it?"

It's a Phoenix, in the dead center of my back with outstretched wings, but rather than rising from the blaze, the bird *is* the fire—sooty black edges encasing a smoldering ember that becomes a live fire with the shifting of my muscles and skin.

"The day I turned twenty," I tell him quietly.

His fingers trace the lines of her wings to where they end at the curve of my ribs before coasting around to the front. His thumbs graze the underside of my breasts over the fabric of my dress as he flattens his hands, one on top of the other, gently pulling me back until I'm flush against his chest. My hands naturally rest on his. The coarse hair of his beard tickles when he drops his mouth to the crook of my neck. I angle my head to grant him better access as he skates his lips to my ear, flicking my pierced lobe with his tongue. I'm instantly wet.

"Is this okay?" Ro breathes the words, and I shiver.

"Yes," I answer, my voice barely audible over the thundering of my heart. I more than want this, but it feels so intimate, and I don't know how to do that.

"I'm clean, and I have protection," he mumbles into my hair.

"Same."

"I want to take my time with you, Li." He sucks on a tender spot under my ear before beginning his descent to my shoulder. "Watching you in this bleedin' dress has had me aching for you all night."

The wine-red spaghetti strap dress I wore to the wedding is tight fitting, with a lace overlay and high-low hem. It's the nicest dress I've ever owned, and it was hand-made by Norah. While I wasn't a part of the wedding ceremony, she said the pattern screamed my name at her. I loved it immediately, but right now? I could kiss her with gratitude.

Rowan removes a hand from my torso, bringing it to the thin strap, and slowly slides it off my shoulder before kissing the lunar phases tattoo there. He repeats the motion on the other side, kissing the symbol of Capricorn I had inked when I turned eighteen. When his hands leave my body, I want to whine in protest until I feel ghosting fingers begin to pull on the zipper at my lower back, dragging it over the curve of my ass. I hear the low rumble of approval when Ro discovers I have nothing on under the dress.

"Fuck," he growls. "Not sure if I'm happy that you're bare under this fabric or disappointed that I don't get to unwrap the rest of you."

"Do you want me to go get something?" My voice is breathy. At this point I'll do anything he asks just as long as it means we finish what we've started.

"No," he grinds out as he grips my hips firmly, yanking me so that my ass is rubbing up against his very hard cock. "The only way you're leaving this room is if it's on fire."

"Then you better hurry up and get this fucking dress off me."

A low chuckle vibrates in his chest as his hands glide up and down my sides. He begins turning us until we're facing the large mirror on the adjacent wall. While holding my gaze, Ro peels the dress from my body, letting it fall into a crimson puddle at my high-heeled feet. With the additional three inches the shoes provide, our faces are level, meaning that when his eyes leave mine to take in my naked reflection, I can feel his breath cascade over my skin as he exhales

"Look at you. Fucking perfect." Ro's golden eyes devour every inch of me, a promise in them that this is only the beginning. "Can I touch you, Li?"

A huff of a laugh escapes me. "You had better touch me, Rowan, or so help me…"

Curving his body around mine, he brings his shaky hands to my breasts, watching in the mirror as he cups them gently.

Arching my back slightly, I force myself into his palms as my head drops back onto his shoulder. I love that he's trying to prolong this, but I'm so turned on, it's uncomfortable. He takes the hint and squeezes me before brushing his thumbs roughly over my nipples. I suck a breath through my teeth, whimpering slightly.

"Are you wet for me, darlin'?" Ro murmurs into my neck.

We both watch in rapture as his hand snakes downward, tracing the triple goddess tattoo that begins between my breasts before spreading beneath them.

"Yes," I breathe out, rubbing my thighs together, searching for some sort of relief.

"Do you need me, a chéadsearc?"

I think he just called me *cade shark,* but my confusion flies away the moment he slips a finger through the soft curls at the apex of my thighs, pressing my clit briefly before sinking into my pussy.

"Fuck," he groans at the same time a moan sounds from me. "You're dripping, Li." Ro's voice has a primal edge to it and that has me squirming against him.

"Rowan," I gasp when he inserts a second finger and begins pumping slowly in and out of me. "Please…"

The leisurely pace he's set with his fingers is maddening. Edging is great, but I don't want to be edged right now. I want this man to claim me. My hips roll, grinding against his rock hard cock as I try to get myself off on the heel of his hand. He removes his fingers, making me growl in frustration.

I'm about to take matters into my own hands when he steps around me, dropping to his knees and holding me captive with burning eyes.

"Watch the mirror."

"Wha…*oh God,*" I choke out, hands dropping to his shoulders as he simultaneously grabs my ass with both hands and presses his face into me.

He licks a slow path from my entrance to my clit, then mumbles into me, "Are you watching the mirror?"

Wobbling on unsteady legs, I curl my fingers into the fabric covering his broad shoulders. He nips me gently in a place I've never been nipped, making me whimper, but I raise my eyes to the mirror. The sight of him on his knees before me, face buried in my pussy and gripping my ass for dear life, nearly sends me over the edge. This is an out of body experience as I watch one of my hands leave his shoulder and cup the back of his head, pulling him even closer. I feel, more than hear, his rumble of approval and it sends a shiver through me. With every unhurried swipe of his tongue, a brick in the walls around my heart begin to fall.

It's not just sex. It's the way he's waited for this. The way he wants to savor every moment. The way his hands are still gentle, even though he's holding me firmly.

My legs begin to tremble, threatening to go out from under me at any point. "Ro, I'm going to fall."

His mouth leaves me, amber eyes meeting mine. His beard is soaked with a mixture of my arousal and his own saliva, and it's hot as fuck. The hands on my backside loosen and slide to the back of my thighs.

"I'm not going to let you fall." He says it so earnestly, like he means more than just keeping me steady while he devours me.

Swallowing the lump in my throat, I cup his cheek and whisper, "I know, Rowan."

He nods in understanding before moving back to his ministrations, but I pull on his lapels to bring him to a stop. His hands move up my body as he stands, locking eyes with me. One by one, my fingers deftly unfasten each button. His jaw clenches when I reach the bottom. The last button is tucked into his slacks, leaving his shirt gaping open, exposing the distinct lines of the muscles that make up his torso. Dragging a finger down his sternum until I reach the belt buckle, I begin pulling the rest of his shirt from his pants to release the last button. Stepping closer, my palms slide under the material to push it from his shoulders.

Jesus, he's beautiful. I imagine he was a tall and gangly kid at one point, but he definitely isn't gangly now. And the tattoos! He could rival me on the amount of ink covering his skin. On his right pectoral is a rabbit looking upward, made up of Celtic swirls. The lines are intricate, weaving throughout the animal's body. It's fascinating. Giving into the temptation, I trace the lines with my fingertips, noting the steady rise and fall of his chest. Placing my other hand over his heart, I find that it's racing just as fast as my own.

We've danced around each other for years, flirting and fighting, but never letting ourselves take that final step to meet in the middle of the dance floor. Whenever I imagined sex with Rowan—and I've imagined it countless times—I never once thought it would be so overwhelmingly intimate. Ripping our clothes off and fucking, quick and dirty, certainly, but to undress one another so attentively? So reverently? I think that scares both of us as much as it excites.

He lays a warm hand over the one I have resting above his heart, and my eyes dart to his.

"I want you," he tells me hoarsely. "I want all of you."

Chapter Nine

Continued...

Rowan

The words have barely left my mouth before Alicia is pressing her lips to mine. The kiss starts slow and sweet, but the moment she glides her tongue along the seam of my lips, the trepidation I've been feeling disappears. I lay claim to her mouth. I don't remember moving them, but my hands are no longer on her waist. One is grabbing her arse, yanking her against me until I can feel the heat of her against my cock—even through these fucking trousers—while the other is tangled in her onyx tresses at the base of her skull. I keep her pressed against me, reveling in the feel of her bare skin against mine as I walk her backward. I don't stop until she's wedged between me and the mirror. She gasps as the cool glass touches her skin, and I swallow the sound.

Her fingernails scrape down my stomach until she reaches the waistband of my trousers. The nearly non-existent space between us causes her hands to fumble as she tries to loosen my belt. I shift my body enough to give her the smallest amount of room. Alicia takes full advantage of the slight space, making the slacks fall from my hips. Reluctantly, I leave her mouth to trace the tattoo on her shoulder with my tongue. My hand fists in her hair, and I pull her head to the side so I can lick a path back to her ear. Alicia palms my cock over my briefs, and the memory of her hand on me in the jacks that one night makes me groan.

"Fuck," I hiss.

That's it. My control has snapped completely, and if I'm not inside this woman in the next five seconds, I think I might actually die. Forcing my hands to release her body goes against every fiber of my being, but I have to get these damned clothes off. Wrenching myself back, I drop my hands to the waist of my briefs, tugging them down quickly. My cock springs free, slapping my stomach as I step out of the shorts and trousers.

"Holy shit…" Alicia exhales.

My eyes snap to her face but she's not looking at me. Not my face anyway. Oh no, her gaze is zeroed in on the erection *she* caused. Those perfect tits with the roses tattooed above them heave with each panting breath. Her cheeks are flushed, and her lips are swollen. She's so gorgeous.

"Do you like what you see, love?" I ask, fisting my cock and pumping it slowly, loving the way she's watching me.

Her tongue traces her bottom lip. "Fuck, yes."

The desire I have to tell her to get on her knees and show me how much is almost overpowering, but that will come later.

"Get on the bed, Li." I order. "I need to get a condom."

"Don't," she blurts out, freezing me in place. "I get the shot, and I've already passed the ovulation part of my cycle."

My head tilts questioningly. "You want me bare, Alicia?"

The breath catches in my lungs as she nods. I've only fucked one girl bare, and that's because I was a sixteen year old eejit that didn't know any better.

We got lucky.

"Bed. Now."

In the span of a heartbeat, she's gone from the mirror to reclining on her elbows in the center of the comforter. She's still wearing those fuck-me heels—watching me intently as I stalk toward her, hand gliding over my cock. I fucking love how her eyes roam over my body. I can practically feel her trailing every line of ink. Her eyes dip past the Celtic Hare on my chest and slowly travel south, until she's watching me fuck my own hand for her. She sinks her teeth into her bottom lip and lets her legs fall open, exposing the very place I need to be.

"Jaysus, Mary, and Joseph." I'm not a praying man, but even I can hear the desperate supplication in my voice.

I set a knee on the bed, then the other, before wrapping my hand around the back of her calf muscle and pulling her foot to my chest. Thank fuck these are the heels with laces rather than those tiny buckles. Keeping my eyes locked on hers, I loosen the bow around her ankle and slip the shoe from her delicate foot, letting it fall to the floor with a low thump. Before moving to the other side, I kiss the arch of her foot. Once both shoes are discarded, I'm crawling over her. I want to kiss every tattoo on her body, but we've waited long enough.

Still propped on her elbows, I capture Alicia's mouth, gently pushing her back onto the mattress. Her arms wrap around my neck, legs bending to bracket my hips as our tongues battle for dominance. Little does she know that I'm so gone for her, I'll submit to anything she wants.

"Ro, I need you," she mumbles against my mouth. "I can't wait anymore."

My response comes easy as I meet her gaze. "No, love. We're done waiting."

Fisting my cock, I position it at her entrance and slowly slide into her, inch by inch until I'm fully seated before stopping. She feels so right that if I don't take a deep breath, I'll blow.

"What are you—" Alicia protests.

I rest my forehead against hers. "Give me a minute, or this will be over before it starts."

Her warm breath coasts over my face when she sighs dramatically. "Can we compromise and do five seconds? Because if you don't keep going, I'll have to finish myself off."

Chuckling, I pull out to the tip. "If that's what you want..."

"No!" Alicia clamps her legs around my waist, locking her feet over my arse.

"There's a good lass," I growl, then punch my hips forward before she can utter any more empty threats.

We both moan at the sensation before falling into a steady rhythm of deep thrusts and slow rolls of our hips. I can't take my eyes off of her face. Every quiet gasp and whispered plea for more has me in a choke hold. When those gasps become moans, and the grip she has in my hair tightens, I know she's close. Moving my hand down her body, I find her clit and apply pressure with the pad of my thumb, then circle it. I keep each thrust deep, but increase the pace. Alicia's moans become hoarse cries as she gets closer to detonating. Then she slams her eyes shut, and I can't have that.

"Eyes on me, a chéadsearc," I command her.

I've called her this twice tonight. *First love.* Not that I've ever had a shining example of love, or even really know what it is, but I can say with every confidence that I've never felt for anyone the way I feel for Alicia.

Those sapphire eyes pop open just as she crests, and I've never witnessed anything more exquisite and intense in my entire life. The way her lips part around my name as she shatters sends me into overdrive. I pound into her harder, growling a string of Gaelic nonsense until I come so hard, it makes me dizzy. The world spins around me for a moment before focusing on Alicia's flushed face. She's looking at me wide-eyed, her mouth parted as she pants.

"Beautiful," I whisper, brushing strands of hair from her face.

A slow smile creeps across her face. "Why did we wait so long?"

It's a valid question. One that's been playing in the back of my mind for days. Why *did* we wait? Why did *I* wait so long to grow a pair and tell her what I wanted?

"Because I'm a feckin' eejit, is why," I tell her.

"Hmm." Alicia purses her lips and narrows her eyes. "That's a good point."

"Hey!" I snap playfully, then roll us so we're on our sides, facing each other.

She breathes a husky laugh before pushing on my shoulder, forcing me onto my back. Leaning over me, her hair falling in a dark curtain around us, and she kisses me softly.

"You're not the only one, Ro. I haven't made things easy on either of us."

I cup her face in both hands, forcing her to pay attention as I repeat her words from earlier. "Let's try again."

She doesn't answer, just kisses me once more before swinging a leg over my hips to straddle me. No more words are spoken after that. It would be several hours, and many more orgasms, before we exhaust ourselves enough to fall asleep.

When I wake up, it's to a cold, empty bed. If not for the lingering scent of Alicia all over the sheets, I'd think I'd dreamed it all.

Chapter Ten

Rowan

"Here! Marcos, here!"

The wanker's been ignoring me since the first half. We're down two to four against St. Louis on their turf, and that's unacceptable. Especially when my old teammate, Mac, scored one of those goals. Marcos has been playin' like shite the entire game, refusing to pass when he has an opening. Coach is goin' to eat the head off him after the game, if not before. The only time we ever get our arses handed to us by Coach during a game is when we really fuck up.

"DIAZ!" Coach screams from the side of the field when Marcos makes an attempt on goal rather than passing. Again.

And he misses. Again.

The ref blows the whistle, signaling a substitution. Absolutely no one is surprised when Coach pulls Marcos and benches him. Nathan Willis, another midfielder, takes his position on the pitch and gives me a nod. Thankfully, he and I are open communicators, so we play well together. So well, in fact, that we manage to tie the game before going to penalties. We end up losing by one and leave the St. Louis field in piss poor moods. The trek to the locker room is somber as we await our lecture from Coach. There's no doubt that Marcos is going to get the worst of it, but we're a team. We're all responsible for the ball.

"Bro, what the hell was all that?" I hear our goalie, Jameson McKnight, call out as Diaz stalks toward his bag.

"Fuck off," he mutters.

"No, you fuck off." Jameson points a finger at him, and I take a step in his direction. He's a great goalie, but hotheaded. This is going to escalate. "We could have won tonight if not for your hero complex, or whatever shit you were trying to pull out there."

Marcos doesn't respond.

"Hey, did you hear me, Diaz?"

"Jay," I chide. "Enough, mate. We're all sore over the loss, but attacking each other isn't going to solve any problems, yeah?"

"He's right," Coach barks from behind me and all of our heads snap in his direction. "Diaz, you fucked up tonight, it's true, but the only one that gets to ream you over it is me. Got it, McKnight?" He shoots a hard look toward Jameson, who at least has the brains enough to duck his head at the reprimand.

"Yes, sir."

"Right. Now, first thing's first. Gallagher and Willis, good work bringing us back up. That's the kind of communication I want to see." He looks pointedly at Marcos, who casts his eyes to the floor. "Second, St. Louis plays dirty, but you all handled yourselves well. Play hard, don't take anyone's shit, but still conduct yourselves honorably. The crown on your kits holds us to a higher standard. They don't call us the Royal Family for nothing."

Coach covers a few more issues before making us huddle up for the ritual we do before, and after, every game. Locking arms over shoulders, we lean in, waiting for our Captain, JR, to ask the single question we answer before and after every match.

"How do we play?"

In unison, but without much gusto, we reply, "We play as one!"

"Pitiful. You can do better than that, boys. How do we play?" JR demands.

"We play as one!"

"Again!"

"We play as one!"

* * *

The mood among us is pitiful as we leave the stadium, so we decide to look for a pub close to our hotel. Is it wise to venture into a drinking establishment that's likely filled with fans of the team we just lost against? No, not at all, but it's safer than if we were to have pulled a win. If we're lucky and keep our heads down, we could have a drink or two unscathed. I've learned to never go out in my kit or wearing any team merch. Instead, I remove my contact lenses, put on my black, half-frame glasses and trade my jersey for a black cable-knit sweater, black jeans, and my leather jacket, which—surprise, surprise—is also black. I rub a small amount of pomade onto my hands then comb my fingers through my hair, slicking it away from my forehead. Styling my hair is reserved for when I need to be incognito or have some posh event, perhaps a wedding or the like. I check my reflection in the mirror one more time and then make my way to the lobby where the team is meeting up.

The pub is within walking distance of our hotel, and it's surprisingly not too cold for a February evening. Some of the blokes from warmer climates are grousing about freezing their bollocks off, but it feels like a night out in Galway to me. Crisp, cool air brushes the exposed skin of my face, and I breathe it in. I don't often miss my home country, but every so often I get a bit nostalgic, wishing I could be walking the cobbled streets, listening to buskers on the corners as I search for my next drink. While the majority of my mates wanted to roost in Naughtons, my favorite spot was

McSwiggan's. A newer establishment as far as pubs in Ireland go, but the live music couldn't be beat. I'd take music over televisions blasting football any day.

I don't have many good memories of my mum, but one thing I'll never forget is her voice. She'd always be singing songs I'd never heard, but when I asked her about them, she'd just tell me they were from a time long past. Being a young lad, I didn't think too much on it. It was only after she left that my Gran told me she'd been a brilliant singer and songwriter. She'd planned on moving to Dublin to attend the Royal Irish Academy of Music, but met my da the summer before, and had me nine months later. He'd swept her off her feet with his deceptive charm and promises of a beautiful life together. He'd told her he was about to become a wealthy man and would make sure her dreams came true. He was convincing enough to rob her of her innocence as well as her future. Once she found out she was pregnant, her da forced her to marry mine, threatening him with his life if he didn't man up and make an honest woman out of her.

A quick, courthouse wedding was the end of her music career. I think she resented da most of all. She was never cruel to me and my brothers like he was, but she always seemed detached, just going through the motions of life. After I was born, Da stopped covering up his drug use and all pretenses of being a charmer. He started drinking heavier when my first brother was born, then started leaving marks on Mum. The fights. Christ, the fights. Screaming at one another into the wee hours of the morning until he'd backhand her into silence. Barry and Cian huddled together under the covers, a pillow over their ears.

Looking back, I can see now that she was depressed, and I can't really blame her. Yeah, it makes my blood boil knowing that she could just abandon her children without a second thought, but it wasn't the life she'd planned or wanted. Had she been able to follow the path she'd set her heart on, maybe it would have been different. I've always hated the mindset that if you get pregnant, you have to get married to make it "right". Statistically, getting married after an accidental pregnancy ends in disaster. Don't even get me started on the whole "making an honest woman out of her" shite. Absolute bollocks.

My musings are cut short when we arrive at the pub. I'm apprehensive as the door opens, spilling not only the sounds of a bawdy Irish ballad, but also three obviously drunk St. Louis fans who nearly knock us all over like bowling pins.

"Whoa," I chuckle, gripping the arm of the bloke who just stepped on my foot to steady him. "Easy there, mate."

I can feel the tension rolling off my teammates behind me. These are the moments we try to avoid when we're away from our home turf. You never know if you'll get a cheerful drunk or an angry one. Thankfully, this fella seems happy enough.

"Ope, sorry, man!" The guy doesn't look much older than twenty-one, his blond hair plastered to his brow with sweat, eyes wide and wild thanks to the alcohol in his system.

"No worries. Just be careful, yeah?" I give him a conspiratorial smile.

"Hey! Are you Irish?" One of his mates asks, coming to grip his friend's other arm.

"Aye, guilty," I tell him, releasing the first guy and stuffing my hands into the pockets of my jacket.

"That's so dope! And you're coming to an Irish pub! Do you live here?"

"Nah." I shrug. "Just visiting for the night."

It's not a lie.

"Well, you'll enjoy this place. They're legit. The bartender tonight is a hot Irish chick. Maybe you two can hit it off." The eejit winks at me like he's doing me a favor.

First, just because we're both Irish doesn't mean we're destined to be together. Second, there's only one hot bartender I have any interest in hitting things off with, and she's hundreds of miles away.

"Yeah, alright, mate. I'll check her out." That's all I'll give him. I'm ready to cut the conversation short with a glass of whiskey. "Have a safe night, boyos."

With a wave, I join my team as we enter the bar. It's darker in here than Paddy's, so it takes a moment for my eyes to adjust. I squint through my glasses as I scan my surroundings. It's a mirror image of O'Nelly's Pub. The dark cherry bar top on my left gleams under the pendant lights, and on my right is seating and a small stage. There are even the same swinging doors I've watched Alicia dart through a thousand times, always popping them open with her hip. For a minute, I think I've actually conjured her into existence when the doors open, and a tattooed arm balancing a tray comes through. Squinting again, I realize that it's definitely not Alicia, because the tattoos on this lass are less edgy and more cutesy. I take in the rest of her, any hint of interest completely fading when I see she's the polar opposite of my dark haired lass. Blonde hair in a high, curly ponytail, bright pink t-shirt with "Lucky's" stamped across her ample bosom, unnaturally tanned skinned, and she's too...happy.

I don't realize I'm scrutinizing her so obviously until she chirps cheerfully, "Heya, handsome. Is there something I can *do* for ya?"

Even though the bloke told me the bartender was Irish, her accent still throws me off. Dublin area, if I'm not mistaken.

I feel a teammate elbow me in the side. "Gallagher, if you don't wanna hit that, tag me in, bro."

Jay. Of course it's Jay.

"Ah, no. Sorry, lass. Thought you were someone else," I lie, rubbing the back of my neck in embarrassment.

The blonde' eyes widen. "Is that a Galway accent I'm hearing?"

I nod in confirmation. "Aye, good ear."

Her pale blue eyes travel down my body, lingering at my waist, before meeting my gaze again. "That's not all that's good on me, love. If you're missing a taste of home, I'd be happy to be tasted."

I raise my brows at her brazenness. Normally, this is exactly the type of lass I'd pursue. I'd wait at the bar, flirting with her as a form of foreplay, until her shift ended. I'd walk her out a back door, slam her against the wall, and finger fuck her until she screamed my name. Then I'd have her take me to her place where I'd fuck her with my tongue and my cock until she passed out, leaving me to sneak out, never to be seen again. My heart sinks as I realize that's exactly what Li did to me in September. Now, I feel like absolute shite for leaving all of those women high and dry like that.

Opening my mouth to politely decline the offer, she cuts me off and extends a hand. "What's your name, Irishman?"

"Rowan," I tell her apprehensively before clasping my fingers around hers. They're soft and manicured, unlike Alicia's calloused hands from years of hard work.

"Hiya, Rowan. I'm Fiona Donlevy, from Dublin. Take a seat at the bar and I'll take care of you and your mates, yeah?"

"Uh, sure, yeah. Thanks, Fiona."

She gives me a saucy wink before strutting down the length of the bar to deposit a plate of food in front of an older couple.

When I turn, the boys are all smirking at me. Luis, a winger from Guatemala, is the first to speak.

"Gallagher, you seem to be struggling with the ladies lately. This could be your chance to get back in the saddle, if you catch my drift."

"Fuck off. I'm not struggling."

Another lie. I haven't had sex since Galway. Not because I don't want to. Jaysus, how I want to. A man can only go solo so long before it loses it's appeal. No matter how dirty the fantasy, it just doesn't compare.

But how can I be with any other lass when I've already had the perfect woman in my arms?

Chapter Eleven

Alicia

“Ms. Petersen, I don’t think you realize the severity of Bridget’s situation. She’s missed an entire week of classes, is behind on all of her assignments, and has been involved in two altercations with other students in the last month. We have a very strict no fighting policy. The truancy and missed assignments are concerning, but the fighting will not be tolerated. A third strike could result in her being expelled.”

My heart sinks all the way to my feet. I knew she was struggling, but her grades were still passing. When Mrs. Jones, the school counselor, called to set up an appointment, I was expecting to hear that Bridget’s ADHD was getting worse or that she smarted off to her math teacher again. A medicine adjustment will help the former, and I don’t give a shit about the latter. That teacher creeps me the fuck out, and the last thing I’m going to do is make my baby sister put up with his antics.

"I had no idea," I mutter. "Not one of her teachers has contacted me, and the school app never alerted me to her absences."

Mrs. Jones furrows her brow then turns to her computer, clicking around the screen for a minute.

"Hmm. I see here that the teachers only contacted myself, and the app has been spotty. I apologize for the miscommunication and will be sure to address this with Bridget's teachers." She turns back to me, folding her hands together on the desk. "In the meantime, how are things at home? More often than not, when there's an issue with a student, it stems from troubles at home."

My spine stiffens, but before I can become too irate, she continues. "I'm not implying that the fault is yours, Ms. Petersen, but I am required to ask."

Sighing, I look down at my hands. Lying about how hard it's been is my first thought, but that's not going to help Bridget.

"Honestly, it's been rough. I'm working two jobs, so I'm barely home. I can't quit either of them because money is tight and my car needs some work. When I am home, Bridget locks herself in her room and won't speak to me. We had an incident recently. My neighbor caught her drinking in the park near our complex while I was at work one night."

Mrs. Jones hums. "What happened after that?"

"Nothing." I shrug. "I gave myself time to cool off before discussing it with her, but every time I try, she shuts me out. I honestly can't remember the last time we even had an actual conversation."

She reaches for a pen and paper and begins writing. "I realize this is easier said than done, but I'd encourage family counseling to help bridge the gap between the two of you. She's going through so many biological and chemical changes right now, and your plate is full. A mediator can do wonders for any relationship." She hands me the piece of paper with a name and phone number scribbled across it. "This is one of my colleagues. Her first session is free and makes payment arrangements after that. If she can't help you, she can surely point you in the direction of someone who can."

I take the paper, folding it in half and sticking it in my purse. "Thank you,

Mrs. Jones. I really appreciate you calling me. Will you please continue to keep me up to date with Bridget?"

Mrs. Jones nods. "Of course, but I can only do so much before the school board takes action. One more incident and I'm afraid that will be it for Bridget here."

My throat bobs. "I understand. Thank you."

I leave the school with my shoulders feeling heavier than when I arrived. How am I supposed to get through to a teenage girl that refuses to talk to me, let alone listen? Providing the necessities has been my number one priority. Emotional connections aren't my area of expertise, but it's looking more and more like that's the direction I need to take. Fuck. The feeling of failure settles into my bones.

Being home more would do wonders, I'm sure, but I can't afford to quit either job. The one that I want to quit is the one that pays the most, but the thought of ever leaving O'Nelly's makes me sick to my stomach. I may give Paddy a hard time, but I love the old man and my job there.

* * *

My boss at the Briar Ridge Country Club was definitely not happy about me showing up half an hour late. He certainly doesn't care about why, either. I'm now busting my ass to get through the lunch rush to make up for it. I keep a smile plastered on my face as I weave between tables, filling glasses, relaying our lunch special, and serving meals. Only a handful of people treat me with any kind of respect. The dark-haired woman sitting to the right of a Senator looks to be around my age and completely uncomfortable. She smiles and thanks me every time I refill her water or the bread basket. She's polite when she orders and doesn't require special alterations to her food.

When she's finishes her meal, she excuses herself and makes her way toward the bathrooms. As she passes by, she slips a twenty dollar bill into my hand and whispers, "For the way this asshole talked to you and stared at your tits. It's not much, but it's the least I can do."

I wrinkle my nose. "Uh, thanks."

"You and I are just the hired help. We have to stick together." Her voice is quiet, and before I can respond, she's slipped into the restroom.

We're nearing the later part of the lunch rush when a large man enters the dining room. He approaches the hostess, smiling at her in a way that makes my skin crawl. I hold my breath as she leads him through the room, praying he's not in my section. The big man upstairs doesn't listen because she leads him not just to a table in my section, but to the private room for large parties. I should have checked the reservation list when I got in, but since I was already late, I didn't think about it.

When the hostess comes back to her podium, I slink up beside her. "Hailey, how big is the party going into that room?"

Hailey eyes me over her shoulder before flipping through the list in front of her. "Looks like eighteen. Doug Tenner. Know him?"

I shake my head. "Never heard of him. Do I have help in there or is it just me?"

She gives me a sympathetic look. "Just you. There's a party of thirty coming in about half an hour for room one. Boss man has the other servers scheduled for that one."

Dammit.

It's not that I can't handle it, I do it all the time. But this whole day has been just one shit storm after another, and there's a feeling in the pit of my stomach that this won't be any different.

Chapter Twelve

Rowan

I fecking hate wearing a bleeding suit. *Especially* to a meal. Who decided that eating food while dressed to the nines was a good idea? If I'm going to enjoy what I'm eating, I should be comfortable, yeah?

Apparently, the owner of CFC does not agree. When Coach told us that the big wig wanted to have lunch with him at his fancy country club, I was the only one that groaned in despair. Having lived in the slums and stolen more meals than I can count, the idea of sitting at a fussy table with fussy men sipping their drinks pinky-out is enough to make a bloke sick. Also, why are there so many forks at the place settings?

But here I am, in the navy blue suit I bought on clearance last year after Coach suggested we each own at least one for press conferences and the like. I refuse to wear a tie, though. They'll just have to accept my white button down and brown loafers. Even though I feel ridiculous in it, it does tend to boost a man's confidence when the ladies' heads turn as I walk to the private room reserved for us.

Doug Tenner, owner of Tenner Sports Entertainment and the Charlotte Football Club, is a large fella who reminds me of Harry's Uncle Dursley. His cheeks are red and veined, hinting that he consumes large quantities of alcohol. My da has the same look about him. The tweed suit jacket he's sporting is straining across his back and shoulders. Even though sweat beads at his brow, and he keeps fanning himself with the menu, he doesn't remove it. All the while, he's speaking to Coach about last season's MVPs and ignoring the rest of us. Glancing around the room, I'm surprised to find a fully stocked bar built into the corner. Just the thought of how much the bottles on that top shelf cost makes my stomach hurt.

Leaning toward the teammate to my left, I start to ask him about the menu when I hear a low, familiar voice to my right.

"Yes, sir. We carry several top shelf whiskeys. Would you like the menu?"

Whipping my head in that direction, I'm first delighted to see Alicia, but then confused by what exactly I'm seeing. Dressed in black slacks and a stiff, white button-up, she's pouring water into Tenner's glass. I can tell by the furrow in her brow that she's less than pleased and trying her best to stay professional.

"Sugar, why don't you bring a bottle of Macallan out for these boys here," Tenner demands, staring at her tits the entire time.

Bristling at the arsehole's condescending tone and wandering eyes, I clear my throat in an attempt to divert his attention, but rather than his, I get Alicia's. Her eyes slip to mine and widen when she realizes it's me. She blushes, embarrassment written all over her face. There's no way she'd be working here unless she absolutely had to.

I hold her gaze and silently mouth, "You okay?".

She gives me a subtle nod before turning from the table. I watch her say something to the bartender before sneaking through the door to where the bathrooms are. I give her about ten seconds before excusing myself with a sudden need to piss. Nobody is paying attention to me, so I'm not worried about being gone for a while.

Casually strolling toward the jacks, my eyes inspect the space, finding it empty. A muffled voice comes from the ladies' room. I can't hear much, but it sounds like Alicia is ranting to herself. Leaning against the opposite wall, I stuff my hands in the pockets of my trousers and cross one foot over the over to wait her out. I'm considering texting her when the door swings open and Alicia walks out, eyes red-rimmed. She freezes, staring at me with her jaw clenched.

"Is there anyone else in there?" I nod toward the door she just exited.

"No, why..." she starts then gasps as I close the distance in two quick steps, her hands immediately latching onto my biceps. "Rowan, what are you doing?"

With my hands on her hips, I direct Alicia back into the restroom and lock the door behind us. We stand there, just staring at each other. I'm immediately assaulted by memories of us in the jacks at the club over a year ago, and if the blush fanning across her delicate face is any indication, she's thinking about it too. For half a moment, I'm sorely tempted to pick up where we left off that night, but I remind myself why I really came back here.

"How long?" I ask, keeping my gaze locked on those sapphire eyes.

"How long, what?" Her breath fans across my face as I realize we're both still holding onto each other, mere inches separating our bodies.

Sighing, I give her an incredulous look.

Turning her face away and shoulders sagging, she mutters, "A while."

I hate that she can't look at me to answer the question, but I get it. It's difficult to admit when you're struggling, especially when you're Alicia Petersen. She doesn't ask for—or accept—help.

"Why?" I don't have the right to ask her, but I'm so curious.

Her eyes snap back to mine and narrow.

She's gearing up for a fight and taking my question as an insult, so I rush forward, squeezing her hips gently. "No judgment, love. It just doesn't seem like the kind of place you'd enjoy. A bunch of demanding old geezers leerin' at ya like they've found their next meal?" I purposefully run my gaze over her body. "Not that I blame them—ouch!" Releasing her long enough to grab the hand that just pinched the underside of my arm, I hold it firmly against my chest, surprised that she's not pulling away. "Hey, play nice! Look at yerself! Those tight trousers and the way that button-up is plastered over every inch of ya? Ya might as well be walking around naked!"

Her lips quirk to the side, fighting the smile I knew my teasing would coax from her. "You're such an ass, Rowan."

My head tips back on a laugh. "Ach. C'mon now, darlin'. You know I'm just slagging you." When I meet Alicia's eyes again, she smiles begrudgingly at me. "There's a good girl. Did Paddy cut your hours or something?"

"No, of course not!" She shakes her head, but doesn't continue.

My fingers flex against her hips again, pulling her a little bit closer. "If you're struggling, you can tell me. There's no shame in it."

Her cheeks flame, and I can see the tears starting to gather. Ducking her head, her response is barely more than a whisper. "There is."

"Hey, now." I tip her chin up with my knuckle, forcing her to look at me. "Did I ever tell you that I grew up in the slums?" She shakes her head again, so I continue. "Aye, my da is an addict. A right arsehole, too. My mum took off when my brothers and I were just wee wans. Da refused to do any sort of work, so I learned to beg and steal at a young age. To this day, paying full price for anything makes me a bit sick, to be honest."

Alicia stares at me a moment before blurting incredulously, "What the hell are you doing here, then?"

Rolling my eyes, I tell her the truth. "Tenner owns CFC and wanted to show off how big his pockets are. Honestly, I tried to get out of coming, but he wanted us all here."

"Well." She drags the word out slowly while her hands slide up to my shoulders to brush off imaginary dust before settling on them. "This suit is pretty nice."

"Yeah? Think so?" I give her a grin. "Got it on clearance. Not sure if it's my color or not, though."

"It is," Alicia says quickly.

I raise a brow at her. "Was that...*two* compliments, darlin'?"

She laughs, shoving against my shoulders in a half-hearted attempt to escape, but I band my arms around her middle, pulling her flush against me. Her hands loop around my neck, but she either doesn't realize it or doesn't care. I'm reveling in the feel of her in my arms again. She fits so perfectly, and while I've ached for her these last months, it's almost like she never left.

The laughter dies when she realizes just how close we are. Eyes wide, her head tips back slightly, the end of her long ponytail brushing the backs of my hands that are now resting above the curve of her arse. I'd barely have to dip my face an inch to press my lips to hers. Shallow breaths pass between us for what feels like a lifetime, but she's not pulling away… and she doesn't appear to be angry at our proximity. I decide to take my shot and close the distance. Just as my lips brush hers, there's a loud knock at the door.

Alicia wrenches herself from my arms, turning her back to me.

Fucking hell.

"Hey, Alicia?" A soft, female voice floats from the other side of the door. "Are you coming back? Your table in the banquet room is starting to get restless."

"Shit," Alicia hisses quietly before speaking louder. "Uh, yeah, Hailey. I'm on my way."

How long have we been in here? It couldn't have been for more than a few minutes? Impatient fuckers.

"I'll take care of it," I assure.

Finally, she looks at me. "How? Are you going to tell them you trapped me in here?"

"'Course not. Unless you think that will work." The look she gives lets me know she thinks I'm an eejit. "I'll go out first, you go to the bar that's not in the banquet room and grab a bottle of whatever you don't carry in that room. When you come back to the table, I'll tell them I had a hankering for it and demanded you find it for me."

"Rowan," she starts.

"Go on, lass. I'll take care of you."

She gives me one more long look before nodding and turning to leave. Just for fun, I slap her arse right as she opens the door, grinning when she cuts me a look over her shoulder.

Chapter Thirteen

Alicia

By the time I've composed myself and return to the table, Rowan has everyone there rolling with laughter. They don't even notice my arrival until I stop next to him and clear my throat.

"Here's your bottle of Barefoot Rosé, Mr. Gallagher." I present the bottle of cheap wine with a flourish.

I almost lose it when his eyes become as wide as saucers. He didn't specify a price range, just that it had to be something not behind the bar in this room. He hates rosé.

"I'm so sorry it took so long to find. It's not highly sought after in this establishment, but thankfully, a recent bridal party requested a few cases and this one was leftover."

His teammates chuckle around him, and the look he gives me promises retribution. Since I'm standing close enough to him, and his back is to the wall, no one sees when his hand slides up the back of my thigh and pinches my ass. I cough to cover the squeak I almost let out.

"Shall I pour it for you, sir, or would you like the honors?" I ask, giving him a sweet smile.

Clearing his throat, he sits up a little taller and straightens his jacket. "Right. You can pour, love."

I pour the glass then look at him expectantly. "Please let me know if it's to your liking, Mr. Gallagher."

He doesn't break eye contact as he plucks the glass by the stem and raises it to his lips. With a wink, he takes a healthy sip.

"Delicious, love. Reminds me of a lass I once had the pleasure of...*kissing*."

"Wonderful." I turn abruptly to face the other men at the table, who are smirking at their teammate. "Now, is everyone ready to order or do I need to go over the specials?"

I make my way around the table, writing down every order and request. I can feel Rowan's eyes on me the entire time, but I don't give him the satisfaction of seeing me flustered. I've been a bartender long enough that I know how to play the game. He finishes his first glass of wine then pours a second, which he sips slowly throughout their meal. When I come to refill his water, he touches my wrist lightly, catching my attention.

"Could you re-cork this bottle and bag it up for me, darlin'? I'd hate for it to go to waste."

I smirk at him. "Of course, sir. I'll do that right away."

"And please put it on a separate tab," he murmurs quietly. "There's no way I'm letting the owner pay for this shite."

After they've all completed their meal, I bring Rowan his bill and circle the table to give Tenner his. When I return, Ro hands the small folder to me, telling me to keep the change. That bottle of wine would cost next to nothing at the grocery store, but here the price has been quadrupled, which still makes it relatively cheap. When I take the tickets back to the register, I realize that he put a one hundred dollar bill in there, with a note on the receipt.

Li,

Call me when you get off work. My number is still the same.

Yours,

Ro

I glance up at their table, but he's already striding through the door to the exit.

* * *

Rowan: *You didn't call.*

Alicia: *Got off work late. Headed to O'Nelly's now.*

Rowan: *A heads up would have been nice.*

Alicia: *I'm telling you now.*

Rowan: **eye roll emoji**

Rowan: *What if I had something time sensitive to talk about?*

Alicia: *You could have called me. *shrugging emoji**

Rowan: *Li...*

Alicia: *Ro...*

Alicia: *I'll be at the pub all night.*

Rowan: *I can't come tonight.*

Alicia: Sounds like a personal problem, Gallagher.

Rowan: *Fucks sake.*

Alicia: *Gotta go. Good luck with all that.*

* * *

"Lower."

"I am lower."

"You're not low enough!"

I turn to throw a glare over my shoulder at Paddy who's been directing me on how to hang this stupid Saint Patrick's Day garland over the bar for ten minutes now. Offering to stay after my shift to help set the pub up for the upcoming holiday didn't seem like a bad idea at the time. I should have known better.

Then I see it.

"Pat!" I point at the chair he's leaning on. "It's never going to look right while you're not standing up straight!"

At least he has the decency to look sheepish.

"Ach, sorry, Alicia , love," he apologizes. "The hip's been botherin' me something fierce."

My brows furrow in concern. I know he's no longer a spring chicken, but any sign of him slowing down makes a lump form in my throat.

"What did you do?"

His cheeks turn bright red and he refuses to meet my eyes. "Nothin' you need to be concerned about, lass."

Oh. My. God.

I tilt my head to the side while giving him a scrutinizing look. "Patrick O'Nelly, are you telling me there's a special someone you've been spending your time away from the pub with?"

I laugh when his face becomes impossibly redder and he pulls the collar of his shirt away from his neck like it's fitting a little too tight.

"You dog! Who's the lucky lady? Or I guess it could be a lucky man." I'll give him hell every day, but I'm completely thrilled for him.

"Ya think yer clever, don't ya?" His hands rest on his hips as he tilts his head down to look at me over the top of his glasses.

Giving him my best smile, I hop down from the stepladder, garland forgotten, and say, "I don't think it, I know it. Now 'fess up. Who is it? Do I know them? How'd you meet?"

"Hold yer horses," Pat grumbles. "One question at a time. And this information goes nowhere, ya hear? This is a…newer…development."

I cross my hand over my chest. "Cross my heart. I won't tell a soul."

He gives me a hard look, but then his lips start to tip up in a smile. Next thing I know, he's positively beaming at me.

"Her name is Sondra, and she's my next door neighbor. She moved here from Indiana last month, and I s'pose ya could say we've hit it off rather well, so we have."

"I'd say! Especially if just the mention of her makes you blush like a school girl!"

I've never seen Paddy so flustered and yet, so happy. He deserves it.

"When can I meet her? She knows we're practically family, right?" The look I give him implies that she had better know.

Pat chuckles and turns to shuffle back toward the bar. "Aye, she knows. And they'll be in this next week."

"They?"

"Sondra's grandson is coming to visit her," he informs me, hoisting himself onto a bar stool. "I asked her to bring him by some evenin' so I could meet the lad. They're very close. I'm going to ask Norah and Eamon to swing by as well."

Pat claimed Eamon, Norah, and me as his own from the very beginning, always calling us his kids. Despite what he says, this must be serious, or moving in that direction, if he wants to introduce us to his lady love.

"I'm happy for you, Paddy," I tell him with a soft smile, which he returns before casting a glance at the picture of him and late wife, Ellie, hung above the bar.

"Ach, I know she'd want me to be happy too. But I can't tell ya how many times I've almost ended things with Sondra outta fear of disrespecting my sweet Ellie's memory." He pulls a handkerchief from his pocket to dab at his eyes.

Stepping up behind him, I throw my arms around his neck, hugging him tight and resting my cheek to the top of his head. His weathered hand lifts to rest on my forearm. Paddy loved Ellie more than life itself. She passed away in Ireland, and he left for the States just a few years later to be nearer to their two sons that came over for med school. Eamon and Norah's wedding was the first time he'd set foot in Ireland since.

The day he decided to visit her grave, I offered to go with him, but he wanted to make the trek alone. I can't say that I blame him. I imagine it would feel almost like a reunion. The thought gets me choked up just thinking about it.

Ireland is special, I'll admit it. While the people play a huge part, it's more than that. The land itself is magic. You can feel it in the briny sea air, hear it pass through the tall grass in an open field, and smell it in the ever present rain. I've only been one time, but the moment I stepped out of the airport, I knew I'd keep a part of it, however small, with me for the rest of my life.

Chapter Fourteen

Rowan

My mind is still spinning over my encounter with Alicia at the fecking country club. She never did tell me why she took a job there, but the clues all point to her struggling with money. I figured that was the case after her fussin' about not leaving O'Nelly's to get her sister because of wages. She's the hardest worker I've ever met, and yet making ends meet is still a challenge. It's bollocks. I will find a way to help her, but I'll have to be so careful in how I do so. She'll not take charity.

I left the lunch with the team's owner and immediately sought out Eamon and Teagan. I miss them more than I'll ever let on, so when I'm in town, I try to meet up with them at least once. Today, we're meeting at the school Eamon's been teaching and coaching at. Never thought he'd actually stop playing footy, but coaching seems to suit him.

By the time I arrive, Teagan is already there, observing the kids practicing on the pitch. He steps in from time to time to work with their goalies because he's good to his core. Both of my mates are. I can't say that I've ever had a strong desire to be around kids like they do. I don't hate kids by any means, I just spent all of my time since leaving Ireland focusing on my own pursuits. Anything to separate me from the life I left behind.

"There he is!" Teagan calls when he sees me.

I'm walking the perimeter of the pitch, watching the players' footwork and mentally noting small ways they could change it up to get the results they're working toward. Nothing huge. Eamon's doing grand with them.

"What's the craic, boyos?" I greet them, clasping hands and giving quick hugs. "Ready for me to teach the young wans how to really play footy yet?"

I love giving people shite.

"Fuck off," Eamon quips. "What, you think because you're some big shot pro footballer you know a thing or two?"

"Aye, to be sure. I'm no rookie, Kennedy."

"That St. Louis game was brutal," Teagan interjects. "You and Willis played grand, but Marcos was way off. I've heard Layla yell at her brother before, but she never gets worked up when we watch him on the telly. How he didn't hear her through the screen is beyond me."

I huff a laugh thinking of Teag's mot eatin' the head off my teammate next time we're all together. Can't say he doesn't deserve it.

"Yeah, not sure where his head was, but it definitely wasn't on the pitch. Probably has to do with that lass of his he's been grovelin' after," I offer, deciding to fuck with them a bit., "Seems like something you lads do when a wagon's involved."

"Oy!" They both answer in unison, turning to glare at me.

"Tell me I'm wrong. Go on. You both know you'd be crawlin' on your bellies if Norah and Layla asked you to."

My mates grumble their agreement, and I think I've won until Eamon opens his mouth. "Speaking of women we grovel for, what's the status with Alicia?"

I'm inclined to tell him to feck off, but realize that I actually do want to get their take on the situation. Not here, though.

Keeping my eyes zoned in on the kids on the pitch, I let my mates in. "I, uh, I wouldn't mind gettin' your advice on that, actually. Can we meet up for a pint later?"

I feel the way their eyes land on me, the shock rolling off of them in waves. I can count on one hand the amount of times I've been serious with them about, well, anything.

Teagan clears his throat. "Sure, yeah, we can do that. Meet at Paddy's?"

Eamon and I both turn to look at him, and I snap. "Will we, yeah? Go to the pub where the lass in question works and discuss her? That's bleedin' brilliant, O'Brien."

"Oh," he says sheepishly as Eamon laughs loudly. "Right. Fair play to ya."

Shaking my head, I clasp a hand on his shoulder and give him a friendly squeeze. "No worries, mate. We can meet at my place. I'll grab the messages when I leave here."

We chat a bit longer, discussing different plays for Eamon's team when a commotion has all three of us whipping our heads around to the bleachers behind us. A fight has broken out between a group of girls. From the looks of it, there are three ganging up on the one in the middle—though, she's giving it back just as hard as she's getting it. For half a heartbeat, the girl's face comes into view. Black as night hair, angular face with sharp cheekbones, but instead of the blue eyes I'm used to seeing in that face, hers are green.

I'm sprinting before I can fully comprehend what I'm doing, vaguely aware of Eamon and Teagan on my heels. We reach the fight, my mates yelling and breaking up the outer circle as I immediately loop my arms around the waist of the girl with green eyes and hoist her out. She's spittin' mad, limbs still swinging, cussing up a storm.

"Alright, lass, that's enough," I murmur against her hair.

"Put me down!" There's venom in her voice as she pushes against me.

"I will, yeah? Once you calm down and I know you're not going to tear their hair out."

She fights a second longer before dropping her arms. A bob of her head lets me know she's agreeable.

"Good lass."

"Alright, you lot," Eamon demands, hands planted on his hips as he stares the group down. "Who wants to tell me what's going on here?"

Every single one of the girls looks down at their feet, not one of them caring to answer.

"Right." He gives them all a hard look. "We'll just head into the principal's office and see if we can't get this sorted."

* * *

"Sorry you're stuck here, mate." Eamon keeps his voice low. "They need witness accounts."

We've been sitting outside of the school office for the last half hour while the principal gets the story from everyone involved in the scuffle. All of the kids have been put in separate rooms in an attempt to keep them from collaborating.

"No worries," I tell him honestly. "Hey, the one I pulled out. What's her name?"

Eamon narrows his eyes as he thinks, then shrugs. "Honestly, I don't know. She's not in any of my classes. Why?"

"No reason. She just looks familiar is all."

I feel a shift on my left, and Teagan leans forward, placing his elbows on his knees. "You know, now that you mention it? She does look a bit like—"

"Alicia?" Eamon says in surprise.

Teag and I both look at him only to find the woman in question hurrying down the hall, attention focused toward the desk. As soon as she sees us, she stops in her tracks, and there's confusion written all over her face.

"What are you guys doing here?"

I rise to my feet, taking a few steps toward her until we're close enough to speak quietly. "I came by to see Eamon, and a fight broke out between some lasses. We helped break it up and are here to give testimony."

Alicia's eyes close while she takes a deep breath. When she opens them again, she looks bone weary.

"One of them was Bridget," she mumbles. "My sister. This is strike three."

Angling my head, I dig deeper. "What do you mean?"

"I was here this morning meeting with the school counselor. They told me if Bridget stepped out of line one more time, she was going to be expelled."

She drops her face into her hands and sniffles. On instinct, I wrap my arms around her, drawing her head to my chest. Her shoulders shake with silent tears, and it damn near breaks me.

"Shhh, Li. It's alright. We'll get this sorted, yeah? Don't worry, love." I run my hand down her ponytail and place a kiss to the top of her head. We stand there for who knows how long as she cries, and I try to shield her from the rest of the world. Alicia is so strong. She never wants to show a single weakness, so I know that being vulnerable right now is eating her alive. I don't know how to fix this though.

"Ms. Petersen?" The secretary steps into the hallway, eyeing us suspiciously.

Alicia pulls away quickly, wiping beneath her eyes with her fingers. Squaring her shoulders, she faces the woman. "Hi, Mrs. Stanley."

"Ms. Bowland will see you now. Bridget is already in there." She purses her lips, shaking her head slightly in disappointment.

I'm about to make a scene when Alicia shocks the shite out of me by reaching behind her to grab my hand. "Can my...Rowan be in there too?"

Stepping to her side, I intertwine our fingers and try to appear like this is completely normal.

Mrs. Stanley's eyes dart between us, then down to our hands. "I suppose so. Go on in."

Alicia lets out a breath before leading us back to the principal's office. When we enter, Bridget is sitting in a chair to our left. She doesn't look up, but there's already a bruise forming on her delicate cheek bone and her lip is split. I feel Alicia tense, rage simmering along her skin. I give her hand a gentle squeeze to remind her she's not alone.

"Ms. Petersen." A tall, elegant Black woman sitting behind the desk rises and extends a hand toward Alicia. She has to release my hand to return the greeting, so I rest it at the small of her back. The movement doesn't go unnoticed. "And Mr....?"

"Gallagher," I answer, offering my hand. "Rowan Gallagher."

Bridget's head finally whips toward us.

"Ah." She gives me a small smile, then motions for us to take the seats on our right. "Mr. Kennedy tells me you helped put an end to the altercation. I wasn't aware that you knew Bridget."

I let out an awkward chuckle as we sit. "Actually, we've never met. I'm acquainted with her sister, though." I look over to Alicia, but her eyes are glued to Bridget.

Ms. Bowland raises an eyebrow at us. Acquaintance isn't the right word, but for this situation, that's all I'm giving her.

"Right," she says, "Well, Ms. Petersen, this is an unfortunate situation. As you know, Bridget was caught fighting with some other students this afternoon out by the soccer fields. According to the other students, Bridget instigated."

Bridget bristles in her chair, but Ms. Bowland raises a hand to stop her.

"I am aware that this isn't the first time you've fought with them, and I know that blame does not fall on just one side. I'm giving you the opportunity to tell me your side of it before we make a decision. You and I both know that you're in a precarious place, young lady."

The girl hangs her head, fists clenching in her lap. I see so much of myself in her right now. Before really getting into football, I was brawling with anybody that looked sideways at me.

"I didn't start it," Bridget mumbles. "They were messing with me and I told them to fuck off—"

"Language," the principal reminds her sternly, making Alicia bristle. I reach over and lace our fingers together. Her eyes dart to mine, so I give her a reassuring smile and start to rub my thumb over the back of her hand.

"Sorry, Ms. Bowland. I was just giving you the full story. Anyway," Bridget continues, voice low and resigned. "I told them to...leave me alone, but they kept saying shi...stuff and shoving me back and forth between them. One of them ripped my jacket, and it just made me so mad, that I took a swing at her. Then, it all just got worse from there."

"Oh, B," Alicia whispers, then turns to the principal. "What story did the others give?"

"According to them, one of the girls bumped into Bridget on accident, and in an attempt to keep from falling, she grabbed Bridget's arm. The sleeve tore as she fell. They claim that Bridget just started hitting her, so they intervened, trying to pull the girls apart."

"Now hold on," I interject. "I didn't see the fight start, but what I did see was a group of kids gangin' up on one girl, holdin' her down while the others took turns, swingin' and kickin' at her. When Eamon—I mean, Mr. Kennedy—Mr. O'Brien, and myself reached them, it took both grown men to hold them back and I had to physically remove this lass," I motion to Bridget, "from the fray. And while she did get in a few good punches, she's the one that's come away bruised and bloody."

I feel both Petersens staring at me, but I don't care. I've seen and lived this scenario many times.

"Mr. Gallagher, I understand your concern, and I can assure you that those students will also receive punishment for their actions. However, they weren't already sitting on the edge of expulsion for other behavioral issues."

"Ro," Alicia whispers next to me. "She's right."

I look down at her, seeing the defeat in her eyes, and it makes my blood rage.

"Aye, that may be true," I begin, giving my attention back to the principal. "but what I fail to understand is how this incident can be counted against her when it's obvious that she didn't start it."

"Mr. Gallagher, we have a strict no fighting policy at this school, no matter the situation. All parties will be disciplined, and—"

"Stall the ball," I interrupt, leaning forward in my chair. "So, Bridget is being punished for not rolling over and taking the beatin'? A lass isn't allowed to defend herself when not one, not two, but three others are kickin' the shite out of her?"

"Mr. Gallagher, language please!"

"Ms. Bowland," Alicia pleads. "I know Bridget's record isn't great, and that's my fault. I'm not home enough. I'm working two jobs to make ends meet, but clearly I need to be spending more time with her. Maybe I need to quit my night job."

Her voice breaks, and both her sister and I look at her in alarm. Quit workin' for Paddy? Over my rottin' corpse.

"Li," I start.

"I could put in my notice today. I'm sure Pat won't make me give a full two weeks, so hopefully I can implement this change sooner. Just...*please,* Ms. Bowland. Please give Bridget one more chance."

A tear streams down her face. The love she has for her sister runs deep, and if nobody can see that, they're fecking blind.

Ms. Bowland stares at our group for a long moment before sighing heavily. "Alright, Ms. Petersen. One more chance. In the meantime, I'd like to provide you with some resources that might make things a little easier at home, financially."

Alicia's eyes drop to her hands and her cheeks redden in what I assume is embarrassment. When the principal hands a packet of papers across the desk, Li snatches them and quickly stuffs them in her purse.

"Thank you so much," she mumbles.

"However. And this is a big however," Ms. Bowland cautions, looking over her glasses at Bridget. "One toe out of line, young lady, and my hands will be tied. Don't disappoint me."

"Yes, Ms. Bowland," she mutters softly. "I'm sorry."

"You may go now."

"Hold on," I say. "What will happen with the wans who started the fight?" I give her a hard look to ensure she knows I mean business.

"Mr. Gallagher, I can't disclose that information with you, but I can assure you they will be dealt with in an appropriate manner."

This answer doesn't assure me of anything. I'm about to say as much, when Alicia stands.

"Thank you, again, Ms. Bowland. I really appreciate you being so understanding."

"You're welcome, Ms. Petersen. Please look into the information in that packet, and let me know if you have any questions."

Alicia only nods, but I know the last thing she wants to do is accept any kind of assistance from the state or otherwise.

Chapter Fifteen

Rowan

When we exit the office, Eamon and Teagan are still sitting, waiting for their turn to speak with Ms. Bowland. Even though she's giving Bridget another chance, I'm hoping my mates will be able to add a little more info to swing things in her favor.

"Mr. Kennedy and Mr. O'Brien?" Mrs. Stanley pokes her head out of the doorway. "Ms. Bowland will see you now."

The old bird bats her lashes at Eamon. He smiles politely, but I can tell he's about to crawl out of his skin. I file this away to use later when I want to bring out Norah's fire sprite. There's nothing better than getting a fellow redhead riled.

"Call me later, yeah?" I mumble as they pass by me. They both nod and slip into the office.

I turn to find Alicia and Bridget a few paces down the hallway. Alicia is trying desperately to get her sister to say something, but the lass isn't having it. She keeps looking at her shoes like they'll portal her to another world if she just clicks her heels together three times. I lean against the wall to give them a moment, replaying the whole day over in my head. Not ideal, but I did get to touch Alicia more in a handful of hours than I have in months. Is it too much to hope that her allowing it means she's ready to give this a go? Maybe she's missed me as much as I've missed her.

Completely lost in my own thoughts, I don't hear her approach me until she speaks.

"Hey."

Smiling, I ask quietly, "You okay?"

There's a bit of relief in her eyes, but she still seems like she's on the edge of a breakdown.

"Yeah. Thanks for...everything."

I nod solemnly. "I'd like to do more. If you'll let me."

She breaks eye contact and looks down the hall. "I don't know what more you could do, Ro. You literally saved my sister from a group of teenage cunts who likely wouldn't have stopped until she was unconscious."

"Aye, but I'd like to think anyone would—should—do that. You don't need to thank me for it."

"Yeah, I guess." Finally, she looks back at me, forehead furrowed in confusion. "You fought for her. You don't even know her, and you fought for her. There's a good chance she started the whole thing. The principal wasn't lying about her record. Bridget is on thin ice."

Nodding, I reach out, taking her hand in mine, and she doesn't pull away. "She reminds me a lot of myself when I was a lad. Nobody ever fought for me until my first football coach. Rather than tossin' me out of school on my arse, he made me come to the pitch before and after school. He'd have me running for what felt like ages before making me line up shot after shot to kick. He saw I had a bit of talent and convinced me to join the team. I owe everything to that man."

"So." Alicia's lips tip into a smirk. "Are you saying that I need to put her in soccer?"

I give her a cheeky grin. "Never know. Could work wonders. I bet Eamon could help sort her out. He's a good man, and a good coach."

"So are you, Ro." She cups the side of my face with one hand then stretches onto her toes to kiss my cheek. Instinctively, my hand goes to her hip.

Her breath tickles the shell of my ear when she whispers, "Thank you."

I swallow thickly, fighting the desire to pull her into me and never let go, but I release her, nodding in reply. My eyes never leave Alicia as she meets Bridget at the end of the hall.

* * *

"So, what was the verdict?" I take a healthy swig of my beer and wait to hear the outcome of my mates' meeting with the principal. After leaving the school in somewhat of a daze, I picked up a few different types of beer and headed to my flat. I should probably drive back to Charlotte tonight so I don't have to get up so early for practice in the morning, but I'm genuinely dreading leaving. I want to stay in Wilmington, just in case I'm needed.

Eamon sinks into the other end of the second hand leather sofa I found at an estate sale and runs a hand over his face. Teagan should be here soon. Said he had to do something at home, which likely means Layla.

"Bowland ended up suspending the three who initiated the fight all of next week. Said Bridget had quite the champion." He raises his dark brows at me.

I shrug. "Couldn't let her take the blame when it was clear she wasn't at fault."

"Did you know she was Alicia's sister beforehand?"

Glancing over at Eamon, I see he's watching me closely. "No, mate. Honest to Christ, I didn't. I mean, when I first saw her she reminded me of Li, but I didn't even consider they might be related. She doesn't speak of her sister often, so I think I forgot."

"I wish I'd known," he remarks, regret tinging his words. "I would have kept an eye on her. Tried to help."

"Actually…"

"What?" He narrows his eyes.

"I, uh, told Alicia that maybe it would do Bridget some good to have an outlet for her aggression, and suggested maybe she get into footy."

"Okay, so how does this involve me?"

"You're a good coach, Kennedy." I focus on the label around my beer bottle. "Maybe you could work with her."

There's a stretch of silence that's making me anxious. Eventually, I look over and find Eamon grinning.

"What?" I ask innocently.

"Gallagher, did you just pay me a compliment?"

I roll my eyes dramatically. "Feck off. Don't be a wanker about it."

He laughs loudly and I fight a smile.

"This is a big day for you, isn't it, mate? First, you ask for relationship advice, then you rescue the love of your life's wee sister, and now you're complimenting me. Who are you and what have you done with Rowan Gallagher?"

"Ah, here!" I cry in mock outrage. "Go on with ya, ya tosspot."

There's a quick rap on the door before it opens, revealing a rather disheveled Teagan. His hair is all mussed and the buttons on his shirt are all cockeyed. If I'm not mistaken, there appears to be some red lipstick smeared on his neck. Eamon and I must both be giving him a look, because he stops mid-step.

"What? Why are you looking at me like that?"

I motion to his shirt. "Did ya get dressed in the dark, O'Brien?"

He looks down, swears, and starts fixing his buttons. Eamon chuckles as he rises from the sofa and heads to the kitchen.

"Beer, Teag?" he asks, pulling open the fridge.

"Aye, thanks a million. Sorry I'm late."

I snort in amusement. "Seems like it was for a worthy cause. As long as your lady is pleased, we'll forgive you this time."

Teagan gives me a cheeky grin. "Oh, she's pleased alright. I don't leave her wanting."

"Good man," I commend, tipping my bottle at him. "I take it things are still going well with Layla then?"

"Yeah, more than well, thanks very much." He runs his fingers through his hair in an attempt to tame it before asking, "So, uh, what's going on with you and Alicia? I was surprised when she had you go with her to talk to the principal."

"You're not the only one," I confess. "I didn't even realize the lass was her sister until she showed up. Don't get me wrong, I'm glad I was able to help a bit, but the last thing I expected was for her to bring me in there with her."

Eamon stalks over, hands Teagan his beer, then reclaims his spot on the sofa, throwing an arm over the back of it. "I've never seen her so upset before. She doesn't usually show her cards like that."

I drain my beer before saying anything, even though I know they're both waiting for me to elaborate on it all. Deep down, I know they're going to give legitimate advice, and there's no one else I'd rather receive relationship advice from than these two. But opening up? Especially in regards to *this,* goes against every fiber of my being. Bolstering my courage, I lean forward to set the bottle on the black coffee table.

"Right, so Alicia and I hooked up after your wedding." Might as well get that out of the way first thing.

There's a beat of silence before Teagan lifts his arms in the air and lets out a whoop of excitement. "Fucking finally, mate! Good on ya!"

"Wait," Eamon starts. "When exactly did this happen?"

The bloke is too observant for his own good.

Suddenly very interested in the label on my beer, I spin it in my fingers like I'm reading every word. "That night. We left the reception and went to my room."

"So that's where you disappeared to. I was wondering, but figured you had a good reason," Eamon muses. "I was right."

All I can do is nod.

"So what happened after that?" Teagan questions. "Have you been secretly dating this whole time?"

I laugh because he's an eejit. "What do you think, mate? You think I would have been so surprised to see her if that were the case? Nah, she was gone before I woke up the next day. We've barely spoken since."

They already knew about our near hookup at the club over a year ago, and had tried to orchestrate a little meeting between us, but it backfired. I fill them in on the details of that night and every interaction since. Neither one of them interrupts me or makes smart arse comments like I would. They just listen as I pour it all out—not just the condensed version, but how I was all in, ready to give her the world. How I thought we were on the same page, but apparently, we weren't even in the same story.

"And you tried to get a hold of her after, right?" Teagan asks when he sprawls out in the arm chair across from us.

"Yeah, 'course I did. I called, texted, everything. I even tried to see her at Paddy's but she'd disappear into the back the moment she saw me. Before I knew it, it was time to head to Charlotte for training."

"It's hard to say what spooked her when we don't know much about her life," Eamon muses. "What was her childhood like?"

"That's the thing," I tell them, running a hand through my hair in frustration. "The only thing I know is she's been the primary caretaker for her sister for a long time, but no clue why or when it began. These were all things I'd hoped to learn after Ireland. She never gave me the chance though."

My knee starts bouncing the more I think about it, so I stand to pace the room instead.

"I don't want to demand answers, but today gave me mixed signals. It's like jumping back and forth between an ice bucket and a hot tub."

"I can ask Norah if she knows anything," Eamon offers, leaning forward to put his bottle on the coffee table next to mine. "They've become closer over the last year."

It's good that Li's found someone like Norah to confide in. I only wish she'd feel that safe with me, too.

Chapter Sixteen

Alicia

"Bridget, I have to go!" I yell over the music blaring behind her locked door.

Even though her ass was just saved from being expelled earlier this week, she still refuses to talk to me. This is normal teenage behavior, right? I was too busy raising her and providing for us to actually have a full teen experience. I didn't have to sneak out because I was the only one there most of the time, so I could just walk out the front door. I didn't drink until after high school. I don't do drugs. I guess I did have sex for the first time when I was sixteen, but that's a memory I'd like to lose.

Knocking a little louder, I try one more time to get a response. "Bridge, please open the door. Just for a second."

Finally, the music quiets and I hear the thudding of feet before the lock clicks. It pulls open a fraction, and a single green eye glares at me through the crack.

"What?" Bridget growls the word, making my blood pressure rise. It would be nice if we could have just one conversation without her giving me attitude.

"I have to leave for work."

"So? What else is new?" She starts to shut the door, but I shove my boot through the crack.

"Could you just *not* for a minute?" I plead with a heavy sigh. "I'm doing the best I can, B. What more can I do?"

She looks down at where my foot is lodged between the door and the frame. "I dunno."

"Listen," I start quietly. "Tonight is going to be insane at work, but if you want to come and hang out—just to get out of the house—you can sit at the bar, and I'll make you a drink or two."

Her emerald eyes shoot back to mine and widen in shock.

"*Virgin* drinks," I clarify, earning an eye roll in return. "You know I can't sneak you booze at my place of employment. If it were just the two of us at home, then maybe I'd make you a *very weak* margarita or something."

"Nah, I'll pass."

My shoulders droop and I release another heavy sigh. "Okay. If you change your mind, the offer stands. Kat said she'd be home tonight if you need a ride. Otherwise, I won't be home until really late."

She raises a brow like I'm not telling her anything exciting or new, which I guess is true.

"There's leftover lasagna in the fridge."

"Okay," she replies blandly. "Bye."

I remove my foot, letting her shut the door.

"Bye," I mumble, standing there for a brief moment before turning away.

The sound of her door opening has me spinning on a heel, my ponytail whipping around my face. She's leaning against the frame, gangly arms crossed over her chest. I give her a questioning glance and wait.

"Um, have a good night."

You could knock me over with a feather. My first instinct is to gasp and make some comment about her being able to actually respond in a friendly manner, but I know that will only make her dart back in her shell. So I give her a small smile and thank her. "Thanks, B."

Maybe there's a chance we can actually communicate now. My gut tells me to tread carefully, but my heart feels lighter than it has in months. It feels like finally releasing a breath that you've been holding for far longer than is safe.

* * *

Saint Patrick's Day at O'Nelly's is the busiest night of the year, for obvious reasons. It's been so swamped that I've barely uttered a word to anyone other than Pat. He's been taking orders while I fill them. I've mainly been stationed at the Guinness tap for the last two hours, pouring pint after pint of the famous stout.

A loud cheer rings out as the front door opens and Eamon, Teagan, and Ro file in, dressed in green and instruments strapped to their backs. Norah is tucked under Eamon's arm, while Teagan has a hold of Layla's hand. The two couples are so disgustingly cute together I could puke. I watch as they approach Pat, careful to not let my gaze linger on Rowan and the over-sized green top hat sitting on his head. The Kelly green button-up and white bow tie he's sporting look better than they ought. I'm distracted not by the way his dark wash jeans stretch over his muscular thighs, but by the giant shamrock belt buckle that reads, "Kiss me, I'm Irish" in flashing light up letters. I snort at how ridiculous it is, but am immediately swept back to our night in Galway when we showered together, and I dropped to my knees before him. The way his hand knotted in my wet hair as I sucked and gagged on his cock. I still get myself off to the memory of the way he groaned my name when he spilled his release down my throat.

Cold liquid spills onto my hand, jerking me from my dirty thoughts. "Fuck," I mutter, dumping the beer down the drain so I can start the pour over. Tonight is not the night for me to waste Guinness, but it's undrinkable if you don't get the timing right.

"Alicia, love!" Pat's voice calls over the noise.

Lifting my eyes to his in question, he waves me over to where Norah and Layla are standing. I finish the beer I'm pouring, passing it to the patron waiting patiently on the other side of the bar.

"Be right back," I tell the guy next to him, giving him a flirty wink.

Am I attracted to him? Nope. Will it distract him enough to keep from getting upset at my sudden departure before he gets his drink? Hell yeah. He'll spend that time checking out my ass as I walk away. I can feel his eyes following me as I make my way over to the girls.

"Hey babes," I greet them cheerfully. "*Erin go bragh* and all that stuff."

Pat harrumphs at my flippant tone, but he knows I'm just messing with him. I actually really enjoy the holiday, but teasing my Irish boss makes life more fun.

"I'll forgive yer disrespectful nonsense if ye'll go grab something' outta the office for me."

I raise a brow at him, then throw a thumb over my shoulder at the line of people waiting for their drinks. "Little busy at the moment, Pat. Wouldn't it be easier for you to get it yourself seeing as you're just standing there and I still have ten more beers to pour? No offense, girls." I wink and they grin back at me.

Pat's round cheeks flush, but he doesn't relent. "Nonsense. I'll pour the rest of the drinks. You need a break anyway. Music's getting ready to start so it'll settle down back here soon enough."

He's up to something. I don't know if it involves Norah and Layla, but he's definitely got something up his sleeve. Knowing I'm not going to get out of it, I roll my eyes.

"Fine. What am I getting and where in the office is it?"

"A mate of mine back in Ireland has a small distillery and he sent me a bottle of his newest batch. It's in the box on me desk. I'd like to crack it open for our friends here." He pulls the key to the office from his pocket and hands it to me.

Plucking it from his fingers, I take a quick glance around, checking to see if Rowan is missing. Paddy is notorious for putting people into forced proximity when he's playing matchmaker. Eamon and Norah are proof of that. Fortunately, Ro is on the stage with the other two Irishmen, setting up their instruments for tonight. Breathing a sigh of relief, I turn toward the swinging doors that lead to the back of house. Paddy's office is to my left, down a short corridor, across from a single bathroom. I unlock the door, ready to snag the box and go, but there's no box on the desk.

"Of course there's not a box on the desk," I mutter under my breath as I push the door stopper under the base with my foot, wishing for the hundredth time that he would fix this damn door. Last month, Paddy installed some fancy doorknob that locks automatically once closed. It has to be unlocked with the key no matter which side you're on. I hate it.

I begin rooting around the various drawers and shelves, only finding boxes of coasters or business cards. Squatting down, I look under the desk, remembering there's a hidden compartment. As I'm tapping around trying to find it, I hear footsteps.

"Paddy, I swear to God, if this was some kind of trick I'm quitting. Right this fucking minute."

When I don't get a response, I lift my head to look over the desk. Ro is leaning against the door frame, hands stuffed in his pockets, just watching me with pensive eyes. That absurd hat still balanced on his head. The silence stretches between us until I can't take it anymore.

"Need something, Ro?"

His brows pinch together and lips purse before he declares, "Yeah. I do."

I wait for him to expand on this thought, but he just keeps staring.

"Do you want to share with the class?" I prod.

In one swift movement, he's kicking the door stopper out of the way and letting the door swing shut.

"Ro, no! The door…" I trail off as the lock clicks. "…locks automatically."

He whirls around, gripping the handle, but it's too late. The key Paddy gave me is still in the lock on the opposite side. I groan and he turns back to me.

"Who the fuck thought this was a good idea?" He jabs a finger at the doorknob.

"Who do you think? It sure as hell wasn't me."

"Is Paddy daft? Why would he do this? Is there not a spare key in here?"

It's like a light bulb clicked on in my head. Of course. We hung a spare up on a hook by the filing cabinet. I stand, rounding the desk, and head for the cabinet to Ro's right. My heart sinks when I find the hook empty.

"For fucks sake, Pat." I growl, reaching for my cell phone only to find my pockets just as empty as the damn hook. "Ro, do you have your cell on you?"

He pats his pockets, only to discover he doesn't have his either. He mumbles a curse under his breath. "I put it in my fiddle case during set up."

"Great, so we're stuck here," I grumble. "Wait, why are *you* back here?"

Ro shrugs. "Eamon sent me to get an extension cord. Said they were in a box on the desk."

Mother. Fuckers. They were all in on it.

"Well," I say, moving back to the desk and flopping into the chair. "Might as well make yourself comfortable. I have a feeling we'll be here for a while."

Chapter Seventeen

Alicia

Rowan takes a seat on the opposite side, legs spread wide as he sinks down into a slouch. After removing the hat and tossing it onto the desk, he releases a heavy sigh as his head drops to rest on the back of the chair. I watch his eyes close and throat bob as he swallows. From there, I follow the lines of rose tattoos on his neck until they dip below the collar of his shirt. The white bow tie is slightly crooked, and my fingers itch to set it straight. His broad chest and shoulders rise and fall with each steady breath. As my gaze travels down his torso, I attempt to block the images of his sculpted abs, but I fail miserably. I remember every detail-every dip and line of the muscles he's worked so hard for, the way my fingernails lightly scraped over his skin and how the dips of him felt under my tongue.

When his lips had ghosted across mine in the bathroom at the country club, my heart rate spiked, and the desire I've fought to keep at bay rattled against the bars of the cage I stuffed it in after Ireland. If I had allowed myself to remember the way our mouths fused—and the way he tastes—it would have been all over.

"Eyes are up here, hen."

There's no hiding the way my face heats at being caught, but I roll my eyes and nod toward his waist. "Hard to ignore the flashing billboard on that belt."

Ro glances down at his belt buckle before the corner of his mouth tips up in a smirk. "Then it's doing its job."

I scoff. "Drawing attention to your dick?"

"Worked on you, didn't it?"

Yes.

"You wish." The words snap between us as I cross my arms over my chest. Ro's gaze settles on the exposed skin there, and it takes everything to hold a shiver at bay.

"Aye. I do."

Choosing to ignore that, I blurt out the first thing that comes to mind. "Saw you had a good time in St. Louis last week." Regret washes over me as I see his reaction.

"If by *good time* you mean us losin' the match," his amber eyes shoot to mine. "Then sure, yeah. It was grand." His voice drips with sarcasm.

"No," I start. I really should keep my mouth shut, but this whole situation has my anxiety spiking. "Afterwards. At the bar. Someone posted pictures of you and a blonde all cozy."

The notification hit my phone late that night. I was working during the game, but I always check the highlights and look for footage online. It's a weakness I'll never admit to. That and how I have my phone set to notify me anytime Rowan's name comes up on the internet. It's not healthy, I know. The image showed him sitting at a bar, looking absolutely fuckable in all black... and a pair of glasses I didn't even know he owned. His elbows were propped on the counter, grinning wickedly at some tattooed blonde with huge tits, who was leaning toward him, manicured fingers brushing the top of his hand.

Rowan angles his head to the side, brows furrowing as he searches my face. "You mean Fiona?"

Scowling, I examine the chipped paint on my own nails. "I don't know her name. And I don't care. I'm just making conversation."

There's a long pause. I can feel his eyes boring into me from across the desk, but I refuse to look up because I know my emotions are running wild tonight. After seeing Ro at work earlier, the incident with Bridget, and the way I broke down in front of him, I don't trust myself to keep the walls up.

"Right. Well, she was a good Irish lass who knew her way around a tap." There's a hint of mischief in his voice that has me doing exactly what I was determined not to do—look at him.

My eyes burn, either from anger or devastation, I don't know, but the mirth in his own fades quickly. He doesn't owe me anything. Just because we spent one night together doesn't mean that either of us will be celibate for the rest of our lives. We're both free to sleep with whomever we want to, but damn if it doesn't tear my heart out.

"Ah, shite." Rowan leans forward in the chair, propping his elbows on his knees. "No, I didn't mean my…I meant an actual tap. She poured the second best Guinness I've had since coming to the States."

I wave a hand in his direction, trying to play it off as nothing, while also breathing a huge sigh of relief.

A fake grin is plastered on my face as I try to diffuse the situation. "It's fine, Ro. As long as I still pour the first best Guinness, I'm cool."

He pins me with a look I can only describe as anguished. "You'll always be the first, a chéadsearc."

There's that name again.

I still don't know what it means. Forget about searching the internet for the definition; I don't even know how to spell it.

We stare at each other for a long moment, my heart racing in my chest. The conversation I know we need to have is looming over us, but I can't make myself speak the words. I don't even know what I'd say.

Hey, remember that time we fucked in Ireland, and I left you high and dry?

Yeah, the truth is that I realized I'm in love with you and probably always have been and that scares the ever-loving shit out of me. I'm broken and don't know how to love you the way you deserve. I don't even love myself. And rather than risk hurting either of us, it's just easier for me to keep you at arms' length.

Turns out I don't need to say anything, "Will you talk to me now? Please?" Rowan keeps his voice soft as he asks for my input.

I open and close my mouth several times as I try to formulate the words, but I can't do it. I look away like the coward that I am. A heavy sigh leaves him, and the old chair creeks as he adjusts his body. Or at least that's what I think he's doing, when suddenly the chair I'm sitting in spins, and I'm face to face with that godawful belt buckle.

"Ro —".

"No, Alicia," he snaps, squatting down and leveling me with his hard gaze before releasing the chair. One hand goes to run down his face while the other clenches at his side. "I've given you space and time to sort through whatever it is that scared you off, but I'm not waiting any longer. I thought that night was a turning point for us." His large palm rubs his defined jaw. "Fuck, I *knew* it was. So imagine my disbelief when I woke up to a cold bed. Do you even know how terrifying and painful it was? Especially when you wouldn't return my calls?"

I wince because the thought has plagued me with guilt for months now. I knew leaving would hurt him, but not as much as being with me would. My eyes close because I can't stand to see the pain in his eyes.

"Then yesterday," he confides gently as he sinks to his knees in front of me, cracking something inside me as he does. "Yesterday was the first time I've been able to touch you. Hold you. And it felt…it felt like *home*, Li."

My eyelids snap open, and our gazes lock. It *did* feel like home. Being wrapped in his embrace felt like finally stepping foot onto solid ground after holding on to a lifeboat during a hurricane.

A dormant ember flares in my chest, the burn is both excruciating and euphoric. The feeling is similar to the way I feel when I'm getting a tattoo. The needle pierces the skin, injecting ink into the wound, and while it stings, it makes you feel almost powerful because you know that it serves a purpose.

You know that this pain is creating something beautiful.

Swallowing my pride and nearly choking on it, I whisper, "I know."

Rowan's ginger brows lift in shock. "Sorry?"

"It felt like home to me too."

A myriad of emotions flashes over his handsome face before settling on relief.

"Thank fuck," he breathes, then his hands are cupping my face and his lips are on mine.

If I thought being in his arms felt like home, it's nothing compared to this. A needy moan slips from me when Rowan forces my mouth open and our tongues meet. It's been too long, but feels like we never stopped.

Chapter Eighteen

Rowan

When I walked into Paddy's tonight, I expected to play some music, drink a pint or two, laugh with my mates, and maybe find a minute to talk to Alicia. The very last thing I expected to find was myself locked in the office kissing her.

Rationally, I know this isn't the time for all the ways I want to consume her, but fuck if I can remember the reasons why. I'm not gentle as I pry her red lips apart and possess her mouth. My tongue battles with hers, Alicia doesn't surrender—she fights—and that gets me fired up. When her nails dig into my hair, abrading my scalp, I drop my hands from her face to slide them under her arse, lifting her from the chair to plant her on the desk. Not once do her lips fall from mine.

Thank fuck for the cropped tank she's wearing, because it provides easy access for my hand to slide under the fabric. She's not wearing a bra. *Fucking hell.* I palm her breast, brushing my thumb over her nipple, only to find something cold and metallic. My cock jumps, and I jerk back.

"Is that a nipple piercing?"

Alicia's lips tip up into a smirk. "Surprise?"

I yank the bottom of the top up, ample breasts spilling into view. *Fuck me.* Both of them are pierced—a silver barbell through each nipple.

"Christ. It's not even my birthday."

Bending slightly, I latch onto a rosy nipple with my teeth, pulling until I meet the resistance of the piercing. Alicia moans, and the sound is so sweet and sinful. Her head falls back as I lavish her, alternating between sucking, licking, and biting. I'm about to rest her spine against the desk so I can remind myself just how sweet her pussy tastes when she shoves at my chest, slipping between us. She sinks to her knees in front of me, tits still hanging out. Those barbells glint from my saliva, and my cock throbs painfully behind my zipper at the sight.

Alicia doesn't say a word as she swiftly undoes the belt buckle that's still flashing like the fucking billboards in Vegas. Once she finally frees my erection, her tongue darts out to lap up the pre-cum beading on my tip before opening her mouth wide to swallow my cock. I curse under my breath when I bump the back of her throat, wrapping her long ponytail around my hand. When her eyes drift shut, I give it a sharp tug.

"Eyes on me, hen." My voice is low and unrecognizable. Something about getting this lass on her knees after all of the fighting she's done makes me feral.

When she narrows her eyes at me, using her teeth to scrape along the underside of my cock, it's nearly my undoing. Inhaling deeply through my nose, I tighten my hold on her hair and start fucking that cheeky mouth of hers with wild abandon. She's gagging around me, eyes watering, but she gives as much as she gets.

"That's a good lass," I praise her roughly. "I love the way that bratty mouth feels wrapped around my cock."

Alicia whines, and I see her hand slip down toward her core. Any other time, I'd tell her to work that pussy like I'm working her mouth. But if she's going to get off tonight, it's going to be the result of my fingers, mouth, or cock. Preferably all three.

"Don't you dare touch yourself, darlin'. Put your hands on me and leave them there."

Her eyes blaze with challenge before I feel fingernails dragging up my inner thigh. I grunt when I feel her cup my balls in her hand, squeezing a little harder than necessary. Releasing her hair to brace the back of her head, I hold her to me while pumping into her mouth.

I'm so close.

"I'm going to come," I grind out. "So if you don't want it shooting down your throat, you better tell me now."

She snakes a hand around to grab my arse, pulling me closer like I just did to her. That's all it takes. With an incoherent shout, I spill my release, mesmerized by the way she swallows while still keeping her eyes pinned on me. With a pop, she pulls herself off my cock, but I don't give her a chance to do anything else before I'm hoisting her from the ground and depositing her on the desk. We grapple with the button of her pants, and once it's loose, she wiggles her hips as I yank both the pants and the scrap of fabric she calls underwear down to her ankles. I can't fully remove them because of her boots, so I duck my head underneath, coming through the middle of her legs. She spreads them as far apart as she can before digging her fingers in my hair, guiding me to her pussy.

Yes ma'am.

The moment my tongue touches her clit, she starts moaning. "Oh, god, yes. Yes, Ro!"

I feast on her like a man starved, lapping, sucking, and nibbling. In a way, I am. I've been starving for her for months, and now that the taste of her is on my tongue, I never want to stop. She's squirming against my face, pulling me as close to her as I can possibly get as she chases her orgasm. I don't take my eyes off her for a moment, enraptured with the way her face contorts as it builds and the way her still exposed breasts sway with her movements.

"Fuck, Rowan. I'm so close. Please don't stop!" She sobs the words, begging for me to give her what she wants.

I couldn't stop even if I wanted to—which I definitely do not. A bomb going off couldn't pull me from Alicia right now. Her thighs are starting to quiver, a dead give away that she's on the edge. I work two fingers into her pussy as I suck on her clit. Curling them inward, I rub her G-spot and she detonates, screaming my name as she comes. I don't stop until her body sags, and she's gasping for breath. With a final lick, I shimmy out from beneath her legs then stand to kiss her, capturing her mouth with mine so she can taste herself on my tongue.

When I finally pull away, she's staring at me with wide blue eyes, flushed cheeks, and swollen lips. She's so fucking gorgeous. Silence seeps into the room as I help her back into her pants. I'm stunned when she slides off the desk, loops her arms over my shoulders, and buries her face in my neck. Hugging her back, I savor the way she relaxes into me. We stand there for long moments, just holding each other.

"I've missed you," Alicia finally whispers.

Swallowing thickly, I squeeze her a little tighter. "Aye, I've missed you too."

There's a pause before she asks, "Now what?"

"What do you mean, love?"

She pulls back enough to peer up at me, brows furrowed. "What does this mean for us?"

Loose strands of hair frame her face and I brush some behind her ear as I gather my thoughts. I could take the easy way out and ask what she wants, but not tonight.

"This, darlin'," I start slowly, bringing my hand to grip her chin between my thumb and forefinger, "means that I'm done letting you run from me."

Chapter Nineteen

Alicia

Sometimes I think back on those early years and realize that I probably should thank my father for being put in prison, and my mother for abandoning us, leaving me to care for a sister twelve years younger than myself. At least with Mom gone, the house was relatively peaceful, and for the first time in eighteen years, I actually felt safe within its walls. Was it easy raising a six-year old while trying to graduate high school and working two jobs to pay the bills? Absolutely not. But we at least had a fighting chance at a somewhat normal life. We consistently had a pantry full of food, the house was clean and in good repair, and the routine we had in place worked well for us.

Bridget came into the world red-faced and inconsolable. She was so tiny—too tiny, even for an infant. Mom told the doctor she was a month early and that's why she was such a small baby, but we all knew it was because she'd been using since before she was pregnant. When Mom used, she didn't eat. The most I ever saw her eat throughout her entire pregnancy was for the two weeks after she found out she was pregnant. She swore up and down that she was quitting for good and going to turn her life around. Since Dad was back in jail, drugs weren't as prominent in the house, so it was easier for her. The first few days were great. She was engaged and fun. We baked cookies, played outside, and watched movies together. Then the withdrawals started, and it was hell. By the end of the second week, even I wanted her to do drugs just so she'd stop screaming at me.

Mom didn't go to the doctor once. She never had an ultrasound or exams, so the sex of the baby was a surprise. I knew in my heart I was getting a sister, and that as soon as she was born, she'd be *my* baby. Mom couldn't take care of herself, let alone two kids. I was used to providing for myself, though. By the time I was six years old, I could make macaroni and cheese, do laundry, and get myself ready for school. I'm sure it was just so she'd have hours of uninterrupted time to get high, but the one thing my mother did do right was put me in school. I rarely missed a day. Not only because I was guaranteed two meals, but the environment was safe. I thrived in the classroom and never had my fill of books. Learning to read was the greatest blessing of my life. Until Bridget.

During the days of detoxing the drugs from my baby sister's system, the only person who could quiet her screams, coax her to take a bottle, and soothe her to sleep was me. The moment I picked her up and cradled her in my arms, the wailing would turn to whimpers before her eyes would drift closed. I would sing "You Are My Sunshine" to her so many times a day that it became involuntary. I wouldn't even realize I was singing until Mom would yell at me to shut up.

Bridget was fortunate to not have any serious or obvious complications from the narcotics that coursed through her body while in the womb. Apart from the expected withdrawals, all of her behavior during the first two years of her life was relatively normal. Maybe she had a few more tantrums than the average toddler, and her speech took a little longer to make its appearance, but nothing seemed out of the standard brackets for her age group. It wasn't until she reached age four that I began to notice changes in her demeanor. She was constantly in motion, fidgeting or pacing around the room when she was agitated, along with increased impulsivity and heightened emotional reactions. I'd learned enough about ADHD from fellow students and the internet to suspect that my sister fell into that category. We didn't have insurance though, so seeking help was out of the question. After copious amounts of research, I had an arsenal of tips and tricks to help Bridget; it seemed to help for a while. Then puberty hit, and with the onslaught of hormones, everything changed. Gone was the sweet little girl that followed me everywhere, letting me read stories to her every night. In her place was a rage-filled and impulsive preteen who seemed to live to make life harder for both of us.

Everything was a battle. Showering. Eating. Picking up around the house. Going to school, *staying* in school, and keeping up with homework. The first time the school called to question the string of unexcused absences, I felt utterly hopeless. Trying to check my anger, I calmly asked Bridget about missing her classes, and she lied right to my face. We never lied to each other. It was our *thing*—being honest, always. That day, a crack formed in the foundation of our relationship. I should have handled things better. Filled the gap with love and understanding. But instead, I flew off the handle, and like a jackhammer, I made the crack bigger.

As I stand here in Rowan's arms, hearing him say he's no longer letting me run from him, my first instinct is to bristle and tell him that he doesn't *let* me do anything. But a niggling voice in my brain tells me he's doing what no one has ever done before: he's fighting *for* me, rather than against me.

I don't know what to do with that, so I fall back on sarcasm.

"Does that mean you're going to tie me up?"

Ro doesn't miss a beat. "I knew you would be into bondage."

Snorting indelicately, I slide my arms from around his neck, placing my hands against his broad chest. He releases my face, taking one of my hands in his and turning it to place a kiss to my inner wrist like he did the other day. It's such a tender gesture, completely opposite of what that skilled mouth just did to my pussy.

I'm about to make another smart ass comment when the door to the office comes flying open and Paddy bursts in, mischief written all over his face. I start to break out of Ro's arms, but he holds me tight. My face heats when Paddy's eyes land on the desk where what used to be a neatly stacked pile of papers is now strewn all over.

"Alicia, love. I just remembered that I took that bottle home with me the other day! Apologies, lass, for sending you on a wild goose chase!"

I glare at him.

"Rowan, lad, that was mighty kind of you to offer your assistance. I only wish it hadn't been a fruitless endeavor," Paddy goes on.

"Aye, always happy to help when and where I can." Ro smirks, playing along. "I wouldn't say it was a fruitless though. I ended up finding something a wee bit better anyway."

I could kill him.

"Is that right? Well, then not a total waste then, yeah?" Paddy winks at us.

"Not a bit," Ro agrees.

"Grand! I'll need ya back on the tap now, love. It's starting to get a bit rowdy out there. This old fella can only pour so many pints before he needs a bit of a rest."

He's so full of it, but I roll my eyes and untangle myself from Rowan. As I pass by my boss, I let him have a piece of my mind. "I would have been out sooner if someone hadn't taken the extra key from the hook."

He just chuckles and squeezes my elbow. Once I'm in the hallway, I hear him say under his breath to Rowan, "Be good to her, lad."

"Aye, you have my word."

* * *

By the time I make it back to the bar, it's absolute chaos in the pub. People are packed in like sardines, surely breaking some fire code. There's a line formed by the register of people wanting to close out their tabs and another line waiting to have their orders taken.

"Fuck my life," I mutter under my breath as I assess where to begin. Thankfully, everyone seems to be in good spirits.

Putting aside what just happened in the office with Ro, I switch into work mode. I alternate between taking orders, pouring copious amounts of beer, and cashing out tabs until finally Paddy joins me. Mixing and pulling drinks is something I could do in my sleep, but I'm relieved when he takes over the register.

I feel when Rowan emerges from the swinging doors. Glancing over, I give him a small smile, noticing that his hair is still mussed from the work of my hands. He grins and winks at me before taking to the stage again. I'm expecting Eamon and Teagan to join him, but am surprised to find Ro picking up Eamon's guitar and slinging the strap over his head. He strums the strings and adjusts the tuning before stepping up to the mic. Nervous energy courses through me. I didn't know he could play anything but the fiddle, but he appears just as comfortable with the guitar as he does the other.

Clearing his throat, he address the crowd. "Good evenin', folks. Are we havin' a good time?" A deafening cheer rings out that can probably be heard from space. He chuckles lowly before continuing. "Aye, I'd say we're doin' grand, yeah? Alright, for those that don't know, I'm Rowan Gallagher—"

Another loud cheer with a few whistles from a group of girls close to the stage sound, sending a wave of possessiveness over me that makes me nearly drop the martini I'm handing to the man across from me.

"Sorry," I mutter, reaching for a towel to wipe up the bit that splashed over the side. Once he turns, I direct my glare back to the group of blondes making grabby hands for my...Rowan.

"Right," Ro goes on, refusing to acknowledge them, which is almost as shocking as my reaction considering his love for attention. "Normally, you'll find me playin' the fiddle and maybe doin' some backup vocals for my mate, Eamon, but tonight I've got somethin' else for you all. You see, there's a song that needs to be sung for a lass here tonight. I won't tell you who, or she'd have my bollocks, and I rather like 'em where they are, yeah?"

I chuckle along with the crowd this time, because he's right. I absolutely would cut his balls off and hang them from my rear view mirror.

Ro looks directly at me and winks before saying, "So without further ado, this is *My Wild Irish Rose*."

Chapter Twenty

Rowan

"If you listen, I'll sing you a sweet little song,
Of a flower that's now drooped and dead.
Yet dearer to me than all of its mates,
Though each holds aloft its proud head.
Twas given to me by a girl that I know,
Since I've met her I've known no repose."

As with any good Irish song, there are different versions. The adaptation I grew up on speaks openly of loving the lass in question. While my heart tells me to yell it from the rooftops, my head is telling me to stall the ball. Before I go and start dropping the L-word, I need to figure out exactly what that means. What does it mean to love someone romantically?

Christ, I don't even know what being in a relationship is like. Sure, I've watched Eamon and Teagan with their mots, witnessed the moony looks in their eyes, the soft caresses, heated stares, and even their arguments. While that all feels surface level to me, when I look at my mates, I know beyond a shadow of a doubt that they fully and intently love their lasses. They willingly put themselves into vulnerable positions to prove their feelings, even though they've both been hurt by past relationships.

In football, you don't take the shot unless you're certain it's going to go in, but even then, once that ball is in the air, anything could intercept it and knock it off course. It's easy to convince yourself that you shouldn't make an attempt because it could backfire, but ultimately you have to trust that your aim is true and you've done all that you can to get it to the goal. If it doesn't, then you feel like a gobshite. But when it does hit the back of the net? It was all worth the risk.

Alicia is standing statuesque behind the bar, arms hugging her middle. Her eyes are pinned on me, and even though I'm more nervous than I've ever been in my entire life, I keep her in my sights as I gear up to take my shot.

"My wild Irish rose, the dearest flower that grows.
You may search everywhere,
But none can compare
With my Wild Irish Rose."

The crowd disappears and all I see is her. It's like being on the pitch when I'm taking a penalty shot—the arena is empty, and the only light visible is the one that illuminates the net and the outline of the goalie.

"Her glances are shy, when e'er I pass by,
The bower, where my true love grows.
And my one wish has been that some day I may win
The heart of my Wild Irish Rose."

I'm still staring at her when the song ends and the audience begins cheering. It's impossible to gauge her reaction from here, but neither of us makes a move to break eye contact until some wanker steps in front of her to order a beer. She slowly tears her eyes from mine to take care of the customer, and I'm brought back to earth by Eamon and Teagan joining me on stage. The crowd is chanting "Galway Girl" over and over, and even though we've already played it tonight, who am I to object when the only black-haired and blue-eyed lass I need is in the room?

The crowd keeps us playing until last call. By the time we put our instruments away, I think we're all ready to call it a night. I have to drive back to Charlotte tomorrow and get ready for our away game in Seattle against the Sounders. The thought of leaving so soon after making progress with Alicia is a cruel form of torture. What I want to do is take her back to my flat and finish what we started in Paddy's office. We might have both gotten off, but I am in no way done with her. It'll be another week before I'm back in Wilmington.

That's enough for me to abandon what I'm doing and bound off the stage, making a beeline for where Alicia's wiping down the bar. Once I approach, I snatch the towel from her hand, tossing it somewhere over my shoulder.

"Ro, what the hell...?" She starts, but I cut her off.

"Come with me." I grab her hand and pull her behind me toward the kitchen. Eamon is back with Norah, doing dishes, just like Pat said they would be, but it looks like they got into some sort of water fight because they're both dripping. I don't have the time or desire to find out right now though. As soon as we burst through the back door, I have her up against the wall and my mouth on hers. She stiffens initially but quickly goes languid, gripping the front of my shirt. I kiss her like it's the last time I'll ever taste her lips. My hands stay where I put them on her hip and the side of her neck. If I let them wander, this will turn into another nightclub bathroom ordeal. Aye, I want to fuck her, but not in the bleedin' alleyway. At least not tonight anyway. Plus, I'm aching to explore her new jewelry again.

As the inferno inside me begins to cool, I slow the kiss until I'm lightly brushing my lips against hers.

Alicia clears her throat as she releases my shirt, though she doesn't remove her hands from my chest. "Not that I'm complaining, but what was that about?"

A chuckle rumbles through me as I kiss her mouth one more time before answering. "I leave for Seattle tomorrow and won't be back until next week."

Her shoulders droop and frown lines form on her forehead. "Oh."

The disappointment in her voice is almost enough for me to call Coach and tell him I'm breaking my contract because I'll be damned if I'm the one that causes Alicia any kind of sorrow.

"Sorry, darlin'," I tell her truthfully. "There's nothing I want more than to stay."

She shakes her head, refusing to meet my eyes. "It's fine, Ro."

Gripping her chin, I pull her gaze back to mine. "Don't do that."

"Do what?"

"Put that wall up. We're past that now, aye? No more avoidin' me. If there's somethin' on your mind, we're going to talk about it. Y'hear?"

I stare her down until she nods. Anxiety is rolling off her in waves, like a skittish animal.

"Good. Now let's talk this out," I demand. "I'll go first. Travelin' is part of my job, yeah? And the season's only just begun, but I *will* be back, and we will talk every day until I come home. Yes?"

Alicia rolls her eyes. "I'm not that pathetic, Gallagher. I can go a week without talking to you."

"Aye, I know you can, hen," I tell her. "but *I* can't and don't want to go that long without hearing your voice."

One side of her mouth starts to tip up in a smile, but she fights it back. "You're not going to be one of those stage-five clingers, are you?"

"Ach, don't be a brat." The hand I have on her hip slides around to cup her arse, making her squeak. "Brats get spanked."

Her pupils blow wide as she presses her body into mine and purrs, "Maybe I like being spanked."

My cock twitches and I'm sorely tempted to test out that claim right here. "Aye, of that I have no doubt. I'm more than willing to leave my handprint on your arse, so keep it up and you'll get your wish."

I watch her debating with herself, curious to see if I'm bluffing.

I'm not.

Finally, she sighs and walks her fingers up to my shoulders before sinking them into my hair. "I'm not going to be checking my phone obsessively waiting for your call or text. Are you going to be a pain in the ass if I don't respond right away?"

Maybe.

I shrug. "Depends on how long it takes you to answer."

She snorts. "So, what are we doing?"

Blinking at her, it feels right to give her a bit of sass right back. "Well, love, we're currently standin' in the alley behind the pub while I decide if I want to fuck you against this wall." I slow down, letting my accent thicken. "Or give you a week of edging so you'll come the moment you see me."

Alicia's jaw drops and her cheeks turn pink. She sputters for a moment before giving my hair a sharp tug. "That's not what I meant, you cad."

This pulls a loud laugh from me. I kiss her forehead and pull her into my chest. "What do you want us to be?" I hold my breath as I wait for her response, a part of me scared she's going to want to keep it casual. At this point, I'll take whatever scraps she gives me, but I'm in this for the long haul.

"Are we dating?"

"Aye, if that's what you want."

I feel her nod. "Good," I tell her, relief settling in my bones.

She asks the next question timidly, which is so out of character for her it stuns me. "Are we exclusive?" She must think I'm hesitating to give an answer because she backpedals. "It's okay if you don't want that. I don't want to put any pressure on you, I'm just trying to figure it all out."

I'm shaking my head before she's finished speaking. "No, no, no. Hang on there."

She pulls back, peering up at me with a concerned look.

"Listen," I begin, cupping her cheek. "If we're doing this, if we're going to be together, there will be no one else for either of us. I'm only yours, a chéadsearc."

The smile she's been trying to keep at bay cracks a little more. "That's not very progressive of you, Rowan."

"I don't give a flying fuck. If you think I'm going to share you with anyone else after waiting this long, you've another thing comin'."

Chapter Twenty-One

Alicia

Today's the day Paddy's new lady comes to visit. He's had me cleaning out nooks and crannies that literally no one will ever see while he flits around the pub aimlessly. He's nervous.

"Pat," I call out to him. "Would you sit down before you have some sort of medical episode?"

He harrumphs, taking a seat at the bar opposite of me. I pour him a couple fingers of his favorite whiskey and hand it to him.

"Here. Drink this, and breathe."

Nodding, he takes a healthy swallow from the glass followed by a deep breath. "You're a good lass, Alicia love. I don't tell you that enough. This place would damn near turn to rubble without you."

My eyes widen at his admission. He's complimented me before and has often joked about how I keep the pub up and running, but he's dead serious right now. There's not even a hint of teasing in his voice.

"Thanks, Paddy," I mumble before snagging his glass and downing the last of his liquor.

"Now see here! Just because I paid you a compliment doesn't mean you get to pilfer a man's drink!"

There it is.

"Good thing you're the owner and can just pour yourself another glass." I give him my best smile.

"Ach, not sure how much longer I'll be able to keep up as the owner, if I'm being honest. I'm no young buck anymore."

I think I might be the one having a medical episode right now because my heart just stopped, then tried to leap through my sternum. Taking a deep breath to calm myself, I grab a lime from the container next to the cutting board and begin quartering it.

"Is there something I need to know, Pat?" I ask cautiously.

He's staring down at his hands, completely oblivious to what I just asked.

"Pat?"

"Hmm? Oh, sorry, love. What did you ask?"

"Is there something I need to know? Is there a reason you brought up not running O'Nelly's for much longer?" Refusing to make eye contact, I keep cutting limes until there are no more.

"Nah, just an old man talking nonsense, is all." He waves a hand dismissively, but it's not very reassuring.

I'm about to pry, when the door to the pub opens, the little bell attached to the top frame jingling as it does. The sunlight has them backlit, so I can only see the silhouettes of two people, but the grin on Pat's face confirms that Sondra has arrived. He hops down from the stool and makes his way toward her. The moment they're close enough, he takes her hands in his, kissing her knuckles and every bit the enamored gentleman.

Once the door closes and my eyes adjust to the dim lighting of the pub, I finally get a good look at the woman who's stolen Paddy's heart. She's about my height, but far curvier in a way that makes me a little jealous. She's an elegant beauty with deep brown skin and nearly silver box braids pulled up into a stylish bun. Fine lines adorn her face, but they just add to her beauty. When Paddy leans in to kiss her cheek, you can tell she's just as crazy about him as he is with her.

"Hello, a stór,—my treasure. I'm so glad you're here."

Ugh, it's too sweet.

"I'm glad to be here, my dear," she tells him, then turns to look over her shoulder. "You remember my grandson, Isaac."

Isaac is tall, broad, and devastatingly handsome. He reminds me of a younger Idris Elba—high cheekbones, strong nose, and bedroom eyes. Stepping around his grandmother, he extends a hand to Paddy and lighting up the entire room with his smile. I'm not sure how long he'll be visiting, but I'm expecting him to attract a lot of attention if he comes to the pub during normal business hours. *Especially* if he keeps wearing those designer jeans that hug him in all the right places.

"Aye, of course. Nice to see you again, son," Pat greets, then turns, waving me forward. "And this is Alicia, my right-hand lass."

"Hi, nice to meet you both." I extend a hand toward Sondra, who gently grasps my fingers.

"Lovely to meet you, as well. My Paddy has told me so much about you."

I laugh. "Hopefully all good."

"Only the truth," Pat says mischievously.

I shoot him a look before offering my hand to Isaac, who surprises me by dipping his head and bringing my knuckles to his lips like a proper Southern gentleman.

"Alicia, it's a pleasure." His baritone voice is smooth like velvet.

He winks at me before righting himself and making a show of examining me from top to bottom. Years of fending off the advances of good-looking men has taught me how to hide my facial expressions well, but the attention is no less flattering, especially when they're tall, dark, and handsome.

Extracting my hand, I cross my arms over my chest, not missing the way his gaze darts down to the swell of my breasts for half a second before looking me in the eye. Sondra doesn't miss it either.

"Isaac Brookes," she reprimands, giving him a stern look when he turns. "Behave."

"Sorry, Gran." He has the decency to look ashamed, but the moment she gives her attention back to Paddy, he grins at me with a devilish smile.

He's trouble.

"Can I get either of you a drink?" I ask, throwing a thumb over my shoulder. "Wine, beer, cocktail, soda?"

"Nothing for me, sugar, but thank you," Sondra declines politely, ever the proper lady.

Isaac asks, "What's your specialty?"

"Well," I reply slowly, then give a conspiratorial look . "I don't like to say this in front of the boss, but I've been told I pour the best Guinness."

"Ach! Who told you that?" Pat asks indignantly, crossing his arms and pouting.

I give Isaac a look that clearly says, *"See?"*

Sondra giggles and reaches out to squeeze Pat's arm. The scowl melts from his face at her touch, and he lays his hand on top of hers.

"Well, I won't be a very good judge then. And, please don't be offended when I say this, but I'm not a Guinness fan." He grimaces like he's just insulted the entire O'Nelly family line.

I snort a laugh at the choked sound my boss makes. "Alright, fair enough. What's your poison then?"

"I love a good IPA." His deep voice follows me as I turn. "There's a brewery back home that makes this incredible pineapple coconut IPA. They sell out of what's on tap almost nightly in the summer."

He watches me as I walk behind the bar, propping his elbows on the surface and lacing his fingers together.

"That sounds pretty amazing," I admit. "Do you know if they distribute? Might have to talk Paddy into adding it to the menu."

Isaac grins broadly. "You get that here, and I'll move to Wilmington tomorrow."

I give him a curious look. "Wouldn't you miss your life in Indy?"

"Nah, there's nothing really holding me there anymore. Especially now that Gran's moved."

The light in his eyes fades a little, so I reach for a glass and put it under the tap of our best selling IPA, filling it to the brim. "That sounds like a broken heart to me." I slide the beer to him. "Want to drink about it?"

A smile returns to his face as he picks up his beer and holds it up in salute. "I see what you did there."

"What can I say? I'm gifted." I shrug. "Let me know how you like that one. It's from a semi-local brewery and one of our top sellers."

Isaac takes a healthy drink and ponders it for a moment before nodding slowly. "Yeah, that's good stuff."

"Good enough to leave Indiana behind?"

He gives me a shrewd look as he takes another drink, eyes studying my face. Setting the glass down, he leans forward a little. "Maybe."

The bell over the door jingles and my eyes flit over automatically, then I beam as Norah and Eamon walk in.

"There they are!" Pat blurts, pulling Sondra by the hand to intercept the couple. I watch in amusement as he shows her off like she's the greatest thing to have ever walked the earth, and maybe she is to him. The Kennedys exchange greetings and handshakes, Norah radiating joy while Eamon smiles gently.

I don't have a lot of close friends, which is my own fault, but if there was one person I know I could go to for anything, it's Norah. She's been trying to get me to hang out for weeks now, but our schedules never seem to line up.

"Friends of yours?"

"What?" I jump because I might have forgotten Isaac was standing there. "Oh, yeah. Norah and Eamon. He's Irish too. Pat is kind of responsible for them being together. Or so he likes to tell everyone. I'm technically the one that introduced them and fueled their meet cute, but whatever keeps the old man happy."

Isaac chuckles, standing as Pat leads the Kennedys over. Norah grins at me, and Eamon nods his head in greeting.

"Isaac, meet Norah and Eamon Kennedy. They're only recently married because of yours truly." Pat puffs his chest, looking mighty proud of himself.

I raise my brows at Isaac when he glances my way. "See what I mean?"

He laughs again, extending a hand toward Norah first, then Eamon. "Nice to meet you both. Congrats on your recent nuptials."

"Thank you!" Norah gushes, not so casually bringing her left hand up to Eamon's chest to show off her wedding rings. "Paddy walked me down the aisle."

Leaving them to get acquainted, I slip down the bar to where Sondra is sitting quietly. "Are you sure I can't get you something?"

She smiles and shakes her head. "I'm just fine, honey. It looks like my Isaac has taken a liking to you. I haven't seen him smile a genuine smile in a few weeks."

This revelation makes me a little uncomfortable. I don't want either of them thinking I'm on the market, but I also don't want to be rude. So instead of blurting out that I'm involved with someone, I admit something easy. "He seems like a great guy. What stole his smiles, if you don't mind me asking?"

She glances his way, pursing her lips for a moment, before answering. "A girl, of course. Isaac was dating this young lady for a short while, but was quite smitten with her. She ended things about a month ago."

I nod my head knowingly. Break up stories are par for the course at a bar, and usually the number one reason for any fall down drunk customers. That, or when Norah Kennedy challenges someone to a drinking contest.

"I'm sorry to hear that. He won't stay lonely long, I'm sure. He's young, handsome, and charming. He'll be snatched up in no time."

Sondra grins, eyes twinkling and I can practically see her wheels turning. I've seen Paddy give that look whenever he plays matchmaker. Her lips part like she's getting ready to say something, probably asking me if I'm single, but Norah saves the day.

"Hey, Li!" she chirps. "How are you? It's been too long since we've caught up."

"I know," I tell her with a pout. "I was just thinking about you earlier, so I'm glad you're here now. How's work?"

Norah is a costume designer and seamstress for the theater department at UNCW. She gained a small amount of limelight after creating costumes for a modern-day production of Beauty and the Beast. And rightfully so, because they were stunning.

"It's good! We just started working on costumes for the spring production, but I was able to talk the department into adding a few extra people to our team, so it shouldn't be quite as chaotic."

I turn to Sondra. "Norah is a master seamstress and designer at the University. She made me a dress to wear to her wedding too, and it's still my favorite article of clothing."

They don't need to know that it's because it was the dress Ro stripped off of me the first time we slept together.

Norah blushes, embarrassed by the praise, but she's earned it. "Thanks, Li."

"What a wonderful talent to have," Sondra tells her. "I can do some basic stitching, but to create entire dresses? That's quite the achievement. I'd love to see your work sometime."

Norah pulls her phone from her pocket. "I have a few on my phone if you want to see those."

"I'd be delighted!"

They quickly get lost in the collection of photos, so I pivot, nearly walking right into Pat.

"Jesus, Pat!" I whoosh out. "When did you sneak over here?"

He chuckles. "Sorry, lass." Then he steps closer and whispers, "So? What do you think?"

I smile softly. "I think she's great, and if she makes you this happy, then how could I not love her?"

A giant grin breaks over his face. "Good. My sons have met her, but they're rarely around. It's you three," he gestures to me and the Kennedys, "who matter the most."

"I think it's safe to say she's a keeper for all of us," I tell him honestly. "You deserve all the good things."

Those aren't empty words. Pat has been a constant and steady presence in all of our lives for a handful of years, and I know I speak for all of us when I say he's worthy of every joy this world has to offer.

Chapter Twenty-Two

Alicia

The man has no shame.

Gallagher: *What are you wearing?*

Alicia: *Wouldn't you like to know...*

Gallagher: *Course I do. That's why I asked.*

Alicia: *Doesn't mean I'm going to answer.*

Gallagher: *Careful, love. My palm is itching to paint that pretty arse of yours red.*

Alicia: *Good thing I'm not wearing underwear.*

Smirking, I silence my phone and stick it back in my pocket before clocking in. I'm not supposed to keep it on me at the country club, but since Bridget's fight, I can't afford to miss any phone calls. Thankfully, it's been peaceful on that front. The school counselor has been meeting with her twice a week, and all of her teachers have been instructed to email me with all of her assignments. I don't love having an extra thing to keep track of, but if she's going to pass her classes, I don't have any other options. Eamon has also been going out of his way to keep an eye on her. She hasn't joined the soccer team, but he did mention that he's seen her hanging out on the bleachers after school watching the team practice. I'm taking that as a good sign.

Rowan is supposed to be back in Wilmington tomorrow night. Admitting that I miss him feels so foreign. After years of banter and bickering that have become muscle memory, convincing my brain and my heart to behave otherwise is more difficult than I thought. Now that we're…*dating*….I have no idea how to act. The only people we've told are Eamon and Norah, and that's only because we had to sneak back through the kitchen where they were waiting to ambush us.

He's been the one to call and initiate text conversations—which he's done every day, just like he said he would. Texts are flirty and playful, but our conversations? The ones that happen usually late at night after I get off work are more serious. Serious, but still surface level. There's a boundary line drawn that neither of us are brave enough to cross yet. He's aware that I've been raising my sister because our parents are out of the picture, and I know that he left Galway to escape his father and brothers. Apart from that, we don't discuss our pasts. It got close last night though.

* * *

"If money weren't an issue, what would you do with your life?" Rowan yawned as he forced me to dream a bit.

The question caught me off guard, because money has always been an issue. There has never been a time in my life where I didn't have to worry. Even when bills are caught up, and there's a small amount of money in the bank, I'm still thinking ahead to where the next paycheck will go.

"Hmm..." I stalled, trying to think of something quickly but coming up blank. "I don't know. I've never really considered it."

He was quiet for a moment. "Why's that? Didn't you have something you dreamt of doing as a wee lass?"

I let out an incredulous laugh. "No, Rowan. I didn't get to have dreams as a kid."

"That's—"

"What about you?" I interrupted. "What would you do?"

"I'm doing it," Ro stated simply. "Playing football is always what I wanted to do."

"Did you want to play in any specific country?" Maybe if I kept peppering him with questions he would forget about my non-answer.

"Anywhere but Ireland." His voice was like steel.

"Not even in another part of the country?"

"No. I'd be okay if I never set foot in Ireland for the rest of my life." His tone implied he wasn't going to expand on that, so I let it drop. If I wasn't willing to reveal the skeletons in my closet, I couldn't expect him to.

"Alright," I said slowly. "Then if you could pick any team in the world to play for, where would you go?"

"Easy. Manchester United. No question."

The conversation was lighter after that, both of us sensing the other needed a reprieve.

* * *

Gallagher: *If you're wearing knickers when I see you tomorrow, I'm going to eat the head off of ya.*

I roll my eyes at the text waiting for me when I clock out for the day. Irish lingo is so bizarre. Most of the time I have no idea what he's talking about, so I default to being a smart ass. He likes it.

Alicia: *I can think of something else you can eat.*

Gallagher: *Bleedin' hell woman.*

Alicia: *You started it.*

Gallagher: *And I'm damned well going to finish it. Don't make plans.*

Alicia: *I work at O'Nelly's tomorrow night.*

Gallagher: *Didn't stop me last time.*

God, the mouth on this man gets me so hot, even when he's irritating the shit out of me. Maybe I have some serious issues, but I can't wait to fight with him just for the makeup sex. Hell, even the hate-fucking will be good.

Glancing at the time, I have exactly two hours before Bridget gets out of school, which gives me enough time to run some errands and pick up dinner from her favorite Thai place before she gets home. Coaxing conversation out of her is about as easy as giving Lou a bath, but I promised to be more involved, so I keep trying. Eventually something will give, right?

Once I'm in my car, I remove the country club's mandatory white button-up, revealing the black tank underneath, kick off my shoes, and shimmy out of my slacks, tossing them in the backseat. Before I can grab the denim cut-off shorts, my phone pings, indicating a video call from Rowan. My pulse thrums at the thought of seeing him. I answer, then set the phone in the holder on my dash.

"Hi," I greet him.

"Hiya, love. What are..." He makes a choking noise, and the screen goes black. I can hear him swearing in the background. Finally, he rights his phone, eyes peering through the screen at a downward angle. "Where are your trousers? And why the feck are you in your car without them?"

"Oh my god!" I gasp loudly. "Where did my pants go?" I make a show of looking around wildly for them. "I just had them!"

"You and that smart mouth. I'm not sure if I'm going to kiss you or spank you first when I get home."

A thrill jolts through me, and my thighs press together. He doesn't miss it.

"Are you aching, darlin'? Is that why you're squirming in your seat?"

"Nope," I lie, not meeting his eyes.

"Ach, you're a bad liar. I can see the way your chest is flushing. Where are you?"

"In the parking lot of the country club," I answer automatically. "I just got off work and was changing before running errands."

"Is there anyone around you, love?" His voice deepens, and I can practically feel it caress my skin.

I glance around, thankful I parked in the back of the lot where no one else parks. "No. My car is the only one where I'm at."

"Good," he mutters. "Now be a good lass, and do what I say."

My temper flares at his demanding tone, and I narrow my eyes at him. Now that I'm paying attention, it looks like he's in a hotel room, reclined on the bed with his back against the headboard. "Excuse me?"

"Aye, you heard me. You're going to listen and do exactly as I tell you." He reaches behind his head and pulls his shirt off by the collar. My mouth goes dry because not only is he so fucking sexy, but all of the moisture in my body has gone south.

"Say, 'yes, sir.'"

"Fuck you," I snap.

"That will happen when I get back, darlin'," Rowan promises. "For now, slide your seat back and move your phone so I can see all of you."

I want to fight him, but I'm also so turned on that I'm eager to do his bidding. Putting away my pride, I look him right in the eyes, letting my words purr from my lips. "Yes, sir".

He inhales deeply through his nose as his pupils blow wide. "That's a good hen."

Doing as he asked, I slide my seat back as far as it will go, then adjust my phone. "This good?" My voice comes out all throaty, and even I think it sounds sexy.

A rumble of approval sounds through the speaker. "Christ, you're a stunner. Take your hair out that pony tail and let it fall around your face."

Making a show out of raising my arms, I remove the hair tie and shake my tresses out, running my fingers through them until they're relatively smooth.

"Good. Now, grab your tits and pull on those barbells like you want me to when we're together next."

Trailing my hands down my neck, I do one better and pull the top of my tank down, letting my breasts fall out. I only wear a bra when I'm at the country club, and even then, it's more like a bralette. This one happens to be white, lacy, and see-through. I pinch both nipples through the fabric, making sure to tug at the metal, hissing through my teeth.

"Jaysus, Mary, and Joseph," Ro groans ,and I notice one of his arms moving just off the screen.

"I want to see you, too."

"Your wish is my command. Keep teasing those nipples while I get set up. And don't touch anything else."

"Yes, sir." I pull the piercings hard enough to make me gasp. Then I freeze as I see what Rowan is doing. He's propped the phone up on the bed and is standing at the foot of it, legs apart. The need to see and touch those tattoos in person is so strong, I want to cry in frustration.

"What now, love?" He cups himself through the athletic shorts he's wearing.

"Take them off, Gallagher."

"Yes, ma'am." He agrees quickly and shucks his shorts so fast, his cock springs out and slaps his stomach.

"God, I want to touch you," I tell him honestly. I've always found him attractive, but a naked Rowan is quite possibly the most beautiful thing I've ever seen.

"Soon, a chéadsearc," He promises. "Now, it's my turn. As much as I want to see all of you, I don't want to risk anyone else seeing you, so put your top back to rights. Then slip those knickers off."

Pouting, I do pull the tank back over my bralette. A little exhibitionism doesn't bother me, but I'm positive there are cameras in the lot, so better safe than sorry.

As soon as my fingers grip the sides of my thong, Ro tuts. "Slowly, love. Take them off slowly. Spread those pretty legs as far as you can. I want to see how wet you are for me."

My body heats, but not in embarrassment. I'm so aroused, a random breeze could probably make me come. Holding his gaze, I slide the fabric down, lifting my hips then wiggling them. This earns me another deep groan. His hand starts to wrap around his cock.

"Hands off," I snap. "I haven't told you to touch yourself yet."

He chuckles darkly before placing his hands on his hips. "As you wish."

When I'm completely naked from the waist down, I slowly spread my legs, but place my hands over my pussy, just to fuck with him.

"Alicia," he warns. "Let me see you. Right now."

The demand in his voice makes my hips roll involuntarily against my hand. I whimper at the contact and do it again.

"Enough," he orders before slowly growling,, "Let. Me. See. You."

I obey, sliding my hands up to my breasts and pinching my nipples.

"Fuck, look at that pretty little cunt. Dressed up just for me."

I like to keep it trimmed, so there's just a thin layer of hair shaved into the shape of a heart. That was a recent change in anticipation of when he got back.

"I'd tear up my football contract if it meant I could be there with my face between your legs."

"Ro," I sigh, one hand creeping down my torso. "I need to touch myself."

"Aye. Go on then, love. Show me all of it."

Using my first two fingers, I separate the folds, spreading them wide. I'm practically dripping.

"Fuck," he moans again.

"Your turn," I order with a nod in his direction. "Wrap your hand around it and squeeze. Hard."

Ro obeys, his head falling back. "Look at me," I order him sharply. "Don't take your eyes off of me, baby."

I hadn't planned on giving him a pet name, but if the sound he just made is any indication, he approves.

Chapter Twenty-Three

Rowan

"Don't take your eyes off of me, baby."

Christ Jesus. I've never come from words alone, but hearing Alicia call me baby has me close. I need to put the focus back on her before I embarrass myself.

Loosening the grip on my cock, I tilt my head at her. "Show me what makes you feel good, Li. How do you touch yourself when you're all alone and thinking of me?"

I watch in rapture as she keeps her pussy spread with one hand , circling her clit with the middle fingers of her other. She moves it slowly in clockwise circles before switching to counter clockwise. Her body undulates leisurely, like she has all the time in the world.

"That's it, hen. Tell me what you think of when you get yourself off," I demand.

Blue eyes locked with mine. "You, Rowan. Always you."

My heart swells in my chest at the same moment my hand tightens around my cock, making me inhale sharply.

"Do you like hearing me say that?" Her voice comes out in soft pants. "Do you like knowing that I'm imagining your fingers, your tongue, and your cock in my pussy every single time?"

"Yes," I hiss, pumping my erection languidly. "I fucking love it."

"Sometimes," she tells me in a low voice. "Once isn't enough. Sometimes I have to make myself come twice just to get enough relief."

"Fuck." The word drags from me. "I can't wait to make you come all over me. Pretend those fingers are mine and put them where I want them."

Alicia slides her two middle fingers into her cunt, moaning loudly as she does. I'm suddenly so jealous of those fingers, I want to tear through the phone and replace them with my own. This experience is already so hot, but it's made even hotter by the fact that we haven't broken eye contact once.

"I need you to come, baby," she tells me, pumping her fingers inside her harder and faster. She thrusts up against the heel of her hand and swivels her hips. "Watching you go off is so hot."

"You want...you want me to come first?" I ask in disbelief, stroking myself faster.

Alicia nods her head wildly, whimpering with need. It goes against my entire being to not get her off first.

"Please," she whines. "Sometimes I imagine you shooting cum all over my tits, and it blows my mind."

"Holy god," I choke out right before my body seizes. Yelling out some indiscernible noise, my cock pulses, and I come all over the comforter, my hips jerking with each spurt of release.

"Yes, baby," Alicia praises me in a low voice. "That's so good. I'm so close. So fucking close."

I'm still stroking myself slowly, fixated on the way her hand works her cunt. When her thighs start quivering, I know it's just a matter of seconds before she comes. Her mouth falls open as she cries out in pleasure. *Breathtaking.* I want to be right there, kissing the life out of her—or lapping up the release I can see shining on her skin. Her body goes limp and the corner of her mouth tips up in a small smile.

"Wow." She puffs out a breath as she comes back down

All I can do is whisper *aye* as I memorize everything about this moment, burning the image of her coming apart into my brain.

Alicia leans forward, removing the phone from its holder, and brings it closer to her face. Her eyes are bright, like she has some sort of secret she knows I'll want to hear, but has no intention of telling me.

"Travel safe tomorrow, Gallagher."

With a wink, she ends the call, leaving me with an urgency to get home.

* * *

We won our match against Seattle last night by a landslide. I don't know if it's because we finally found our rhythm or if I was just energized from the phone sex with Alicia, but my game was strong. I scored two of our four goals in quick succession, earning me a group tackle and lots of congratulatory slaps to my arse. After we left the stadium, I asked Coach if I could change my flight to a red-eye. He was curious, but didn't object. A phone call to the airlines from the team's agent had me boarding a plane headed directly to Wilmington a couple of hours later.

The moment we touched down in North Carolina, I shot a text off to Alicia, knowing that she'd be getting off work from Paddy's soon.

Rowan: *We won the match. I credit my game to you.*

Alicia: *Congrats. What did I have to do with your game?*

Rowan: *The pre-game warm up did wonders for me, love.*

Alicia: *Maybe we'll make it a pre-game ritual.*

Rowan: *I'm holding you to it. Are you home from work yet? I could go for round two.*

Alicia: *Don't be greedy, Gallagher. I'm getting ready to lock up actually.*

I don't send a reply because I'm in a cab headed directly for the pub. By the time I'm stepping out of the car, Alicia is locking the door. She spins when she hears the car door close.

"Ro?" She blinks a few times like she doesn't trust her own eyes.

I drop my bag on the sidewalk and close the distance between us, holding her shocked face in my hands as I kiss her soundly. She makes an adorable squeaking sound before dropping her own bag and throwing her arms around my neck. We stand there, lost in each other as time passes. Eventually she pulls away, eyes shining.

"What are you doing here? I thought you were coming back tomorrow?"

"I missed you," I tell her honestly, tucking a strand of hair behind her ear.

Alicia doesn't miss a beat. "You're such a sap, Gallagher."

"Aye, when it comes to you, I am." I kiss her again. "Will you come home with me tonight?"

"I have to go home and feed Lou. He'll become violent if I don't."

"Who the fuck is Lou?" I ask indignantly.

Her laugh is low and husky. "My cat, you idiot. Who did you think it was?"

I slap her arse. "There goes that bratty mouth again."

She laughs again, the sound lighting me up from the inside out. "I'll come to your place, if you're okay with me being around your sister." Because I can't help myself, I kiss her again before speaking against her mouth. "You'll have to be quiet when I make you come though."

Alicia pokes me in the stomach. "She stayed the night with a friend, so I can be as loud as I want."

"Grand, so it's decided. I'm coming home with you."

She snorts. "I didn't invite you."

"No, but you're going to." I kiss my way along her jaw until I reach her neck, biting gently.

Her body arches into mine, fingers twining in my hair and pulling sharply. "Mmm, you think so?"

"Aye, because you want to remember how good it feels when I fuck you, darlin'. And I'm going to make it so good for you."

Her body shudders, and a quiet groan is muffled when she buries her face into my neck. I let my hands glide down her back until I'm cupping her arse, pulling her roughly against me so she can feel the outline of the erection she's directly responsible for.

"What do you get in return?"

I bark out a laugh. "Alicia, love. You. I get you."

Chapter Twenty-Four

Alicia

Unlocking the door to my apartment, I throw up a thanks to whatever higher power is up there that my house is clean and I changed the sheets on my bed yesterday.

Rowan steps in, setting his bag down beside the door, and looks around the space slowly. It's not fancy or luxurious, but it's home, and I'm proud of it. The grey sofa is L-shaped and plush, with several throw pillows of all shapes, sizes, and colors. The art on the walls is an eclectic mix of brightly colored paintings done by local artists. The TV sits in the corner, mounted high on the wall with Lou's cat tower below it. I don't see him anywhere, so he's probably asleep in my closet.

"Want something to drink?" I ask nervously. I never bring men home to my apartment.

He turns around to track my movements to the kitchen. "Aye, whatever you're having."

I had planned on just water, but my anxiety is rearing it's head, so I grab a couple of wine glasses and the bottle of Merlot that's been sitting on my counter for the last month. The familiar motions of uncorking and pouring it are soothing. Otherwise, I have no idea what I'd do with my hands.

Holding the glasses firmly, I round the counter to make my way to the sofa. As I pass in front of Ro, I stop and hand him his wine. When he covers my hand with his and holds it there, I glance up at him. We're only inches apart, so close I can make out the gold flecks in his warm eyes. He has a smattering of freckles across the bridge of his nose and cheekbones that I don't think I've ever noticed before.

"Thank you," he says quietly.

Swallowing thickly, I nod. "You're welcome."

Finally, he pulls the glass from my hand and takes a sip, so I follow suit before asking, "Do you want to go sit?"

He smirks, then takes my glass. "No, darlin'. I don't want to sit." Placing our wine on the nearby side table, he slides his hands onto my hips. "I want to take you to bed."

I can't tell if the butterflies in my stomach are nerves or anticipation, so I just nod again then take his hand and lead him down the hall to my room. When we cross the threshold, I release his hand and move to the bedside table and switch on the lamp.

"No black," Ro remarks, his voice laced with amusement.

Cocking my head to the side, I just look at him.

"I expected your room to be dark and mysterious, like you, but everything is so...soft and light."

When I set my room up, I wanted it to be a place of tranquility, somewhere I could come and escape the demons in my head. The creams and sage greens make this small room feel bigger, but still a safe cocoon for me to hide in. Another reason why I've never brought a man back to my apartment. This is a sacred space.

"Even the dark of night misses the light of the moon sometimes." I mumble as I look anywhere but at Rowan.

I hear him take careful steps in my direction then the tips of his shoes appear. He doesn't touch me.

"If this is too much, we can slow down. I'm happy to just be in the same building as you."

My eyes snap to his. "No, it's not too much, I'm just...nervous."

His auburn brows furrow. "About what?"

I'm not even sure if I can pinpoint why. There are so many factors at play, including how monumental this all feels. The first time we had sex was so life-altering that it scared me into running away. I don't want to run away again, but will I be able to resist the fight or flight instinct that is destined to take over? Will he realize how damaged I am? How a relationship with me will never be easy?

"I don't want to ruin us again," I finally admit.

Understanding flickers in his eyes before he brushes my cheek with his knuckles. "I'm not going to let that happen, love. You have my word."

His promise seems genuine, but I don't think I'm capable of trusting anyone's word. I also know that if I push him away now, I'll hate myself even more than I already do.

"Okay."

Slowly, like he's approaching a wild animal, he leans in and lightly brushes his lips over mine, the hair of his beard tickling my skin. Each time I kiss Rowan, it's different than the last. I open for him, granting access to more than just my mouth. Each stroke of his tongue speaks a language all his own that I'm desperate to become fluent in. His hands reiterate every unspoken word as he pulls me into his embrace, flattening one hand at the base of my spine while the other cradles my jaw. I can't tell if this is his way of keeping me from escaping or telling me I'm precious to him. The first is expected, the second is completely foreign.

One moment we're standing there, getting lost in this kiss, the next we're tumbling onto my bed, hands tugging at clothing and sliding onto overheated skin. I don't know when our shirts came off, but the instant his chest presses into mine, it feels like a piece I didn't know was missing has clinked back into place.

When Rowan breaks the kiss to sit back on his heels, I whine in protest until I get distracted by the tattoos all over his torso. The Celtic Hare now has the addition of roses and thorny vines. The artist did a fantastic job of weaving them through the Celtic swirls without it looking too busy. I brush my fingers over one of the roses and realize it's the same as the two on my chest.

"These look familiar," I say smugly.

"Don't go gettin' a big head." He teases, but his eyes are still hooded with lust.

"When did you get this done?"

He hesitates, then answers quietly. "A month after Ireland. It's not the only one I got."

I lift my brows curiously. "What else?"

He extends his right arm and rotates it so I can see the tattoo on his inner bicep. I gasp and sit up, locking my hands around his arm

"That's my Phoenix!" I exclaim.

It's an exact replica, only minuscule. Small enough that in order to really see it, you have to be up close and personal.

Ro chuckles awkwardly. "Aye, it is."

I meet his eyes. "How did you remember all the details?"

Even though it's dimly lit in my room, I can see his cheeks flush. "Can I tell you after we—."

"No way!" I giggle like an idiot. "I won't be able to focus on anything until I know. Please, tell me?" I pout my lips and bat my lashes.

"Christ," Rowan runs a hand over his face. "Fine. That night, after we..., yeah. You were asleep on your stomach, hair all wild around you, and the sheets had slid down. You took my breath away, so I...I took a picture."

Stunned, I just stare at him.

"I had planned on showing you, but never got the chance."

Because I bailed before he had the chance.

"Ro," I start, cupping his jaw. "I'm sorry."

He turns his head slightly to kiss my wrist. "We're past that now, yeah? I got them as a reminder of the best night of my life, not that I really needed help remembering. It's played on repeat ever since."

My eyes burn with the threat of tears, and I don't want to cry right now, so I kiss him and drag my hand down his chest until I find the button of his jeans. At first, I think he's going to stop me because my questions killed the mood, but instead he angles his head to deepen the kiss while cupping my breasts in his hands. As he grazes my nipples with his thumbs, I loosen the button and tug the zipper down. Ro grunts when I slide my hands into the back of his briefs and grip his ass before sliding his pants down to free his cock.

"I don't want to wait anymore," I whisper against his mouth. "I need to feel you."

With the grace and agility of a cat, he leaps off the bed and has his pants removed in the blink of an eye. I open my mouth to comment, but he begins to prowl toward me, pressing a hand to my chest until I'm on my back again. I shiver when his fingers curl into the band of my pants and begin to slowly slide them down my legs, dragging my underwear with them.

"What did I tell you I was going to do if you were wearing your knickers when I came back?" He's trying to sound menacing, but all it's doing is turning me on even more.

"Something about eating me." I shrug like I don't care. "But I think your bark is worse than your bite."

Narrowing his eyes, he grips my thighs with enough force I'm sure I'll bruise and wrenches my legs apart. "You and that bratty mouth. After I keep my promise about eating you, maybe I'll find something better for those lips to do, yeah?"

I don't get a chance to respond before he's licking into my pussy roughly. My hips buck, and I cry out at the sudden sensation. Rowan keeps his word and devours me until I'm screaming and writhing against his mouth. My fingers are knotted into his hair as I hold on for dear life, but the bastard keeps withholding my release, bringing me right to the edge of orgasm then switching it up. I need to come, but I don't really want him to stop either.

"Rowan, please," I eventually beg on a sob. "Baby, I need to come. Please let me come."

One hand releases my thigh, darting up to my breast. Just as he sucks my clit into his mouth, he pinches my nipple behind the piercing, tugging it roughly and I detonate with a sound I've never made before. I orgasm so hard that I think I blackout for a second. All the while, Ro keeps lapping at my pussy and pulling on my nipple. He doesn't stop until my body goes limp and I'm gasping for breath. He grins up at me, placing a kiss to my hip bone where the tiny cat outline tattoo sits.

"Now, are you going to be a good lass and do as your told from now on?"

I snort. "Not if that's my punishment. I'll defy you at every turn."

"'Course you will."

"Ro?"

He smiles. "Aye, love?"

"Stop talking and fuck me, already."

Chapter Twenty-Five

Alicia

When I wake up, the sun is filtering through the curtains, casting shapes onto the floor as dust motes hover in the air. A familiar warmth is pressed into my belly and the loud purring confirms it's Lou. I stroke his soft fur and realize that for the first time since I can remember, I don't feel weighed down or anxious. I'm relaxed and…happy. It takes me a moment to notice not only that I'm naked, but the heat at my back and the muscled arm slung over not just me, but my cat as well, is Rowan. My eyes widen at the way Lou is curled around Ro's hand. Lou only knows me and my sister. Anytime we have friends over—which isn't often—he hisses at them and runs away.

"I think he likes me," Ro says in a deep, gravelly voice. There are so many reasons why I hate myself for leaving that night, but I'm now adding to the list the fact that I've been missing out on his morning voice. It's sexy as hell.

I grin to myself because he's still here. Neither of us ran. Rowan Gallagher spent the night in my bed and he's still here, holding me—and my cat—like it's his job. For just a small second, I allow myself to be hopeful.

"What did you bribe him with?" I ask, snuggling into his embrace, not missing the feel of his cock thickening at my back. I wiggle my ass just a little.

He makes a low growling noise and thrusts his hips in retaliation. Lou holds his head up and glares at us.

"Spoke too soon," I tease. "You're on his shit list now."

Ro props himself up and leans over my shoulder to look at my cat. "Apologies, mate, but unless you want a front row seat to what I'm about to do to your mum, I suggest you leave the room."

"The only way you'll get him out of this bed is by feeding him."

"Bleedin' cat," Ro mutters. "Where do you keep his food?"

I tell him and have the immense pleasure of watching a naked and fully erect Rowan stalk out of my bedroom, calling, "Louie, get your furry arse out here and eat this food."

Lou hears Ro scoop it and perks up. When the sound of the food hitting his bowl sounds, he leaps from the bed with a chirp and runs to the kitchen. I laugh out loud when a muffled cry of, "Ow! What the fuck was that for, ya damn demon?"

Ro stomps back to my room, slamming the door behind him, and throws himself on top of me. I scream in alarm, but we're both soon laughing. The laughter morphs into moans when he starts nipping my jaw and sucking on my neck while his hand creeps down to the juncture of my thighs. I wince a little because of how tender it is down there.

"Sorry, love. I'll stop," he says, beginning to pull away.

I roll with him until he's on his back, and I'm straddling his stomach. "Don't," I say, folding myself over to kiss him. "I'm okay."

He slides his hands up my thighs until he reaches my hips, then rubs his thumbs over the bone that juts out. Apparently, this is an erogenous zone I didn't know I had, because my eyes close as my head lolls back, and I begin rocking my hips.

"Fuck me, your pussy is soaking my stomach. That's so fuckin' sexy." Ro grips me tighter and slides me back until I'm rubbing myself on the length of his cock.

Moaning, I rock faster, my hands braced on his chest so I can grind harder. Calloused fingers begin to trace my nipples before he sits up enough to suck one into his mouth.

"Oh god, "I groan, clamping my hands onto his shoulders. "The things you do with your mouth."

"You like that, yeah?" He sounds so pleased with himself. I have half a mind to bring him down a notch, but then he shifts and his dick is sliding into me at the same time he bites the already sensitive bud.

"Fuck. Yes." I grind out. "I love the way you feel inside of me, baby."

"Aye, you were fucking made for me, darlin'. Feel how perfect we are together, how good your pussy takes my cock?"

His dirty talk has me riding him harder and faster until we're both moaning so loud, I'm afraid my neighbors will call the landlord for noise disturbance. Between the way he had me screaming as he fucked me last night and the moaning and groaning this morning, there's no way we aren't being heard. I should probably feel bad, but right now? I don't give a shit about anything other than the way he keeps impaling me on his cock.

"I'm going to come," I pant into his neck right before I do exactly that. "Ro!" I yell just as he pumps into me one more time before groaning through his own release.

* * *

After another epic fuck fest in the shower, we make our way to the kitchen for food. I'm not used to having another body in here with me, so we keep bumping into one another or brushing against the other. Each time we do, Ro kisses my neck or I reach up on my tiptoes to peck his lips. He's in my way as I go to rinse a dish, so I slide in front of him, pushing my ass into him a little. His hands fall to my waist and mouth to my shoulder just as the front door opens and Bridget walks in, coming to an immediate halt.

Ro whips his head up but leaves his hands on my hips. My face flames, and I just stand there mute.

"Um, what's going on, big sis?" Bridget asks with wide eyes, pulling her braid over her shoulder.

"Oh, uh," I stammer. "You remember Rowan from the other day. He's, um…"

"The boyfriend" Ro states proudly before releasing me to round the corner and extend a hand to my sister.

She takes it cautiously, eyes darting between us. "The boyfriend," she says skeptically. "Since when?"

"Just recently, actually," I admit, finally finding my voice. "We've know each other for a long time, but have been together for about a week."

"Uh-huh." A smirk tugs at her lips. "And you were going to tell me, when?"

I hadn't even thought about it, honestly.

"Today. I was going to tell you today after you got home. And now you're home, so this is me telling you. Surprise! I have a…boyfriend." I ramble and hold my arms out Vana White style as I showcase Rowan.

Bridget looks at Ro, taking in his bare feet, grey sweats, and rumpled white t-shirt. When she sees his tussled hair, her brow quirks. "So, did new boyfriend spend the night, or does he normally look like a hobo?"

"Bridget!" I snap.

Ro barks out a loud laugh. "No, it's alright, love, she has a point. I do look a little rough around the edges today, but," he turns to my brat of a sister, "I did spend the night. And I hope to be doing that whenever I'm in town. Is that alright with you?"

My heart melts a little.

"I don't know." She considers him. "Am I going to have to listen to the two of you going at it through the walls?"

"Oh my god," I mutter, face burning.

Ro just laughs. "I've got a great pair of noise canceling headphones you can have."

"Rowan!" I throw the closest thing to me at him. A sponge. A wet sponge from the sink. It hits him with a thwack before splatting on the ground. He stands there stunned while I gape in disbelief at my own actions.

Then Bridget does something so out of character, I'm confident I'm in the twilight zone. She laughs. Not like she did the other day with our neighbor, Kat, but a full belly laugh that has her doubling over. Then Ro starts to chuckle before roaring out a laugh I've *never* heard from him.

"Oh my god, Alicia, you should have seen your face!" Bridget gasps out, gripping her sides. "I didn't think you even knew how to be embarrassed!"

"I hate both of you," I say unconvincingly, my lips fighting to break into a grin.

"No, you don't," Ro says, walking back to my side and planting a kiss on the top of my head.

"That's what you think, Gallagher." I playfully shove at him and turn like I'm leaving, but one of his hands shoots out to grab me, pulling me back into his arms.

"Ach, where do you think you're goin'?"

"Wherever I damn well please!" My attempts at freeing myself are futile because I don't actually want to be free, but his arms are like vice, not budging an inch. When my eyes dart toward my sister, she's still standing in the doorway with a shit-eating grin on her face. "What?" I snap.

Bridget holds her hands up in defense. "Nothing! Don't mind me. I'll just be in my room." She closes the door before turning back to us and pointing at Rowan. "I'll take those headphones now."

He chuckles, squeezing my hips before releasing me to stalk over to his bag. Bridget steps aside, watching him warily. Like me, trust isn't something that comes naturally to her. While she can easily share a laugh or a few quips with someone, the moment they get too close, her guard snaps into place. I don't say anything, simply observing the way Rowan squats to open his bag to retrieve the headphones. He doesn't stand before handing them to her.

"Here ya go, love."

Gingerly, she takes them. "Should I give them back to you when you leave?"

He smiles softly at her. "No, *mo stóirín.* Keep 'em. I prefer ear buds."

"Thanks!" Bridget beams at him like he's her knight in shining armor.

He has no idea the impact he's made in just one tiny gesture. If he leaves, it's not just my heart he'll be breaking.

Chapter Twenty-Six

Rowan

Bridget reminds me so much of myself. Apart from her sister, no one has ever taken the time to make her a priority or show her how valuable she is. I'm sure her teachers are kind enough to her at school, but the only time she gets individual attention is when she's causing trouble. The only difference between us is that I had an outlet for my anger.

"What does your sister like?" I ask Alicia as we sit cozied up on her sofa.

She's nestled into my side, legs bent underneath her, fingers tracing the tattoos on my arm. I'll take her in whatever form I can get her, but this right here might be my favorite. That hard exterior she usually keeps up is soft and relaxed. Her mouth has had the hint of a smile all day.

"What do you mean?" Alicia asks, tilting her head to peer up at me.

Christ, those eyes. I'm bleeding obsessed with them. They hold some kind of power over me that I can't explain. What I'd like to do is toss her over my shoulder and head back to her bed, but it's important that she knows this is more than just sex.

"What interests her? Does she have hobbies?"

Her forehead creases as she thinks. "She likes music and…well, I don't really know. Communication isn't really our forte these days."

"Let's find out, shall we?" I ask, jumping up from the sofa.

Alicia laughs. "What are you doing?"

"I'm goin' to ask her, obviously." Giving her a cheeky grin, I walk backward down the short hallway.

"Good luck!" She calls after me, shaking her head at my antics.

I knock softly three times and wait before knocking louder. After a beat, the door cracks open and Bridget's green eyes change from annoyed to shock.

"Um, hi?"

"What do you do for fun?" I ask.

"Why?"

Shrugging, I say, "Curious, is all."

There's a long pause before she narrows her eyes. "Why?"

Bleedin' hell, these Petersen women don't make things easy.

"Look," I fire back, crossing my arms over my chest. "I'm planning on being around for the foreseeable future, so it makes sense that I get to know you better. I'm not asking for your darkest secrets. I just want to know what you do for fun."

Bridget peeks around me, so I follow her gaze to see Alicia shrugging.

"For Christ's sake," I mutter. "Alright, that's it. We're going to play a game. Come on."

"But I don't like games."

Sighing heavily, I rub my forehead before squaring my shoulders. "Half an hour. Give me half an hour of your time, and then you can go back to your room, yeah?"

There's nothing quite as daunting a teenage girl's stare. I don't have a lot of experience with teens, but I thought they were supposed to be overly emotional. Bridget's face is blank, only her eyes giving away anything, and it's mostly annoyance. Finally, she nods.

"Fine. Thirty minutes."

I throw my arms in the air like I've just scored a goal as she walks past me to the living room. "Yes! It'll be fun, promise."

Alicia snorts. "Depends on the game."

"Ach, I make everything fun and you know it." She returns my wink with an eye roll.

Bridget sinks into the over-sized armchair close to the couch and pulls her knees up to her chest. "What are we playing?"

"Would You Rather," I announce proudly, resuming my position next to Alicia.

She turns to glare at me. "Are you out of your mind? I've seen the way you play that game, and I'm not about to let you corrupt my little sister."

I clutch my chest dramatically. "You wound me! I've never corrupted a soul in all my life."

She pokes me in the side. "That's debatable."

Pressing my lips to her ear, I murmur, "Careful, darlin'. That mouth is going to get you into trouble."

"Ew," Bridget exclaims. "What are you saying to her that's making her blush like that? No, on second thought, I don't want to know, but if this is how the game is going to go, I'm out."

Alicia's elbow connects with my ribs, making me chuckle.

"Fine, fine. I'll behave," I promise. "Now, I'll go first, yeah?"

Both lasses nod their consent and I lean forward, planting my elbows on my knees. "Bridget, would you rather read a book or watch a movie?"

"Movie," she answers quickly. "My ADHD makes it hard for me to focus on books."

I nod, keeping my face schooled, but I'm actually surprised she admitted that. "Aye, that makes sense. Now, your turn."

"Um," she starts, picking at the frayed edges of the hole in the knee of her jeans. "Li, would you rather eat sushi or Thai food every day of your life?"

Alicia groans. "That's not a fair question!"

Bridget giggles.

"Fine, if I *have* to pick, I'm going with sushi."

Interesting. Did not expect that.

This game serves two purposes: get Bridget to open up and for me to learn more about both of them.

Turning, I wink at Alicia. "Alright, love, your turn."

* * *

Alicia

"Would you rather play soccer…"

There are a million questions I could ask, but the only one in my brain right now is, "Would you rather play soccer professionally or stay in Wilmington with me?".

It's not a fair question, and it's not fair of me to even consider it. He's earned his spot with CFC, and is a damn good player, but when he told my sister that he planned on being around for the *foreseeable future,* I felt almost giddy. Until I realized that regardless of what Rowan Gallagher says, his actions are what speak louder. He's never been in a relationship with anyone and travels all over the country where the opportunities for meaningless hookups are endless. He'll get bored and realize that monogamy while on the road isn't what he wants, so he'll ditch me. Which is understandable, because I'm not a pleasant person the majority of the time. I'm not warm and welcoming.

He looks at me expectantly, waiting for me to finish my question. I don't want to spoil this moment he's created with Bridget, so instead I ask, "Ro, would you rather play soccer or drink Guinness?"

He falls against the back of the couch and laughs like I've told the funniest joke. "Ah, love, I can do both at the same time. Give me a pint and a ball and I'll get it in the net while I'm drinking."

Rolling my eyes, I extend my legs over his lap, making sure to subtly rub my foot right over his dick, which makes him shut up fast. His hand clamps around my ankle in warning as he glares at me. I bat my lashes innocently.

"That's not how the game works," I remind him. "If I can't have both sushi and Thai food, you can't have both soccer and Guinness."

Ro drops his head and groans then begins absently rubbing my feet. "If I had to choose, I guess I'd pick football. I'm not after becoming an alcoholic, which would undoubtedly happen if I had to give it up."

My heart sinks.

"Bridget, your turn." He nods in her direction. "Would you rather play a sport or do something in the arts?"

Looking over, I watch my sister's brow furrow as she ponders her answer. I'm anxious for her response because this is something I don't know about her that I should.

Finally, she answers. "Play a sport. I watch the soccer team practice after school sometimes and it looks kind of fun."

Who is this kid?

"Atta girl," Ro says proudly. "I bet Eamon—or Mr. Kennedy, rather—would let you do some drills with the team."

She's already shaking her head. "No way. I don't know anything about it, so I'm not about to make myself look stupid in front of the boys' soccer team."

The look of absolute horror on her face is comical, like she was asked to parade around naked in front of them rather than kick a ball.

Rowan rubs his thumb and forefinger down the length of his beard. "Right. I'll teach you then. If you want to, that is."

"Really?" Bridget's voice is laced with shock.

"Aye." He nods. "Whenever I'm in town, we can start with the basics. Just let me know when you're ready."

She beams at him before schooling her face into nonchalance. "Yeah, okay. I'll think about it."

"Think about it while you're asking your sister the next question." He presses his thumb into the arch of my foot. I bite back a moan. "And make it a good one. Something she doesn't like to share, but isn't really a secret."

Her eyes twinkle, and I know what's coming.

"You're going to regret this," I promise both of them.

"Li," Bridget sing-songs.

I yank my foot out of Ro's hands and practically leap from the sofa. "Don't do it. If you've ever loved me at all, you will not ask me what I know you're about to ask."

"Don't worry, lass. I'll protect you from her. Go ahead," he croons.

Scowling, I grab a throw pillow and toss it in his face. He just laughs and tosses it back at me.

"Would you rather," my sister begins.

"No."

"Listen to..."

I turn to scowl at her. "Bridget Nicole Petersen, this is your last warning."

Hands yank my hips and I fall into Ro's lap. He quickly locks his arms around me, and I'm helpless to escape, but I give it my best effort, shrieking and thrashing like a rabid animal.

"Shite, it's like trying to wrangle a hellcat." Ro grunts when I bite down on his arm. "Alright, that's enough of that."

Next thing I know he's flipped me onto my stomach over his legs and brings a hand down on my ass.

I gasp loudly and Bridget cackles.

"Rowan whatever-your-middle-name-is Gallagher, I'm going to kill you!"

"No, you won't." He chuckles darkly. "Now, behave before I do it again."

For a millisecond the rage dissolves into lust, and I nearly whimper. I'm not submissive by nature, but thinking of being a good girl for Ro is suddenly very alluring.

"And it's Conor."

"What is?" I snap, attempting to free myself from his hold, while Bridget just keeps laughing.

"My middle name," he grunts when my elbow connects with stomach.

When I wiggle again, he loosens his grip and helps me to my feet before pulling me back down on his lap. Rather than fighting him this time, I relax against his chest, enjoying the satisfied sigh he exhales against my temple.

"Rowan Conor Gallagher. I like it," I tell him. "Very Irish."

He snorts in response.

"Alicia," Bridget says sharply, and I whip my eyes in her direction. "Quick, *NSYNC or Backstreet Boys?"

A choked sound leaves my throat, and I lunge for her before Ro even has a chance to register what's happening. Bridget screams at the top of her lungs and tries to scramble out of the chair, but I land on top of her, pinning her down.

"You're so dead!" I screech as I start tickling her sides. "I hope you pee your pants, you little brat!"

"Get off me! Help!"

"There's no one to save you now!" Whipping my head toward Ro who's slowly advancing in our direction, I snarl, "Don't even think about it."

He lifts his hands in defense and backs up a step. "Alright. Sorry, Bridget lass."

"Traitor!" She yells, making him laugh. "I thought we were friends!"

I don't let up until she's red-faced and gasping for breath. Even then, I'm still sitting on her, staring daggers into her skull. I can't believe she spilled my guilty obsession to Rowan. It's not really a huge deal, just embarrassing since I'm the last person anyone would suspect of not only listening to boy bands, but being enamored by them. Well, not *them*, just one.

Ro approaches and folds his arms across his chest. "Spill."

At the same time I give a firm *no*, Bridget sings, "*NSYNC!"

I make to attack her once more, but Ro scoops me up, throws me over his shoulder like I'm nothing more than a bag of cat food, slaps my ass again, then turns on his heel to stalk down the hall.

"Put your headphones on, Bridget," he calls out.

The last thing I see before entering my room is my little sister's appalled face slowly transform into a grin.

Chapter Twenty-Seven

Alicia

It's barely five o'clock in the evening and Paddy's is already slammed. I had a meeting with my manager at the country club after my lunch shift, so I was late getting to the pub. I've been serving drinks for an hour and still haven't even cut up limes. Usually, by five o'clock, the bar is completely set up, and it's smooth sailing from there.

Tonight is already feeling like we're gearing up for stormy waters.

"What's a guy gotta do to get a drink around here?" The reedy voice immediately triggers memories from years past.

Something about the tone and the way he drawls the word "drink" has me clenching my teeth. Inhaling deeply through my nose, I hold it for four seconds before releasing the breath. I plaster a smile on my face and turn to take care of the asshole demanding his drink.

No.

No fucking way.

"Hey, baby girl."

It's my father.

Older and grayer, but the green eyes he shares with my sister are clear—something I've never seen on his face before. Panic starts to set in as my hands begin shaking, and a cold sweat breaks out on the back of my neck. I'm dangerously close to puking, and for a second, I actually consider letting it fly straight across the bar to the man smiling at me like he wasn't a worthless piece of shit who gave up his wife and kids for drugs.

"What the fuck do you want?" Surprisingly, my voice is steady and emotionless.

He startles, brows flying high on his forehead before furrowing in disapproval. "Now, is that any way to talk to your old man after not seeing each other for so long?"

"I wouldn't know what it's like to speak to a father because I haven't had one. So again, what the fuck do you want?"

"Ally girl," he croons, using the name he called me when I was little.

"Alicia." I correct him. "Now, either order a drink, or get out of my bar."

A line is forming behind the man responsible for half of my DNA. Paddy is in the kitchen, making stew, and our busboy is out sick, so it's just me.

He scowls, showing no sign of budging. "I just want to talk, girl. Can't you spare me a few minutes?"

"No, I can't. Unlike you, I take my career seriously and have a strong work ethic. And, in case you didn't notice, there's a line of people waiting to order their drinks." I nod toward the customers behind him.

Casting a quick glance over his shoulder, I watch as his face transforms into the charming facade he uses when he knows he's been caught.

"Sorry, folks," he addresses the patrons around him. "This here is my daughter, and I haven't seen her for several years. You'll forgive a man for wanting to catch up."

A few people make noises of sympathy, and it makes my blood pressure rise. "No, don't feel sorry for him. What he's not telling you is that he was an absent father because he's a drug addict that never gave two shits about his family, and the reason he's been gone, is because he's been in prison."

Eyes widen at my outburst before narrowing at him. This pisses him off and he whirls to point a finger at my face.

"This conversation isn't over, little girl. I'll wait here all night if I have to, but you will hear what I have to say."

Squaring my shoulders, I lean forward, making sure he can see just how serious I am. "The only way you're staying here is if you are a paying customer, which we both know is highly unlikely, so do us all a favor and leave. Permanently."

I watch as his face becomes mottled with rage. As a child I would have ran and hid, but that little girl is gone now.

"You little..."

"Mister, the lady asked you to leave."

I was so caught up in my father's drama that I didn't even notice Isaac enter the pub, let alone come up to the bar. He stands a good foot taller than my dad, arms crossed over his massive chest, making his biceps bulge. That white t-shirt he's wearing is precariously close to having some ripped seams.

He has to step back in order to fully look into Isaac's face, but when he does, fear flashes in his eyes and his throat bobs. The coward knows he doesn't stand a chance.

"I was just..."

"Leaving," Isaac finishes for him. "You were just leaving."

With one last pleading glance in my direction, my father exits the pub and air whooshes from my lungs in relief. But then the adrenaline kicks in, and I'm shaking all over while tears well.

Warm hands wrap around my shoulders, pulling me into a soft chest and belly. Paddy envelops me, holding me tightly, and I breathe in the scent of his cologne. I've never asked him what he wears, but in this moment I realize how much I've come to associate it with comfort. It's spicy with an undercurrent of wintergreen. I bury my forehead into his chest, breathing deeply to keep the sobs I know I are building up from escaping.

"It's alright, lass. He's gone now." Weathered hands rub my back and he continues to murmur reassuring words into my hair.

Finally, I feel composed enough to lift my head. I'm met with Paddy's hazel eyes, surrounded by wrinkles he's gained not just from age, but laughter.

"There she is." He smiles softly then suggests I take a moment for myself. "Catch your breath, and freshen up, yeah? Let this old man run the front for a bit."

Normally, I'd protest, steel my spine, and get on with it, but seeing my father has shaken me to my core.

Nodding, I take a step back. "Yeah, thanks Pat. I won't be a minute."

"Take your time, love." He winks then calls out to the line. "Alright, you lot, since you've been so patient, for the next half hour, you'll get two pints for the price of one!"

Cheers ring out as I duck through the swinging door, making my way to the bathroom. I give myself a few minutes to calm my breathing, splash some cold water on my face, and wipe the smudged mascara from under my lower lashes. Tossing the paper towel in the trash, I open the door and nearly scream bloody murder when I see a hulking figure leaning against the wall by the door, arms folded over his chest.

"Isaac!" I screech, clutching my hand over my heart. "You scared the hell out of me!"

His radiant smile lights up the hallway. "My apologies. I just wanted to make sure you were alright."

"Thank you," I tell him sincerely, reaching out to give his arm a quick squeeze. "Not just for checking, but for basically coming to my rescue. That had the potential to be very bad."

He shrugs one massive shoulder. "Not a problem. I'm used to dealing with difficult people like that."

I quirk a brow at him. "Do you make it a habit of being surrounded by difficult people?"

Isaac smirks. "Something like that."

"Oh, come on," I tease. "You have to give me more than that, or else I'm going to think the worst."

There's a deep rumble of a laugh before he says, "I'm just fucking with you. I'm a bouncer at a club back in Indiana while finishing up med school. I'm doing clinicals now."

"Med school? That's ambitious. What field?"

"Sports medicine."

He doesn't elaborate, so I ask, "What are you hoping to do with that? Private practice? Work with a specific team?"

He shrugs. "I'm open to anything, honestly. There's not a sport I don't enjoy."

"What about that new dancing soccer thing? I can't remember what it's called, but it's soccer, only you have to dance the entire time."

"Discofoot," Isaac informs me, a trace of amusement in his voice. "And as ridiculous as it is to watch, it's actually pretty intense. Soccer's already a high intensity sport, but add in dancing? There's a lot of room for error, which leads to injuries."

I nod, considering the truth of his words. I'm not an athletic person. Sports and I have never been friends, and frankly, I haven't been interested in anything enough. The only time you'll catch me watching—and cheering for—a sport is when Ro is playing. And how that man plays....

"Good point," I admit, then push away from the wall. "Well, I better get back out there before Pat gets too overwhelmed. Thanks again for coming to my rescue. I owe you one."

His large hand darts out, catching my elbow gently. He's not being aggressive, but it still makes me wary. I look down at where his fingers wrap around my arm, his dark skin a stark contrast to the pale surface of my own.

"Actually." He hesitates, moving a bit closer, and if I'm not mistaken, he sounds nervous. He clears his throat before continuing. "I was wondering if I could take you out sometime."

I jerk my head back in surprise. That's flattering. Isaac is a beautiful man, and I can't remember the last time I was asked out on a date. Not even Ro has taken me out. All of our time together has been...more.

Rowan.

Extricating my arm, I smile politely. "I'm extremely flattered, but I'm actually seeing someone."

"Ah." He takes a step back, folding his arms over his chest again. He studies me a moment before smirking. "Is it serious?"

Snorting in response, I tell him that it's headed that way.

"But it's not there yet?" He cocks his head to the side. "That means there's still a chance."

A sharp laugh bursts from my chest, and I shake my head at him. "No, not really."

"Am I not your type?"

I snort again. "Not sure what you're getting at, but it has nothing to do with your looks. You could be anyone's type."

A smug grin spreads across his face. "So, you find me attractive."

"Oh please," I scoff, rolling my eyes at him. "You know you're hot. It would be stupid to deny it, but I can find someone objectively good-looking without being attracted to them."

"That's only because you haven't spent enough time with me," Isaac counters. "Which is why you should let me take you out."

I freely admit that I'm a flirt. It comes with the job, but it's time to shut this down. Even if my feelings for Ro weren't....whatever they are, a cheater I am not.

"Listen, Isaac," I say flatly. "Again, I'm flattered, and maybe if I wasn't with someone I'd give you a chance, but we're exclusive, and I have no intention of changing that."

He holds his hands up in defeat. "Alright, alright. I hear you. Can't blame a guy for trying though."

He gets another eye roll before I step past him so I can resume tending bar.

"But, Alicia," he calls after me, and I look over my shoulder. "When he doesn't satisfy you, I'll be around to make up for it."

Chapter Twenty-Eight

Rowan

"Ladies and gentlemen, we regret to inform you that Flight 1987 from Salt Lake City to Charlotte has been delayed due to inclement weather."

Of fecking course it has.

It's been pissing down for the last two days, with no end in sight. And not just rain, but it's fierce windy. I've been gone all week, traveling from one side of the country to the other for away matches, and it's putting me in a right foul mood. Normally, I live for the thrill of traveling and seeing new places, but it's all beginning to feel lackluster. When I'm not on the pitch, my mind is swimming with thoughts of Alicia and counting down the hours until I get to see her again.

I should already have her nails in my back as I'm buried deep inside her. I should be listening to her moan and pant as I bring her closer to the edge, our sweat-slick bodies moving in tandem. But no, I'm stuck in fecking Salt Lake City, Utah while it pours fecking buckets, with no fecking clue when I'll be home.

I've been sitting in these shite chairs for too long, my leg bouncing impatiently. I know it's not the fault of the flight attendants or any other person that works here, but my current state has me on the verge of eatin' the head off of all of them. Instead, I pull my phone out to call Alicia, but a text comes through from her at that same moment.

Alicia: *What time will you be back?*

I groan. Last time we talked, I told her I'd be in Wilmington before she got off work, but now it's an hour to closing time at O'Nelly's, and I'm no closer to boarding that fecking plane than I am to dancing a jig on the moon.

Rowan: *I'm so sorry, love. It's pissing rain and our flight was delayed. The whole airport is on standby.*

Alicia: *Ugh. Okay.*

Rowan: *Hen...*

Alicia: *Ro...*

Rowan: *I'm sorry. I'd already be with you if I could help it.*

Alicia: *I know.*

That won't do. Foregoing anymore texts, I call her—if for nothing else than to just hear her voice.

It rings three times before she picks up.

"Hey." She sounds off somehow.

"What's wrong? Are you okay? Is Bridget?" I demand, unease churning in my gut.

"Yeah, we're fine."

"Alicia," I push. "Talk."

There's a long pause before, "It was just a really long day. And I miss you."

Alicia being vulnerable is something I'm still getting used to. Standing from the chair, I stroll away from the boarding area toward a secluded alcove.

"I miss *you*, a chéadsearc. Now, tell me what's going on. What made your day so long?"

Another pause. I want to shake the answer out of her, but that will only make her clam up, so I wait.

Finally, in a broken whisper, she says, "My father came into the pub tonight."

Of all the things I was expecting her to say, this was not it.

"He what?" I choke out in disbelief. "I thought he was in prison?"

She sniffs and I know she's crying. It kills me that I'm so far away from her.

"I thought so too, but he showed up and caused a scene. If not for Isaac, I'm not sure what would have happened."

My eyes narrow. "Who's Isaac?"

"Oh, sorry. I forgot you haven't met Paddy's lady friend, Sondra, and her grandson, Issac."

"Hold on, it feels like I've started reading a book in the middle of a chapter," I tell her. "Pat has a lady friend? When did you meet them? And how did this Isaac fella help?"

Alicia exhales deeply in frustration, making me realize my error.

"Sorry," I apologize quickly. "Not important. Tell me more about what happened with your dad. Are you okay?"

"I'm fine, just a bit shaken."

She goes on to tell me the whole situation. The audacity of this dosser coming into her work and making demands of her has me raging. For more than one reason, I wish I had been there tonight. It shouldn't bother me so much, but this Isaac has me feeling some kind of way, like he's doing my job for me. Alicia is mine to protect and comfort. Any other bloke that thinks he can step in can get fucked.

"I'm so sorry, love," I murmur when she relays how her dad stormed out of O'Nelly's. "When I get home, we'll figure out what to do about it, yeah? Maybe I can have Eamon and Teag be there when I'm out of town."

"I don't need a bodyguard, Ro," she snaps.

"Clearly you do, since Isaac was the one that made him leave. I'd rather have someone I know and trust watching out for you."

A sardonic laugh sounds over the speaker. "I'm sorry, why does it have to be somebody that *you* know and trust? I'm capable of finding my own help—*if I* decide I need or want them. You don't have a say in it."

I can feel my blood starting to boil. She's gearing up for a fight, and my first instinct is to bark back and stake my claim. Pinching the bridge of my nose, I close my eyes and take a deep breath before replying.

"You're right, I'm sorry. I'm not trying to undermine you, hen. I just want to help."

There's a lengthy pause before she responds. "Don't worry about it."

"Li, I'm always going to worry about you. And Bridget." Shite, I didn't even consider how the younger lass is doing. "How'd she take the news?"

Her voice is still stiff when she answers."I haven't told her. It's not like she'll remember him, and it will just hurt her in the long run."

This doesn't sit right with me, but I keep that to myself. "Aye, you know her best."

We talk for a couple more minutes before Alicia remarks on how Pat is likely drowning at the bar and she needs to relieve him. I don't want to end the call, especially since she's still a bit cold toward me, but she needs to know that I'm not going anywhere.

"Aright, we'll talk later. I—".

Without any conscious effort from me, I start to tell her I love her, and barely manage to keep the words from slipping through.

"What?" She asks absently, like she wasn't really paying attention.

"Nothin', just that I miss you."

After I end the call, I stay in the alcove, replaying our conversation and trying to imagine what she could possibly be feeling right now. Had the roles been reversed and my ma showed up out of the blue, I have no idea how I would have handled it in public. Later, I'd probably drink myself into a coma.

"Attention, ladies and gentlemen. Flight 1987 from Salt Lake City to Charlotte will be boarding in an hour and twenty minutes."

Fucking finally.

Chapter Twenty-Nine

Alicia

I've had more bad days than good days in my life, but today is in the top five. As if the ordeal with my father wasn't enough, now I won't see Rowan until at least tomorrow. Obviously, he can't control the weather, but the disappointment I felt when he told me he'd be late was overwhelming. My first reaction—albeit an unfair one—was to take it out on him.

His offer to have the guys hang out at the pub while he's away was sweet, but it pisses me off that I even have to consider that. Why can't people that are supposed to be in prison *stay* in prison? If my father had been picked up for just drugs, I could understand parole, but he's a thief and violent. The world would be a better place without him taking up oxygen. Now he's free and taking up *my* oxygen.

Stepping just inside the door to the main level of the apartment complex,

I stop to check our mailbox, rifling through bills and junk mail. A letter from the landlord with a red-stamped "URGENT" leaves a sinking feeling in the pit of my stomach. I can guarantee what it's going to say before I even open it, but I do so anyway, and skim the first few lines until I find the words I knew would be there: *increased rent payment.*

"God fucking dammit," I curse under my breath while I read through the rest of the missive. When I see how much rent is increasing, I want to puke. "An extra two hundred dollars? How…?"

Groaning, I shove the letter in my purse and trudge down the hall to our apartment. The light is on in the kitchen, but it's otherwise quiet. Bridget is already asleep, if the lack of light coming from under her door is any indication. It's actually a huge relief since I have no idea how I'm going to tell her about our father. I want to shield her from him, but the last thing she needs is for him to blindside her. There's no telling how she'll react though.

* * *

I've been tossing and turning all night, sleep evading me completely. Finally, at around seven o'clock, I give up and force myself out of bed and into the kitchen to make coffee. When it's finished brewing, I pour the life-giving liquid into the Medusa mug Bridget gave me for my birthday last year and trudge to the sliding doors that lead to our microscopic patio. I leave the door cracked to let in the fresh air. There's only enough room for a small bistro table and two folding chairs. I always had plans to spruce it up, but with how little it gets used, I can't justify the money.

The sun is just starting to peek over the horizon, coaxing the midnight blue sky to lavender before resting above a line of vivid pink. It's been a long time since I've witnessed a sunrise, thanks to working late hours. I forgot how beautiful they can be. It hits me then that I haven't taken the time to enjoy my hometown in years. When did I last go to the beach or stroll along the River Walk? Hell, I can't even remember the last time I just watched the clouds roll by. I need a day off. And not one spent running errands or doing housework.

Paddy told me to take tonight off just in case my dad decided to show up again, so my shift at the country club is all I have today. I could easily work that shift then enjoy the evening, but I know I'll be too exhausted to really do anything by the time I get home. Which leaves calling in, something I never do, and probably shouldn't. No, I won't do that. Working a shift while short-staffed sucks, so I don't want to be that person.

My phone chirps from inside with a text message. Setting my mug on the table, I dart in to grab it, then settle back in my chair before opening it.

Rowan: *Mornin' love. Sorry for the early message. I just got back to my flat in Charlotte. Going to sleep a few then drive your way if you're free today.*

A smile warms my face as the universe makes the decision for me.

Alicia: *Hey stranger. I've been up for a while. No plans today. I'm calling in to the club, and Pat gave me tonight off.*

Rowan: *Calling in? Are you sick? I'll head there now.*

Alicia: *No, not sick. Just realizing I need a day off. Weather is supposed to be on the warmer side. Thinking of having a beach day. Want to join me?*

Rowan: *Does that mean you'll be in a bathing suit?*

Alicia: *No, I swim nude.*

Rowan: *In front of God and everyone?! Over my dead body, hen.*

Alicia: *Kidding.*

Rowan: *Funny. Aye, I'll be there. Let me sleep a spell, then I'll be on my way.*

Alicia: *Take your time. XOXO*

Suddenly, I'm feeling wide awake and light as a feather. A beach day with Ro is exactly what I need. Maybe Bridget will want to join us. With that in mind, I call my manager. He won't be happy, but he'll get over it.

* * *

The forecast wasn't kidding when it said today would be on the warmer side. By early afternoon, the temps are already pushing ninety and there's barely a cloud in the sky. It will be another thirty to forty-five minutes before Ro gets here, so I force Bridget to sit in front of me on my beach towel while I french braid her hair back like mine and apply sunblock to her pale skin. This kid really needs to go outside more. But then I can't really say anything, because I'm just as pale as she is.

"Do you ever think about our parents?" Bridget asks suddenly.

My fingers freeze their work for a moment, stunned by her question. I take a deep breath and resume braiding. "Sometimes. Why do you ask?"

She shrugs. "Just curious. Sometimes I think about them and wonder what they're doing, and if they ever think about us too."

"Bridge, I don't think either one of them is capable of thinking of anyone other than themselves. If so, they wouldn't have left us." I've never lied to her about their absence.

"What if..." She pauses. "What if prison helped dad? What if being there is what makes him realize his mistake?"

If I didn't know any better, I'd think she'd been present at the pub last night. Tying off the end of her braid, I place my hands on her shoulders, squeezing them gently. "Hey, where is this coming from?"

Bridget shrugs again, then shocks me once again by leaning back into my chest. Gingerly, I wrap my arms around her and tuck my chin over her shoulder.

"You know you can tell me anything, right? Just because I'm your parental figure doesn't mean my duties as your sister have disappeared. In another life, you and I would still fight, but we'd share everything with each other."

An indelicate snort escapes my sister's nose. "You mean how you told me all about you and Rowan before I walked in on your kitchen cuddle fest?"

"Ugh, I know. I know. This goes both ways. I'm sorry." She's right. I can't expect her to open up to me when I don't do the same. "What do you want to know?"

She makes a humming noise while she considers. "When did you realize you liked him?"

"Honestly?"

"No, I'd prefer if you lied to me. Yes, honestly!" She snaps.

I turn my head and blow a raspberry on her cheek for her sass, earning a disgusted shriek.

"You're such a brat," I tease, smiling broadly. "I thought Ro was hot from the moment I saw him, but I didn't start to like him until maybe a year later. He had—and still has—this way of getting under my skin. He knows exactly what to say to set me off. It annoyed the hell out of me for such a long time. But then one day, he came into O'Nelly's after I'd had a particularly awful shift at the country club. I was not in the mood for his antics. I could tell he was about to start in on me, but the moment he really looked at me, his entire demeanor changed. I can't remember exactly what he said.

"I said that whoever put that look on your face was a right gobshite that didn't deserve to lick the dirt off your boots."

Bridget and I whip our heads around so fast, our necks crack to see the only man who's ever made me weak in the knees while wearing navy blue board shorts and a white tank top.

"Rowan!" We both shout, scrambling to get up.

Because Bridget is younger, she's on her feet first, throwing herself into him, arms locking around his waist. I can't see his eyes behind his sunglasses, but his mouth falls open in surprise at her enthusiastic greeting. He recovers swiftly and returns her embrace, planting a quick kiss on the crown of her head.

"Well, hello there, *mo stóirín*. It's good to see you too."

She pulls back, stepping out of his embrace, looking a little embarrassed by her actions, but still smiling up at him like he hung the moon. He doesn't make a big deal out of it, no doubt trying to keep from making her uncomfortable. Ro gives her a grin, before turning his attention on me.

"A chéadsearc," he murmurs, one hand reaching for me while the other pushes his sunglasses to the top of his head. "I've missed you."

Sinking into his arms, the world feels right again. I'm expecting just a hug, but he pulls me flush against him before tipping his head down to capture my mouth. I can tell he's holding back out of respect for my sister and the other beach goers around, but it's no less sizzling than when he has me under him or against a wall.

Breaking the kiss, he smiles before his eyes drop down my body. I chose my swimsuit with him in mind. It's a simple, black bikini, but the bottoms are high cut. The band rests above my hip bones and only covers half of my butt cheeks. Taking my hand, he twirls me slowly to see the back.

"Christ almighty," he mutters.

I look over my shoulder at him, enjoying the way his eyes devour every inch.

"Gross," Bridget whispers. "I'm getting in the water. You two enjoy."

"Be careful!" I call after her, even though she's more than capable of handling herself in the water.

"She'll be fine," Ro whispers against the shell of my ear, accent thicker with desire. "But I won't be while you're wearing this bleedin' suit, and I can't do anything about it."

Pivoting in the sand, I face him, looping my arms around his neck. "Come swimming with me, and I'll fix that for you."

Chapter Thirty

Rowan

I don't make it a habit of eavesdropping, but I couldn't help myself when I walked up behind Alicia and Bridget talking about when Li realized she liked me. To say I was surprised is an understatement, and while I'm elated, it also makes me a little annoyed that we could have been enjoying each other for years as opposed to weeks. In hindsight though, I was an immature wanker then. I've always been attracted to Alicia, and wanted to be with her physically, but I was nowhere near ready for any sort of relationship.

It's impossible to say what made me realize that I was wasting my time on meaningless hookups. Maybe it was seeing my mates deliriously happy with their mots, or maybe it was moving from Wilmington to Charlotte and not seeing Alicia's face multiple times a week. When you grow used to certain things, you take them for granted until you no longer have easy access to them. You realize that without that one constant, your world is off kilter. It's only when I'm with her that I feel settled.

"Ro? You coming?" Alicia's looking at me expectantly, a dark brow raised halfway up her forehead.

"Aye, sorry. Just thinking about how fucking good you look and how I can't wait to get behind closed doors."

She laughs when I wink at her then reaches for my hand. "Sounds like you need a cold shower."

I let her lead me toward the water, watching the way her arse moves with each step. "Wouldn't help. You forget that I learned to swim in the North Atlantic Ocean. I doubt the water ever got over sixty degrees, love. And there's not a fecking thing that could keep me from wanting you right now."

She turns to face me, walking backward further into the surf, and there's a challenge in her eyes. Mine don't leave hers as we sink deeper into the water. When we're chest deep, she stops and pulls me to her, twining her arms around my neck and locking her legs around my hips. My hands immediately palm her arse to pull her against my hard cock. The contact making me grit my teeth.

"I missed you," Alicia whispers.

"Yeah? What did you miss most?" I ask teasingly, letting my fingers play with the hem of her swim bottoms, sliding just under the edge.

She rolls her lower body as she leans in to kiss my jaw. "All of you, Ro."

"Feeling's mutual."

One of her hands slides from my neck and down my chest until she reaches the top of my swim trunks, then she slips it in to grab my length, slowly pumping from base to tip. I groan, burying my face into her neck.

"Fucking hell," I mutter, licking the salt water from her throat. "I need to be inside you."

"Good thing no one can see us from here, Gallagher."

I keep one hand under her arse to hold her up and let the other sink into the front of her swimsuit to gently circle her clit before plunging two fingers into her cunt.

"Oh my god," she gasps, forehead dropping to my shoulder.

I feel her teeth sink into my skin and the hand around my cock squeeze tighter. My fingers glide in and out of her leisurely, letting the pleasure build until she's writhing against the heel of my hand. When her fingers release me, I start to object until I realize she's freeing my erection.

"Fuck me, Ro," she pants, her breath hot. "Please."

In one smooth motion, I pull my fingers from her, moving her swimsuit aside, then guide my cock to her entrance and punch my hips until I'm fully seated in her. We both moan softly, not moving save for the way the waves rock us back and forth, just relishing in the feeling of being home. Alicia winds her hands around my neck once more and lifts her mouth to mine, kissing me like her life depends on it. The taste of salt and everything that is uniquely her floods my senses, and I get lost in her. Gripping her hips, I move her along my shaft. I'm not going to last. It's been too long since I've had her.

"Christ, you feel like heaven," I mutter against her lips. "You take my cock like it was made for you."

Alicia grins at me with flushed cheeks. "It was, baby. Didn't you know? This cock was always meant to be mine."

The possession in her voice sends me right over the edge.

"Fuck," I growl through gritted teeth, and my hips falter.

"Don't stop!" She whines in my ear. "God, please don't stop. I'm so close."

I find her clit with my thumb, rubbing until her inner walls squeeze my cock and she's gasping my name as her orgasm starts to peak.

"Ro!" she cries softly as it barrels through her, making her body quiver. I stroke her clit through it until she's begging me to stop. "Stop, oh my god, stop. It's too much."

I chuckle, kissing her temple. "I'll stop now, but when we get home, I'm going to make you come so many times, you won't be able to walk or speak."

Alicia whimpers, her body sagging against mine, and I wrap my arms around her tightly, soaking up the feel of her in my arms. I don't want to ever let go.

* * *

"You guys aren't very discreet, you know?" Bridget tells us when we settle onto our beach towels. "Everyone knew exactly what was going on out there."

"Wasn't trying to be," Alicia quips, knocking her sister's shoulder with her own before leaning back onto her elbows.

"Gross. I'm taking a walk." She rises nimbly to her feet.

"Don't you want to get in the water again?" Alicia asks innocently.

"And get your love juices all over me? No thanks."

I laugh out loud at the gagging face she makes. Had it been my brothers, I would have punched them, but this lass seems to have unknowingly carved out a spot in my heart with her name on it.

"Ah, it's nothing but a drop in the ocean, now," I tell her with a wink and Alicia bursts out laughing. I want to bottle it up and take it with me on the road so I can pull it out and listen to the sweet, husky sound whenever the mood strikes.

"I might actually puke," Bridget informs us. "I can't believe you'd say such crude things in front of my virgin ears!"

"Psh. Virgin ears, my ass," Alicia snaps playfully. "I've heard the music you listen to."

Bridget grins in response. "Whatevs. I'm going on that walk now. Don't get arrested for indecent exposure."

"No promises." Alicia waves her off. "Don't go too far, B. Okay?"

The teen gives us a thumbs up before sauntering away. We sit in silence, watching her go. I know she's old enough to walk the beach on her own, but the urge to follow her like a guard dog is damn-near overwhelming. I'm about to suggest a walk, when Alicia lays flat on the towel, arms resting at her sides. She closes her eyes and inhales deeply. Peaceful. She looks peaceful. It's a dilemma trying to decide if I want to keep staring at her beautiful face or let my gaze travel over her perfect body.

The remaining water droplets that the sun hasn't dried up sparkle on her skin. There are a few scattered across her stomach, and I want to lick them off of her. Instead, I lay back, rolling to my side to face her and prop my head on a fist. Starting back at her face, I memorize the slope of her forehead as it connects to the straight line of her dainty nose. Her high cheekbones compliment the angular shape of her face. And those lips that I could kiss all day are soft and pink, perfectly proportioned with a deep Cupid's bow.

Continuing on my visual journey, I skim past the strong column of her neck—knowing that if I linger, I'll end up putting my mouth on her throat—and absorb the details of the designs tattooed on her chest. The roses that rest above the swell of her breasts are as delicate as they are strong, with thick lines making up the stems and thorns, while the petals and leaves are fine-lined and wispy. The top of the triple goddess begins on her sternum before descending to just above her navel. The tender maiden holds space under her right breast, the weathered crone on her left, and the mother, heavy with child, centered in the middle of it all. Stunning.

Unable to keep my hands to myself any longer, I brush my fingertips over the face of the mother. Alicia's stomach tenses in response, then relaxes. That's the effect I want to have on her. I want her to feel safe and free, able to let her guard down and not carry the weight of the world on her shoulders.

"When do you have to leave again?" She asks softly, eyes still closed.

Flattening my hand across her abdomen, I spread my fingers wide in an attempt to touch as much of her as possible. "I'll have to be back in Charlotte on Monday. We have a home game Tuesday."

A defeated sigh leaves her before she rolls to face me, mirroring my position. Her cheeks are pink from the sun exposure. "I wish I didn't have to work, or I'd come watch you. I've yet to see you play in person."

Gasping dramatically, I clutch at my chest. "The audacity of ya to miss my games so you can work to pay bills! Never heard of something so selfish in all my life."

"Shut up." Her husky laugh warms me to my bones.

"Darlin', don't worry that pretty head of yours," I tell her, reaching over to stroke her cheek with my thumb. "My matches don't take priority over your livelihood. Plus, I look just as good on the telly as I do in the flesh."

Alicia rolls her eyes, a smirk dancing across her lips before a frown forms. "Maybe one day it won't be so hard, and I'll have more time to be the supportive partner."

She drops her eyes to space between us, fingers worrying the edge of the towel.

"Hey now." I duck my head while tipping her face back up. "What makes you think you're not supportive?"

Scoffing, she rolls to her back and folds her arms over her face. Not having that, I grab her wrists in one hand and raise her arms above her head, angling my body partially over hers. Those blue eyes fly open in surprise, and she opens her mouth to smart off, most likely. I put a halt to whatever she's going to say when I dip to give her a deep and sloppy kiss. I don't stop until her body arches into mine, and I feel one of her legs hook over mine. Not wanting to be arrested like Bridget warned against, I break away to give my lass a stern look.

"I asked you a question."

She presses her lips together and squeezes her eyes shut. A moment passes before she answers, her voice nothing more than a whisper. "I have nothing to offer you, Ro. So far I've contributed nothing to this relationship while you've been doing all the heavy lifting. It feels like a whole lot of you giving and me taking while giving nothing in return. You'll get tired of that eventually."

"Ach, *a chéadsearc,* that's not true. And even if it were, who gives a flying feck? The only thing I want from you is knowing you're mine and waiting for me when I get home."

I want to tell her that she gives me more joy than I've ever known, and that when I'm with her, time simultaneously stops and moves too fast. I want to tell her that her steadfastness reminds me to keep pushing on and off the pitch. I want her to know that I've always fought *with* people, but have never wanted to fight *for* someone until her and Bridget.

Chapter Thirty-One

Alicia

After we packed up and left the beach, Ro invited me and Bridget to have dinner at his place. I was more than happy to let someone else do the cooking, and I'd never been to his apartment, so I was curious. Bridget opted to stay home, stating she was tired and just wanted to hang out in her room. She seemed off after her beach walk, but I chalked it up to feeling awkward around Rowan and I after our *moment* in the water. After confirming that she was okay with me not staying with her, we dropped her at home and I packed an overnight bag. Just in case.

Now I'm leaning against the breakfast bar in the open kitchen of Ro's apartment. The one that used to be Eamon's, which then became Teagan's. When Eamon moved in with Norah, Teagan was already his roommate, so he took over the lease until he decided to shack up with Layla. Ro had been looking for a new place, so he stepped in. When Charlotte signed him, he could have given it up, but decided last minute to keep it for when he came back to visit.

It's simple, but spacious and in good condition. When you enter the front door, you're met with an open concept kitchen and living room design. The breakfast bar serves as the divider for the space, but there's room for a small dining table and chairs opposite of the door. Past that is a short hallway that leads to two bedrooms—a master with a small bathroom, and the guest room across from the main bathroom. My favorite part of the whole place are the sliding glass doors that overlook Empie Park. It's not the greatest park in the area, but it beats the view from my apartment. At least you can see trees and grass here, rather than the rooftops of other buildings.

"Sorry about that. When Coach calls, you answer," Ro says as he saunters down the hall toward me. His phone rang the moment we walked in the door, and he excused himself to his room, telling me to make myself at home. I haven't moved from the spot he left me in.

"No worries. Is everything okay?"

"Aye, just a shift in this week's practice schedule." He sets his phone on the bar before extending a hand in my direction. When I take it, he tugs me gently until we're chest to chest. I press my face into his shirt, inhaling deeply. He smells like ocean and sunblock and...Ro.

"You smell like the beach," I tell him. It's not an insult.

He chuckles softly. "Maybe we ought to shower."

"We?" My body tingles with anticipation as I smile up at him.

"Aye, if we shower together it's better for the environment. That's what Teagan tells me, anyway. Saves on water or some shite."

"Right," I agree soberly. "It's important to take care of the earth."

"Mhmm," he agrees then bends slightly to grip my ass, hauling me into his arms.

"Rowan!" I squeal, locking my arms around his neck and legs around his waist.

He tips his head to place open-mouthed kisses under my jaw and down my neck. I tangle my fingers in his hair, yanking his head back roughly so I can kiss him. The moment our tongues meet, a frenzy unleashes. He doesn't break his stride as he carries me to the bathroom, only stumbling slightly when I pinch his nipple through his shirt.

"Fucking hell," he mutters, dropping me to my feet and yanking my tank top over my head. Pausing only a moment to stare at my bikini-clad chest, a growl comes from him. "Fucking swimsuit driving me fucking crazy all fucking day."

I quickly shed the top, tossing it into the sink behind us. He doesn't give me a chance to even touch him before his giant hands are on me, kneading and squeezing my breasts. I love the way his fingers pluck my nipples into hard peaks, moaning when he pinches them. I've always enjoyed nipple play during sex, but getting them pierced was the best decision I've ever made.

"Oh god, do that again," I order him as we step backwards into the shower. Rowan is still completely clothed. "Wait, do that again after we're naked."

"Gladly." He turns to crank on the water before kneeling to tear my shorts and swim bottoms down my legs.

He's eye-level with my pussy, and as much as I want his mouth on me, I need his clothes off. The spray of the shower is plastering his shirt to his body. Just as he starts to lean in, I grab a fistful of hair and tug. "Later. Let me take your clothes off."

Disappointment flashes in his eyes, but he obeys, rising to his feet. Wet t-shirt contests are usually associated with women, but there's nothing *not* sexy about a man in a soaking wet shirt. I fumble with the hem of his shirt, peeling it up his torso, but getting stuck around his broad shoulders. Tight, wet clothing doesn't relinquish easily. I growl in frustration, and Ro brackets my wrists in one hand. My eyes dart to his face in confusion.

"Leave it."

"But—," I start to protest.

"Alicia," Ro barks, the sternness causing my spine to go ramrod straight. "Get on your knees, darlin'."

I don't question him, sinking down to the tiled floor of the shower. He rips his shirt over his head, dropping it beside me with a splat.

"Go on," he commands, nodding down at his trunks. "Take them off."

Reaching for the waistband, I tug them. Down his hips and over his very huge, and *very* hard cock. It springs free, and just looking at it has my core throbbing.

I glance up. Rivulets cascade down his chest, becoming a confluence of streams over his abdomen, and running into the V of his Adonis belt. I want to lap up every drop from every inch of his skin. Leaning in, I make to wrap my lips around the thick tip of his cock. Ro reaches out and rests his hand on my head, making a *tsking* sound.

"If you want my cock in your mouth, you'll wait until I tell you to take it."

"What happens if I don't?" I challenge.

His slides his hand to grip my chin. "Brats don't get to come."

The shower continues to pour over us, and I can feel my arousal leaking out of me. It only increases when he wraps his other hand around his length and brings the tip to my mouth, spreading the bead of pre-cum along my upper lip. Because I have given, and will always give, him my bratty side, I extend my tongue to flick the underside of his length, feeling immensely satisfied when his hips jerk, forcing the head of his cock just past my lips. He yanks his hips back and replaces his cock with his thumb, sliding it back to press my tongue down. Closing my mouth around his thumb, I suck, then bite. Rowan smirks.

* * *

Rowan

Alicia looks so pretty on her knees, inked skin dripping, and lips wrapped around my thumb. She plays the role of brat beautifully, and it gets me hard every time she smarts off. I lied though. I told her brats don't get to come, but I will always make certain that she does.

Pulling my thumb from her mouth, I stroke the wet strands of hair from her face, then slide my hand to her neck, squeezing slightly. I feel, more than hear, the moan in her throat, the vibration of her vocal cords a confirmation that she enjoys my hands on her like this. I angle her chin up so she's forced to look me in the eyes.

"Fuckin' gorgeous," I mutter. "Now be a good lass and touch yourself for me."

Alicia's baby blues flare at the order, but she obeys, sliding her hand between her legs. Her lids fall shut in pleasure. I can't see, so I tap one of her knees with my foot.

"Spread 'em wider so I can watch."

I maintain rapt attention as her knees slowly slide apart, baring herself to me.

"Wait," I bark when she starts to dip her fingers inside. Her gaze snaps to mine in irritation. "Touch your clit only. Your cunt is mine."

Her fingers return to where I want them, and she begins to circle the pad of *just* her middle finger over it, a defiant gleam in her eyes.

"Clever, aren't you?" I chuckle darkly. "Now open wide."

She stretches her mouth as wide as she can, extending her tongue. Bringing my cock closer, I trace her lips again with the tip, impressed when she doesn't even try to disobey.

"There's my good lass," I praise, sliding into her mouth slowly, letting her adjust. She gags a little, so I start to pull back, but her hands shoot up to cup my arse, fingernails digging into the skin as she holds me in place, glaring up at me.

Greedy girl.

"You want to choke on it, darlin'?" I push in further until she gags again. "Be my guest."

She curls her tongue around the underside of my shaft, dragging the very tip along the veins. Grunting, I begin to fuck her mouth slowly, but she grows impatient and grabs my arse again. I let her take control, setting the pace. Best decision I've ever made. Releasing her throat, I bury my fingers in her hair as she sucks me off, bringing me closer to the edge.

"That's it," I growl through gritted teeth, head falling back against the shower wall. "Fuck, I love the way your mouth feels around me."

Alicia hums and I feel a hand leave my backside. Fingers ghost along my inner thigh before she's cupping my balls. Jerking my head forward, I find her eyes on my face. The way they burn with desire is the final push.

"I'm about to come," I gasp out, stars dotting my vision. She hums again and I blow, yelling out, "Christ! Oh fuck!"

By the time it's over, my legs are shaking, and Alicia is popping off my cock with a smug grin on her face.

"You okay, baby?" She purrs with a smirk on her swollen lips.

"Never better. C'mere." I pull her to her feet, claiming her mouth the moment she's upright. Saying "thank you for the blowjob" seems a little much, so I pour my gratitude into this kiss. It's not frantic or sloppy, but slow and passionate. We fucked in the ocean, but now I want to do something I've never done in my life. I want to make love to this woman who has turned my world on its head.

Reluctantly, I pull my mouth away, searching her face for some indication of what she might be feeling. Her expression is soft, more serene than I've ever seen on her. I kiss her forehead then reach for the bottle of body wash. I squirt a reasonable amount in my palm, then rub my hands until it lathers. Slowly and meticulously, I begin to wash Alicia's beautiful body in silence. I turn her so her back's to me, spreading the suds over her shoulders. She's tense, so I rub my thumbs along the contours of the trapezius, applying pressure the way the team's sport therapist does after a particularly rough match. He's a great physician, always teaching us basic techniques so we can help one another if he's not around.

A low groan flows from her lips, and I stop.

"Sorry," I murmur, kissing the spot.

"No, it felt amazing," she replies dreamily. "I've never had a massage. Didn't realize what I was missing."

"Let's finish cleaning up and I'll give you a full one, yeah?"

There's a brief pause before she finally says, "Okay. I'd like that."

Sliding my arms around her middle, I pull her against me and press my lips to her shoulder again.

"Thank you," I breathe against her skin, holding her a little tighter.

Alicia turns in my arms, smoothing her hands over my chest. She looks at me curiously. “For what?”

“Letting me take care of you.”

“Ro, it’s just a massage,” she argues.

“No, love, it’s not. You don’t realize what a gift it is to be the one to give you what you need, to provide for you.”

She rolls her eyes. “You’re ridiculous.”

“I’m serious.” I brush my thumb over her cheekbone before cupping her face. “Taking care of you in any capacity is all I want, so for you to trust me with your body…it’s a gift. *You* are a gift, Alicia.”

Chapter Thirty-Two

Alicia

"You doing okay?" I ask my sister, looking up from the stack of bills I've been going through.

After our shower last night, Rowan toweled me off then led me to the bed, instructing me to lay down on my stomach. I expected him to make some comment about my ass, or use the massage to get handsy, but to my absolute shock and delight, he really did give me a massage. My body felt like jello afterwards and I just wanted to sleep, but he made me drink a large glass of water to flush the toxins out, and then proceeded to give me a mind-blowing orgasm involving the partially full bottle of rosé from the country club and his tongue. He wanted me to stay another night, and while the idea was severely tempting, I didn't want to leave Bridget alone that long, so he dropped me off at home a little bit ago before heading to see

Eamon and Teagan. As much as I want to stay wrapped up in him the entire time he's here, I know that's unreasonable for both of us.

"Yeah, why?" She asks quickly, eyes locked on the screen of her phone.

Bridget's been off ever since I got back, barely interacting with me, and obsessively checking her phone more than usual.

"You seem a little distracted." I set the papers down. "Something on your mind?"

"No." She hops from the chair she's been perched in and heads toward her bedroom.

"Bridget," I say warily. "What's going on?"

"Oh my god, Li. Nothing!"

If I wasn't already suspicious, I definitely am now. Teenage attitude is par for the course these days, but things have been pretty great between us recently, so this feels completely out of left field.

Standing, I take cautious steps in her direction. "Bridge, whatever it is you're trying to keep me from finding out, I promise I won't get mad. Just be honest with me. Please?"

She freezes in the hallway and hangs her head. The dark hair, twin to my own, falls to form a curtain around her face.

"Bridget, what's wrong? I can't help you if I don't know what's going on."

"Li," she whimpers. "I think I fucked everything up."

My heart sinks to my stomach. I have no idea what she's referring to, but unease bubbles within me. I take a couple more steps.

"What do you mean?"

"You're going to hate me." Her voice sounds so small and resigned.

"B, I'll never hate you. No matter what."

I wait, and just as I'm about to ask again, she turns to face me.

"He said that it would be okay, that it would help us." I go cold as my sister sobs.

"Who, Bridget?" I ask her hollowly, even though I'm pretty sure I already know the answer.

No. Please God, no.

"Dad." My eyes squeeze shut as despair courses through my body. "He showed up last night, and I let him in. I don't know why. Maybe because I stupidly thought he had really changed, and I just wanted some semblance of a normal family."

"You have to be fucking kidding me," I snap, and she flinches. "In what world would having him around be considered *normal*, Bridget?"

I've gone from horrified that he was in the same room as her to absolutely livid that she'd fall for his shit after everything. Somewhere along the way, the gentleness I was clinging to slipped from my grasp, all rational thought leaving my head.

"I'm sorry, Li. I'm so, so sorry!" She's crying fully now, the heels of her hands pressed into her eyes.

"You need to tell me everything right now, or so help me."

Bridget shuffles her feet and fidgets with the string of her hoodie, still not giving me eye contact.

"I'm waiting." I bark, folding my arms over my chest.

"He said he needed money to help get him set up here, and then once he had a stable job, he'd pay it all back. He said he was here to stay and that he wanted us to be a family again. I didn't know what else to do, so I..." she stammers before rushing out, "I opened the safe in your closet and gave him the money."

"You did *what*?" I choke, hands falling to my sides. My head is swimming, my pulse thrumming in my ears.

"I'm so sorry," she whispers.

"You have no idea how much you just fucked us both over!" I yell, throwing my arms wide. "That piece of shit is long gone now, and we'll never see that money again! Do you know how long I've been saving? How hard I've worked? That money was a down payment for a house, Bridget. And now it's all gone. What were you thinking?"

"I don't know!" She screams back at me. "Is it so bad to want a bigger family? To have someone else to spend my time with rather than *you*? Not that we spend that much time together anyway, since you're always working or with Ro!"

"That's not fair, and you know it." Hurt spears through me, but I'm so angry. "I'm doing the best I can, so please cut me some fucking slack! You think I wanted to become a parent and give up my life?" I stomp into my bedroom, throw open the closet door, and even though I already know it's going to be bad, I fall to my knees and punch in the code on the safe. With a soft beep, the door unlocks and pops open.

It's all gone. Every last cent is just gone. I let my butt hit the floor as the weight of what this means washes over me. I don't know how long I sit there staring at the empty box, but it's dark outside of the window, so it was for at least an hour. Eventually, I close and lock the safe, though I'm not sure why. There's nothing in it anymore.

I trudge into the living room, noting that there are no lights on, not even a sliver of light from under the crack of Bridget's door. Switching on the lamp, I glance around the space until my gaze snags on a piece of paper on the coffee table, my name scribbled onto the front in my sister's handwriting. Gingerly, I pick it up and unfold it.

A,

You can have your life back. I'll go find my own.

-B

The note falls from my fingers to the floor.

I need a drink.

* * *

One glass of Scotch ends up being an entire bottle, plus a beer. I'm so drunk that my body feels numb. Good. That's what I was going for. Something other than pain, fear, or extreme sadness. For once, I don't want to feel a goddamn thing. The years I've spent fighting to make the best of our situation feel so futile.

Maybe I wasn't the best candidate for the job. Maybe I should have surrendered Bridget to the state. Maybe, just maybe, had she been with anyone other than me, she would have had a chance at a better life. I tried so hard to be what she needed, and it's never been enough. *I'm* not enough.

With that thought, I stumble into the kitchen and pull another beer from the fridge. Lou weaves through my feet, making me trip. I barely catch my self on the lip of the counter.

"Fuck, Lou! Are you trying to kill me?" I shout at my cat.

He glares at me, flicks his tail, and stalks out of the room.

Perfect. Now my cat hates me too.

I'm vaguely aware of my phone ringing from my bedroom. Maybe it's Bridget. Moving clumsily, I eventually make it to the doorway, then to my bed. I fall ungracefully onto the mattress and pull the phone from my nightstand. I don't even remember putting it there. It's pitch dark in here, so the light from the screen is blinding. My vision is blurry, no doubt due to the alcohol in my system. Squinting, Ro's name comes into view. One part of me wants to answer and tell him I need him. I want him to hold me and tell me I'm not a fuck up. But the other part of me can't bear the thought of him seeing me like this...or hearing how awful I was to Bridget.

My pride wins out, and I silence the phone then roll to get up. It was the wrong move. Nausea has my stomach churning, and my head feels like it's spinning. I slap a hand over my mouth and lurch for the bathroom. Miraculously, I make it to the toilet before hurling up my guts. The last time I was anywhere near this drunk, was the night Rowan and I almost hooked up in the bathroom.

Eventually, there's nothing left for me to vomit and my body is spent. I slump to the floor and curl up on my side. Bathroom floors are, by nature, disgusting and uncomfortable, but right now it feels like the only place in the world I've ever needed. The phone starts ringing again as I drift into unconsciousness.

Chapter Thirty-Three

Rowan

The line rings and rings until it finally goes to voicemail.

Hi, you've reached Alicia. Leave a message.

That shouldn't concern me since I know she's spending the evening with her sister, but unease coils in my gut for some unknown reason. I'm being ridiculous. If there was a problem, she would call me.

"Everything okay, Ro?" Eamon asks from across the table.

Eamon, Teagan, and I hadn't hung out in what feels like ages, so we met up at O' Nelly's. It's always odd being here when Alicia is off. Paddy is great, but not as pretty to look at.

"Yeah, mate. It's grand." I answer automatically.

"You sure?" Teagan inquires, looking at me strangely. "You seem a little worried."

Looking up, I give him a cheery smile. "All's good. Just thought I'd see if Li and Bridget needed anything, but she's not answering. I'm sure they're just busy."

Eamon smirks before taking a gulp of his beer.

"What?" I narrow my eyes at him.

"Nothing." He shrugs. "Just not used to seeing you lose your head over a lass."

"Fuck off." I smirk. "A man can change, can't he?"

"'Course he can. I'm not getting down on ya. It's a good change, just... different."

"Yeah, Ro," Teag cuts in. "Never thought we'd see the day when you'd actually settle down. I always knew you had it bad for Alicia, but never thought you were this gone for her."

Grinning, I take a drink from my glass—I only drink spirits when Alicia isn't pouring. "I think I always have been. I was just too much of a dumb fuck to realize it. Sort of makes a fella realize he doesn't enjoy travelin' as much when he's on his own."

My mates share a look.

"What was that?" I ask, pointing between the two of them.

They both shrug. I'm about to start tossing coasters at them when Eamon speaks up. "Think you'd ever leave CFC and find a way to be here more?"

He doesn't know that the thought has been in my head more often than not, lately. I love football and playing for the League has been the dream since I was a boy. The thought of not playing in some capacity makes me feel hollow inside, but surprisingly, when I think of not playing professionally, it doesn't sting as much as I thought it would. But the thought of leaving my girls behind so much? That's another story.

"Not sure what other options I have at this point," I tell him instead. "My contract is for a year, so I couldn't leave until after the season anyway."

"True," he muses. "That could give you time to research other options though if you're considering changing up."

I nod, considering. Eamon didn't have a problem saying no to playing professionally when the scouts approached him. He told them he needed time to think about it, but he'll say that he knew his answer immediately. He wasn't going to leave Norah. Even though she was supportive and encouraged him not to turn it down if even a small part of him wanted it, he'd already made up his mind.

"I'll think it over," I told him. "One more round, boyos? It's on me."

They consent happily, so I make my way to the bar, pulling my phone out and dialing Alicia again. Still no answer. I'm about to text her, when the phone buzzes with an incoming call. The unease from earlier stirs again.

"Bridget?" I answer. "Is everything okay?"

* * *

She looks so lost, so young, sitting huddled on the park bench. This wee lass has been through more in her short lifetime than many adults. Being a parent is not something I ever considered. My mind was always focused singularly on football. Then I met Bridget, and something about her pulled at my heartstrings. She's Alicia's sister, yes, but I think even if she weren't, I'd still feel this way. We haven't known each other long, but I want nothing more than to watch her thrive. I want to keep her safe while also showing her that there are adults out there who stick around because they want to. I want her to know that she's wanted.

Alicia loves her sister without a doubt, but she's pouring from an empty glass. She gives and gives, works and works, to make sure that they can simply survive. She was a kid herself when she started caring for Bridget. She's never had the chance to just *be* Alicia. They both need relief.

"Hey, m*o stóirín,*" I call softly as I approach her.

Bridget lifts her head from where it's resting on her knees, and the moment her eyes meet mine, her face scrunches up, and she bursts into tears. My heart breaks.

When she called me, I knew something had to have happened, and I was right. She didn't give me many details, just that she and Alicia got into it and she ran away. I told her to stay where she was, and I'd be right there. I didn't hesitate—just rushed for the door, thanking the blessed virgin that

I'd only had one drink and was okay to drive. I called Eamon once I started the car and explained the situation, promising to update him when I could.

Sitting down beside her, I gently put an arm over her shoulders, tugging her to my side. "Shhh, it's okay, love," I coo, stroking her hair.

"It's not okay," she chokes out through her sobs. "I ruined everything!"

What could a child possibly have ruined?

"I doubt that," I assure her. "Whatever happened, we can fix it, yeah?"

Her head shakes back and forth rapidly. "No, this can't be fixed."

"Do you want to tell me about it? Maybe I can help. I may not look it, but I'm actually a pretty decent problem solver."

I let her cry until it subsides, and she raises her head to wipe at her eyes with the sleeve of her jumper. After another moment, she takes a deep breath and releases it.

"I gave him all of her money."

My mind flits through memories of conversations, trying to think of anything she or Alicia has told me that I can connect to this, but I draw a blank.

"What do you mean? Who did you give whose money to?"

Bridget sniffles. "I gave all of the money in Alicia's safe to our dad."

"Wha...*what?* When? Why?" I stammer in shock.

"Last night. He showed up at our house while you two were gone. I was stupid and let him in. I was so excited to see him. I thought he was coming to be with us, that maybe jail changed him." Her shoulders cave inward. "He told me that he wanted to be with us, but he didn't have any money, and that without money for rent and stuff, he'd have to leave again."

She hiccups, lips quivering.

"Oh, Bridget, love," I murmur. "That was..."

"I know! It was stupid. I get that now. Alicia was so mad when I told her. I've never seen her like that."

Fuck. I need to check on Alicia.

"Okay," I flounder for something to say that will be helpful. "Here's what we're going to do. First, let's call your neighbor and see if you can stay there for the night, then I'll go and talk to Li, okay?"

"She hates me," Bridget whispers sadly.

"No," I argue, grasping her shoulders to turn her in my direction. "Listen to me, *mo stóirín.* Your sister loves you more than anything in the whole world, I can promise you that. There's not a single person on this planet that she cherishes more than you. Right now she's probably feeling scared, and yes, angry, but I promise that who she's really mad at is your father. Frankly, I am too. If I were to see him now, I'd likely knock a few teeth out of him. You didn't hear me say that though. Violence is never the answer."

She huffs a small a laugh, and that's enough for me to know she'll be okay. Pulling her in for a hug, I rest my chin on top of her head.

"Thanks, Ro," she murmurs.

"Anything for you." I tell her, and I mean it.

* * *

Once Bridget is safely stashed at the neighbor's, I pull the spare key from my pocket and let myself inside. It's dark, save for a lamp in the living room. I've barely closed the door behind me when a meow sounds at my feet.

"Ah, hello Lou," I greet the cat quietly, reaching down to scratch his chin. "Where's your mum?"

Meow.

"Not helpful, mate. Think you could learn to talk like that cat from Sabrina?" I look at him hopefully, but he just blinks his big green eyes at me then lunges for my leg, sinking his teeth into fabric of my athletic pants.

"Oy!" I whisper-yell. "Bleedin' menace is what you are."

Lou meows again then saunters to his food bowl, spins in a circle, then sits primly next to it.

"Yeah, alright. Don't get your whiskers in a knot."

Quickly, I fill his bowl with a scoop of food then head toward Li's room. There's a light on in the bathroom and black hair pooling across the floor. My heart sinks and I rush over, dropping to my knees to shake her.

"Alicia. Alicia, love, wake up." I'm trying to stay calm, to assess the situation, but inside I'm in a fucking panic.

Rolling her to her back, she groans, and I finally see the beer bottle next to the toilet. That's when I register the sour scent of alcohol and vomit lingering in the air.

"Fucking hell, hen. What all did you drink?"

Rotating, I find a washcloth in a drawer of the vanity and run it under cold water. I ring it out, then fold it before wiping her face. Her skin is so pale, and the circles under her eye are a mix of exhaustion and smeared makeup. She's still beautiful, even like this.

Once I have her cleaned up, I carefully slide my arms under her, lifting and cradling her body against mine before standing and moving to her bed. Before pulling the covers over her, I strip off her pants, followed by her stained shirt. Pulling mine off, I swiftly thread her arms through the sleeves and tuck it over her head.

When I pull the blanket over her limp body, her eyes flutter.

"Rowan?" She croaks, voice hoarse from throwing up, most likely.

Brushing the hair from her face, I murmur, "Shh. Go back to sleep. I'll be right here."

"Where's Bridget?" She asks weakly.

"She's safe, love. At Kat's for the night. Don't worry."

Alicia slips back into sleep and I watch her for a while, just to make sure she doesn't aspirate. Once I'm sure she's fine, I kick my shoes and pants off, then slide into bed next to her. Wrapping an arm around her waist, I snuggle in close, knowing that tomorrow is going to be rough.

Chapter Thirty-Four

Rowan

Lou wakes me up by lightly tapping his paw on my cheek. Squinting open one eye, I see him perched on my chest, tail curled around his feet, staring intently at me.

Meow.

"I'm getting you an automatic feeder for Christmas," I grumble. Is this a cat thing or just strictly *this* cat?

He leaps from my chest to the floor, trotting into the hall, tail flicking as he goes. I roll to my side and find Alicia still sleeping. Pressing a kiss to her shoulder, I carefully slide from the bed and pull my sweats on before making my way to feed the gremlin.

When I enter the kitchen, there's an empty bottle of Scotch on the counter with the plastic seal next to it. Shite. If she drank all that, she's going to be in ribbons when she wakes. After feeding Lou, I rifle through the cupboards, finding a bottle of aspirin and the fixings for coffee, two things that I know Alicia will not only be wanting, but needing something fierce.

Once the coffee is brewing, I rummage through her fridge, wishing she had the makings for a full Irish breakfast. Nothing cures a hangover better than a fry up. And you have to have it all: fried eggs, sausage, rashers, black and white pudding, beans, tomatoes, mushrooms, and, of course, bread to sop up whatever is left on the plate. The closest thing I find is a carton of eggs, pound of bacon, and sandwich bread. That will have to do.

I start the coffee then go about fixing breakfast. Once the bacon is nice and crispy, I crack the eggs into the grease. The team trainer would have an absolute conniption over that, but we're doing this proper like. And what he doesn't know won't hurt him.

Lou winds between my legs, purring loudly.

"I see what you're doing, ya cute hoor," I tell the cat, narrowing my eyes at him. "Tryin' to act like you're nothing but sweet so that I'll fill your bowl up again. Well you're meowing up the wrong tree, mate."

"Did you just call my cat a whore?"

My head snaps up, eyes locking on Alicia. My t-shirt is massive on her lithe frame, the hem reaching mid-thigh. On any other day, I'd be putting my hands on her, but that's not what she needs today.

"Mornin', love," I greet her, keeping my voice soft. "How are ya feelin'?"

She grimaces. "Like the biggest pile of shit that's been run over by a semi and a school bus back to back."

I blink. "That's...oddly specific."

"Yeah." She fidgets with the bottom of the shirt until Lou starts rubbing against her legs. "So, *did* you call my cat a whore?"

"Hoor," I repeat, pronouncing it slowly. "H-O-O-R. A 'cute hoor' is someone that's sneaky or able to manipulate a situation to get what they want. Ergo, that wee bastard at your feet."

One corner of Alicia's mouth tips up in what I think is the start of a smile. "That tracks. He can be a conniving little shit."

I nod, proud of myself for catching on to his wily cat ways, then snag the aspirin fished from the bottle earlier and a glass of water. "Here." I step out of the kitchen to meet her where she stands. "Take these while I get you some coffee. Then you're going to eat something before we talk."

She lifts a brow, her expression falling somewhere between amused and irritated. "You think so?"

"Aye, I do. Now, go sit."

* * *

"Fuck, love." I rub a palm over my beard, though I'd rather use these hands to throttle Alicia's father, the fucker.

We ate breakfast in silence, but once the table was cleared and dishes put in the dishwasher, I pulled Alicia down on the sofa with me and wrapped my arms around her as she told me everything. I watch as her shoulders droop further and further the more she talks.

"I'll go talk to him. Or hit him," I tell her matter-of-factly. "Whichever will make you feel better."

"No, I don't want you to do either of those," she says wearily, unfolding her legs to rise from the sofa. She pads down the hall to her room, so I follow suit.

"What are you going to do about the money?" I ask carefully, watching as she moves around the room, picking up random clothes littering the floor. "That's theft, Li, and he needs to be reported."

"What good will that do? I won't see that money again." She slides the closet door open, and stares down at the small safe she keeps tucked away there.

"It will at least put his arse back in jail, won't it?" I step behind her, brushing the backs of my fingers down her arms. "He can't bother you behind bars, yeah?"

"I guess."

These non-answers are going to drive me mental. I understand she's going through a sort of grieving process, but this gobshite committed a felony. I have no idea what she needs. Even if I gave her every cent I own, it's not going to fix the gaping hole in her chest right now.

"What is it you want, love?"

"I don't know, Rowan!" She sobs, throwing her hands in the air before turning to lean on the wall beside the closet. Then in a listless voice, she lets another wall down. "I don't know. I'm so tired. My heart hurts, my brain hurts, my body hurts. I don't know if I can keep doing this."

"What do you mean?" The warning bells are going off, urging me to pay attention.

Her head falls back against the wall, eyes closed. Tears streaking down her porcelain skin. "Do you ever feel like you just want to go to sleep and never wake up? Just drift off into the void, or whatever it is out there, just so you can finally rest?"

Fuck.

"I can't even say that I miss when life was easier because mine has always been one giant clusterfuck. I can't remember a time when I wasn't providing for someone else. Even before I was the sole provider for my sister, I was picking up after my parents because they were too drunk or high to take care of themselves, let alone us."

My fucking heart squeezes in my chest at her admission. I've lived the life she's describing. To think my wild rose had to endure a similar childhood guts me. But it explains so much—both her anger and how she freezes people out. She's never had a single person to rely on in her entire life. That ends now.

"It will never be enough," she whispers. "*I'll* never be enough."

"Alicia," I start.

"You should go," she blurts out, refusing to look at me.

She's reinforcing her walls, trying to keep me out.

"Is that what you want?"

"It doesn't matter, because *you* want to. I can see it in your face," she counters, her accusation completely coming out of left field.

I scoff. "Yeah? Hard to see what's on my face when you won't even look at me."

She finally flicks her gaze to mine, and I'm met with cold, blue eyes. If I hadn't spent so much time studying her face, I'd almost believe her, but the fact that she can't maintain eye contact for longer than a couple of seconds is enough for me to know she's angling for an excuse to fight. It will be easier for her to shut down and avoid the hard parts if she can get me to spar with her. If this is what she needs to expel the anger bubbling in her veins, I'll give it to her.

"Go on," I sneer, crossing my arms over my chest. "Tell me what else you can read on my face. Look me in the eye and tell me exactly what it is you think I'm feeling."

"Don't be an asshole." She tries to storm past, but I snatch her arm, yanking her back to trap her between my body and the wall. I take hold of her wrists with both hands and pin them to my bare chest.

"Same ol' song and dance, isn't it, darlin'?"

"If you mean the part where you get tired of being in one place for too long and leave to find a new pussy to fuck, then yeah."

A derisive laugh bursts from me and I press closer. "Aye, I'm the one that leaves, am I? Last time I checked, I wasn't the one that left in the middle of the night and refused to speak to you for months on end. As far as finding another pussy, you should know that yours is the only one I've touched, tasted, and fucked in two bloody years! *Two years*, Alicia."

Fresh tears roll down her cheeks as the ice in her eyes begins to thaw. They give way to a choked sob as she speaks. "Why? I'm nothing, Rowan. Useless. I have nothing to show for my life other than the ability to mix drinks. I have nothing to offer anyone, so what's the point of even trying anymore?"

I can't handle her taking shots at herself, and while I want to raise my voice, I don't think that will help her at all, so I press my forehead to hers. "Alicia, stop."

Chapter Thirty-Five

Alicia

He matches me at every turn. I can lash out, bare my teeth, slash with razor sharp claws, but Rowan doesn't bat an eye. He doesn't back down, doesn't call me crazy, or give up and walk away, even though I just accused him of doing that. He takes every barb and jab without flinching.

It's only when I aim those attacks at myself that he steps in, takes hold of my wrists, and touches his forehead to mine.

"Alicia, stop," he orders quietly, and for one cruel moment, I'm whisked back to when he stopped our bathroom tryst, the catalyst for where we are now. "I'll take whatever you can throw at me, but I refuse to let you hurt yourself, even with your words. I don't care what your brain is telling you. It's nothing but vicious lies. You are not weak. You are not useless. You are not unlovable."

"Then why does everyone leave?" My voice cracks on the last word, and I hang my head in shame.

I've never let myself form the words in my head, let alone out loud. But that's what it comes down to, doesn't it? No one has ever loved me enough to stay. My father wasn't around much, even before he went to prison. Then when he does show up, he's gone the moment he gets what he wants. My mother left the moment she realized I was capable of taking care of myself and Bridget.

And Bridget? She obviously hates me so much, she ran away.

Rowan's strong hand grips my chin firmly, forcing my eyes back to his. Through clenched teeth, he growls out, "I'm right fucking here *a chéadsearc,* and I'm goin' nowhere."

Blinking rapidly to clear the tears, I meet his eyes. "Why?"

His eyes burn with an intensity that both thrills and scares me. Lifting one of my hands, he kisses the inside of my wrist. "Because I love you, Alicia."

"What?" My head jerks back, smacking the wall, but I don't feel a thing because I'm stunned by his words.

There's not an ounce of humor on his face when he repeats himself. "I love you. You're everything I never knew I needed or wanted. I don't feel settled unless I'm with you. You..." He inhales deeply like he's fighting back emotions. "You, darlin', are the reason I believe in love at all. When I call you a chéadsearc, it's not just a pet name. It means 'first love'. There was no love in my family, and I've certainly never loved another lass, until you."

A fresh wave of tears spills over. "Rowan," I whisper. "I...you..."

I can't respond because I don't know how to put what I feel into words. Do I love Ro? How would I know? I love Bridget, but that's different than *this*. Loving a sister seems as easy as breathing. Loving someone romantically? It's work. And it's hard. Isn't it? It doesn't feel difficult being with Ro. Convincing myself that I hated him for so long was the challenge.

I've been standing on a precipice, terrified of plummeting to my inevitable doom. I know that if it doesn't kill me, it's going to be unimaginably painful, breaking me beyond recognition. But then I realize that it's too late because I already fell. I *have* been falling, and the fear is no longer present because I know Rowan Gallagher is my landing place.

He's been trying to show me this all along.

"You don't have to say anything back," he says softly. "I just needed you to know that I've got you, love. You don't have to hold it all, all the time. If you feel like collapsing, go ahead, because I'll be right here to catch you every time. You've spent your entire life holding everything—everyone—up, and now it's time to let someone else carry the brunt of it."

"I love you, Rowan!" The words rush from my mouth, leaving him seemingly stunned, but I can't stop the torrent that follows. "I don't know if I'll do it right, in fact, I'm sure I'll fuck everything up. But what I feel when I'm with you is something I've never experienced, so it has to be love. Right?"

"Depends." The corners of his eyes crinkling as he smiles. "What is it that you feel?"

Of course he's going to make me lay it all out. Tit for tat. I take a steadying breath before doing just that.

"You make me feel strong and anchored, like I can accomplish anything as long as you're next to me. You challenge me, and you're not afraid to call me on my bullshit. It pisses me off, but deep down I love that you do it." We smile at each other knowingly. "I miss you when you're on the road, Ro. I count down the days and hours like some love sick fool. I crave your touch, but feel like I'm going to explode because of how much I want you. When your hands are on me, it's too much and not enough, all at the same time. I love watching you with my cat and my sister. You didn't even hesitate to accept them as an extension of me, and I think it might be the sexiest thing I've ever seen. I love watching you on the field. Your focus and the power behind every shot, the way you encourage your teammates, it fills me with so much pride. When I hear other women talking about you or see them try to flirt with you, it turns me into some possessive psycho that wants to claw their eyes out because you're *mine*. I—."

Ro's lips crash into mine as he releases my wrists, one hand holding my jaw while the other presses against my lower back, dragging me against him. Our mouths part as we attempt to devour the other, as if this is the only way to express the measure of our feelings. My fingers unfurl against his solid chest, coasting across the muscled expanse of skin. I mirror him, placing a hand to the side of his face and sliding the other around his waist to splay it across the middle of his back.

"Say it again," he pleads against my lips before kissing my cheek and moving to my ear. "Tell me I'm yours, Li."

"You're mine," I breathe, moving my hand to cup the back of his head. "You're mine and I love you, Rowan Gallagher."

"Sweetest sound I've ever heard," he rasps against my throat, the coarse hairs of his beard tickling me.

I tip my head back to rest against the wall as he kisses, sucks, and nips every inch of my neck. The hand at my back drifts down to squeeze my ass before lifting me, my legs automatically locking around his hips. Ro pushes forward, pinning me against the wall, the hard ridge of his cock thrusting against my core. I whimper at the sensation and roll my pelvis to chase it.

"What do you need, love?" Amber eyes meet mine as he thrusts again, slowly, and holds himself against me.

Dipping my head slightly, I brush my lips against his. "Just you, baby," I whisper.

Whirling, he crosses the short distance between the wall and the bed, setting me down gently on my feet. I sit on the edge of the mattress and spread my legs, tugging at the waistband of his sweats until he's standing between them. When I look up, he swallows thickly before stroking his thumb down my cheek.

"You're so beautiful," he murmurs. "I love it when you look at me like that."

"Like what?"

"Like you're safe."

My eyes burn, a lump forming in my throat. No one makes me feel as secure as he does. Extending a hand, I place it over his heart. The steady thumping just one more reminder of how unwavering he's been.

"I've never felt safe with anyone but you." I place a kiss on his stomach while dragging his pants and briefs down his legs. "You're my rock, Rowan."

He doesn't say a word as he reaches for the bottom of my shirt and lifts it over my head, leaving me in nothing but black panties.

"Always will be," he promises solemnly. "Now, let me love you right."

Every kiss and caress of his hands over my skin is unhurried and reverent, stoking the fire within that burns brightest for him. When he finally sinks into me, I cling to him like a life raft in a turbulent sea. Each thrust of his hips is deep, hitting that perfect spot and bringing me closer to detonating. When I think I'm just about to crest, he pulls us upright, with him on his knees and my legs wrapped tightly around his waist. He continues driving into me at a slow and steady pace. My hands are planted on his broad shoulders and our eyes stay locked on each other, breath mingling in the minimal space between us as one of his hands keeps me in place, the other trailing up and down my spine. It's the most intimate moment of my life.

"Rowan," I gasp. I'm so close.

His fingers sink into the hair at the nape of my neck, pulling my head back as he rains kisses all over my throat. The slight sting of my hair being pulled makes me moan.

"That's it, darlin'," he growls out, thrusting harder. "Let go for me. Let me hear you."

Releasing his shoulders, I wind my arms around his neck, clutching to him for dear life and screaming out a garbled cry as my release barrels through me.

"So fucking perfect," Ro rasps as he continues to pump into me, his movements becoming more erratic the closer he gets to his own orgasm. "Fuck. You feel so good coming all over my cock like that."

I nip his earlobe then whisper, "Come for me, baby. Show me how good it feels."

Rowan slams into me one last time then stills, a string of curses falling from his lips. I love watching and listening to—and feeling—him come. The satisfaction of knowing that I am the one causing him to lose control and giving him that pleasure is empowering. Knowing that he loves me?

Euphoric.

Chapter Thirty-Six

Alicia

"Tell me about the Phoenix," Ro rumbles against my spine where he's been placing soft kisses.

We've spent the better part of the day in bed—making love slowly or fucking like the world is ending. Eventually, our bodies wore out and we dozed off. I woke up to him tracing the lines of my tattoo with his lips.

I hum in response, trying to formulate words when all I can think about is the feel of him. "I can't think when you're touching me like that."

He chuckles, places one last kiss to my shoulder, then settles back on his side, head propped on his fist. "Sorry, love."

Cracking open an eye, I give him a look. "I didn't say I was mad about it. But if you want the story, you're going to have be a good boy and not distract me."

He grins, not an ounce of shame on his face. "I rather like the sound of you calling me a good boy, so, *for now*, I'll keep my hands to myself."

"We'll see," I tease.

"Cross my heart and all that," he promises, schooling his face into a mask of sincerity. "Please tell me the story of your Phoenix tattoo."

I sigh as I think back to that day.

* * *

"Okay, B. I'll see you after school, okay?" I wave to my eight year old sister as she exits the car and walks into the elementary school.

It's the first day back after the holiday break, and she's been dreading it. Even as a third grader, school is so hard for her, but I'm hoping that with the new ADHD medicine her doctor prescribed, she'll have an easier time. Last semester was disastrous. Her reading level tanked and she's constantly in trouble for not staying in her seat or interrupting the teacher. Getting her to focus on any single task for longer than five minutes has been a challenge not just at school, but at home too. God bless her teacher, though. That woman has the patience of a saint. At our first parent-teacher conference, I was honest and explained our situation. How both parents had been out of the picture for quite some time and I'd been the one raising Bridget for the last eight years. I confessed how I was at my wit's end and had no idea how to help my sister. That's when she said she suspected Bridget had ADHD and would benefit from testing. Initially I fought the idea, but the more she explained it the more sense it made.

It took me a while to eventually make the appointment with our family doctor, but finally, over the holiday break, I got her in and her diagnosis was confirmed. They gave me some resources to help manage the symptoms while also prescribing a low dose of a stimulant. She's been on it for about a week, and so far, I can't tell if the improvements I've seen are from the meds, new routine, or both. Time will tell, I guess.

Speaking of time, it's my twentieth birthday, and I have plans with my tattoo artist, Griff, to finally get started on the Phoenix tattoo I've been saving up for.

The idea came to me shortly after our parents deserted us. I've worked at least two jobs since I was sixteen and learned how to manage money at a young age. Whenever Mom would send me to the store with a list and a rumpled up wad of cash, I always bought the off-brand of what we needed and pocketed whatever money was leftover. Then when we'd get shut off notices in the mail, I'd pull from my stash. At first, I was certain that we'd be doomed without our parents, but quickly realized that I'd been the one holding it together all along, so I was more than capable of doing this now. Probably even better now that I didn't have to manage my good-for-nothing parents. Once I saw that we weren't just surviving, but thriving, I felt like a new person. We'd been in the flames of hell for so long, but we were finally starting to emerge.

My first tattoo was a Capricorn symbol, and that's all it took for me to know that my addiction wouldn't be drugs or alcohol, but the buzzing of a needle inking a permanent mural into my skin. So I saved and saved, knowing that eventually I'd want a large piece (or two) and it wouldn't be cheap. The Phoenix may be cliché, but it's the best representation of my life I could think of. Life is hard as fuck, but I've always managed to rise from the ashes and start fresh. It also reminds me to not just get back up, but to stay strong. And maybe be a little intimidating in the process.

* * *

"So, there you have it. Not anything exciting really." I shrug my shoulders, still laying flat on my stomach.

"Not exciting, like skydiving, but still a compelling story of resilience and strength. For someone that young to already carry so much weight, it's remarkable, love." Ro leans in to place a gentle kiss on the corner of my mouth. "*You* are remarkable. And in case no one's said it, I'm so proud of you."

I turn my face to bury it into my pillow, not from embarrassment, but to hide the wave of emotions that hit me with his declaration. No one has *ever* said those words to me. I've heard "good job", but never that someone is *proud* of me. For one shining moment, I feel weightless and free. I'm not a fucked up bartender who is barely scraping by while trying to create a better life for her little sister. I feel worthy of good things, of a good life. It's fleeting, but an image flashes in my mind of what life could be for us, and I want to grab it with both hands.

A house. No, not a house, but a home. Nothing huge, or fancy; a nice home full of love and laughter. A safe space for all who enter. And inside, at a kitchen table, sits a dark-haired teen who, for the first time, looks peaceful and genuinely happy. She's laughing at something a beautiful man with red hair is saying. Then there's me, standing in the kitchen, taking it all in. It's my family. It's a future I want more than I've ever wanted anything in my entire life.

Rowan

"Move into my flat."

The words jump from my gob before I can stop them. Not that I regret them, because I don't, but now may not be the right time for this conversation. Too late to take them back now though.

Alicia lifts her head and stares at me wide-eyed, then bursts into laughter. "Whoa there, buddy."

"What?" I ask, falling onto my back and throwing an arm over my eyes, offended and embarrassed.

I feel the bed shift before her hand gently rests on my chest. Peeking out from under my arm I find her staring at me intently, worrying her bottom lip with her teeth.

"Ro," she whispers.

Like the sophisticated man I am, I grunt and shut my eyes.

"Baby," she pleads. "Hey, will you look at me, please?"

"Forget I said anything. I don't know what I was thinking."

Next thing I know she's straddling my waist and prying my arm away.

"Gallagher," she says sharply, the switch in tone snapping my eyes open and making my cock twitch. Plus she's still gloriously naked, which means the view from here is only fueling the fire. She smirks. "There he is."

The sigh that leaves me is supposed to be inaudible, but Alicia hears it and peers at me like I'm a petulant child. "Are you ready to talk to me like an adult now?"

Shame spreads through me, because I am acting like an eejit. My pride was wounded, when it's my own fecking fault for springing it on her like that. That's not something you just throw out there without some sort of preamble.

Sitting up, I drag myself to lean against the headboard, pulling her with me. Once settled, I wind my arms around her waist, bringing her close enough for our chests to press together, her piercings grazing across my pecs. I can't imagine I'll ever get tired of feeling her skin against mine.

"You're right," I murmur, leaning in to brush my lips against her jaw. "I'm sorry, love. I'm being a right gobdaw." I place a kiss just below her ear, making her shiver.

With a husky laugh, and the slight rocking of her hips, she admits, "I don't know what that means, but I agree."

My cock stirs, hardening against her arse. I'd love to impale her on me, watch as she rides me to her release, but that will come later. Right now, we need to talk. Reluctantly, I pull back to look directly in her eyes.

"I'm sorry—truly—but this is something I think we should discuss, Li."

She cocks her head to the side, a curtain of onyx hair spilling over her shoulder. "You think we should discuss me moving in with you? Even though we've only been officially together for a matter of weeks?"

"Aye, I do," I tell her honestly. "We may have only been courtin' a short while, but we've known each other for far longer. And hear me out before you jump down my throat, but I know you're struggling with money, especially after your poor excuse for a da took what didn't belong to him. You hate working at the country club, so just stay at Patty's and move into my flat. It's been paid up through the rest of the year. It's just sitting there empty when I'm on the road anyway. I only stay there when I come back to Wilmington."

Alicia gives me a thoughtful look. "And Bridget?"

"What about her?" I ask disbelievingly. I know she's not suggesting I haven't thought about, and included, the lass in my plans. I'm just as attached to her as I am to the woman in my arms. "There are two bedrooms. She'll have her own space."

Her lips purse. "And where will you sleep when you're back in town if there are only two rooms?"

"Well, darlin'," I croon. "I assumed you and I'd be sharing a bed."

"That's mighty presumptuous of you, Rowan Gallagher. What if I'm not that kind of girl?"

She's fucking with me, but I still give her a what-for. "Christ, woman, do you have to make ructions out of everything?"

A giggle escapes her. "I don't know what the means either, but you can't just spring something like that on me and not expect questions!"

I cup her face between my hands. "Alicia, this doesn't have to be complicated. All I'm asking is for you to let me be there for you. Let me help."

Her sapphire eyes dart back and forth between mine for a moment before she says softly, "Okay."

My shoulders sag in relief. "Good lass," I murmur against her lips, gripping her waist and lifting her slightly to position my cock at her entrance before slamming home. Alicia cries out loudly, digging her nails into my bare shoulders. "Now be extra good and ride me, darlin'."

Chapter Thirty-Seven

Alicia

Taking a deep breath, I roll my shoulders back and knock on Kat's door. Maybe I'm a shitty sister for letting my boyfriend fuck me repeatedly before going to make amends, but not only is Bridget like me and needs time to cool down, but she was also safe. I sent a text to my neighbor when I first woke up to gauge this situation.

Alicia: *Hey Kat. B doing okay?*

Kat: *Hey girl, yeah. She's still asleep. Wanna talk about it?*

Alicia: *I do, but not until I talk to her first. Will you let me know when she wakes up?*

Kat: *You got it.*

Kat: *Just so you know, it's going to be okay. Maybe not the shit with your dad, but you and B will be fine.*

Alicia: *Thanks Kat.*

Her message gave me a little bit of hope, but now that I'm here, I feel more nervous than anything else. Sure, we've fought and had our share of silent treatments, but never to this degree. I'm not even entirely sure what to say. Obviously, I need to apologize for being so harsh, but what she did was reckless. Maybe I haven't done a good enough job of teaching her how to spot manipulation. Just one more failure to add to the list.

The sliding of a deadbolt yanks me from my intrusive thoughts, and Kat's face appears. She gives me a small smile before stepping back to let me in. Cautiously, I cross the threshold, eyes darting around the apartment so similar to my own in structure, but completely different decor wise. Where mine is more bright and eclectic, Kat's is muted and minimalist, probably from having a house full of rowdy boys. Scanning the room, there's a noticeable lack of anything fragile.

Apart from Bridget.

"Hey, B," I murmur. The broken expression on her face guts me, and I want to launch myself at her, holding her like I did when our parents would fight. "Wanna go for a walk with me?"

Her watery green eyes meet my blue, and she nods slightly. I expected her to put up a fight. I nod back then turn to Kat.

"Thanks again for letting her crash here. I owe you one."

She waves a dismissive hand. "Not a problem at all, Li. You're both welcome any time—together or alone."

Bridget slings her backpack over her shoulder and trudges to the door, stopping to give Kat a quick hug and a mumbled thanks. Kat whispers something in her ear that's too low for me to pick up, but my sister nods.

When the door closes behind us, the weight that was momentarily held aloft settles back onto my shoulders. There's so much to unpack.

"Can we go to the beach?" Bridget asks quietly, eyes never leaving her feet.

"Yeah, of course we can. Do you want to change first?" I nod toward the cutoff shorts and band tee she's donning, along with her all black Chuck Taylors.

She shakes her head.

"Alright, let's go."

* * *

The beach is surprisingly empty save for the gulls and sand pipers scuttling over the sand in search of food. The ocean is calm with gentle waves lapping at the shore, providing a soothing soundtrack. I'm not sure if there's another sound in the world that brings me as much peace as the ocean does. I could sit for hours just watching and listening to the rolling and crashing of the surf.

Bridget and I have yet to speak. Even on the drive over, we kept to our own thoughts. It isn't until the beach blanket is spread across the sand and we're settled side by side, knees pulled up with our arms draping over them, that the silence is broken. It isn't me that does it.

"I'm sorry, Li." Her voice cracks, and out of the corner of my eye, I can see her bottom lip wobble. I open my own mouth to speak, but she continues. "I didn't mean what I said. About wanting different family members and about you always being gone."

"But it's true," I whisper. "I am always gone."

"Not because you want to be, though," she argues. "I know I'm just a dumb kid, but I'm not so dumb that I can't see how much you sacrifice for us."

I whip my eyes to look at her. "Bridget, you are not dumb. Not even close. Why would you say that?"

She hangs her head. "When Dad first asked for the money, I told him no. He made it sound teasing, but he said I was just a dumb kid that didn't understand grownup responsibilities or what it meant to be a parent. When I tried to argue with him, he started to get mean—not physically, but like his face changed—and I caved."

"That fucker," I seethe. "Like he has any idea what either of those mean. Bridge, don't take what he says to heart. He's a selfish son of a bitch who will say or do anything to get what he wants."

"I know." She lifts her head again. "And I think I knew it then, but I was just so…shocked…to see him. And even more shocked that you didn't tell me he was back."

"B, I'm sorry. I was trying to protect you," I confess. "I thought for sure that once he found out I wasn't going to give him any money, he'd hightail it out of here. If I thought for even a second that he was going to find you, I would have told you right away. So, yeah, that's on me."

She turns to me, fear shrouding her face. "What are we gonna do, Li? About him? About the money? God, I think I *am* a dumb kid." Bridget starts rocking back and forth, panic taking over.

"Hey, shhh," I soothe, moving to sit behind her, caging her between my legs and wrapping my arms around her. "It's going to be okay."

Shoulder racking sobs spill from her, and I know that this is a storm she needs to ride out. Neither of us are great at processing big feelings, more than content to just stuff if into our metaphorical backpack until it's full, nearly bursting. When the threads start to unravel at the seams, it will only be so long before it explodes. She's been packing it in for so long.

When her sobs turn to sniffles, I begin telling her about the first time I met her. How from the moment I laid eyes on her, I claimed her as my own. Mom would have had me shouldering most of the care no matter what, but I had already made up my mind to give her more than what I received.

"Why are they like that?" Bridget asks, leaning back to rest against me.

Tightening my embrace, I tell her the only answer I have for their behavior. "Addiction changes people, and never for the better."

"Are you going to report him to the police?"

Originally, I wasn't going to, but the more I think about it, the more I want him to be held accountable for his actions. The likelihood of ever seeing a dime of that money is slim, but Rowan is right. He'd at least be behind bars again. Hopefully.

"Yeah, I am." I shift, gently pushing against Bridget's back to get her to sit up. "There's something else I want to talk to you about."

She turns her body so that we're facing each other, and I can see the worry in her eyes. She's afraid I have more bad news.

"Ro asked us to move in with him."

Her eyes widen, but a smile stretches across her face. "What did you tell him?"

"Are you going to disown me if I say the answer was no?" I ask, keeping a straight face.

Bridget's jaw drops right before she yells. "What the fuck is wrong with you, Li? Why would you do that?"

I lose it, bursting out laughing at her outrage.

"Chill, B." I place my hands on her shoulders and relieve her fears. "I didn't tell him no."

The glare I get in return is made of ice, but the corner of her mouth twitches like she's fighting a smile. "You're a jerk."

"I know." I grin, then ask seriously, "So, you're okay with moving into Ro's place? You'll have to change schools since it's in a different district."

"Are you kidding? I'm more than okay with that. Ro lights you up, Li. Your smiles are genuine and you're less tense. As for schools, I'm thrilled to leave." She stops short, backtracking. "I mean, Mr. Kennedy is cool, so that sucks, but I want to start over and meet new people. Preferably ones that don't pick fights with me."

My nose tingles with the threat of tears at seeing the hope in my sister's eyes. Maybe this is the change we've been needing. A clean start, a fresh slate. Maybe letting someone help carry the load isn't as shameful as I always thought.

No, not someone.

Just Rowan.

Ro didn't bat an eye when I brought up Bridget moving in with us. I don't know why I expected him to. Obviously, if he'd said no, then his ass would be on the curb. But he took to her immediately, drawing her into his bubble and not letting go. He's included her, fought for her, and...*loved* her. He even gave her an Irish nickname.

Mo stóirín.

When I asked him what it meant, he grinned. "My little darlin'. Because she's the wee version of you, and you're my first darlin'."

By the time Bridget and I make it back to the apartment, Ro has a stack of empty boxes, packing tape, and a permanent marker sitting in the middle of the living room. As we stare at him, he doesn't even look sheepish about the fact that we hadn't discussed a moving date yet. On the contrary, he's beaming from ear to ear.

"Well? Did ya tell her?"

Instead of replying, Bridget lunges toward him and locks her arms around his torso. He kisses the top of her head while hugging her back, then looks up at me with shining eyes.

* * *

Bridget and I sit awkwardly on the leather sofa facing Dr. Kristina Langston. It's our first therapy session, and we have no idea what to expect. When Mrs. Jones gave me the contact information for a counselor, I put it in my purse and forgot about it until recently.

Dr. Langston smiles warmly at us. "I'm so glad you're both here. I know beginning counseling or therapy can be daunting, but this is a safe space for you to express yourselves, and if need be, find ways to communicate effectively. I'm here to help mediate any challenging conversations and to process any experiences you've faced that trigger difficult emotions."

We both mutter our thanks, not sure what else to say from here.

"So, Alicia," she proceeds. "You mentioned that you both experienced a troubling situation with your father. Would you like to discuss that today?"

"Oh, um, well," I begin nervously. "Our father recently got out of prison and managed to find not only where I work, but where Bridget and I live."

I go on to tell her about it all, letting Bridget add in her part of the story as well. By the end of our hour long session, we're both holding each other and weeping, and Dr. Langston didn't even do any deep diving. She only prodded us gently with innocent questions that forced open the flood gates. We have a long way to go, but we leave the office feeling lighter and ready to start a new chapter in a new place.

Originally, we were going to have Rowan join us, but he insisted that we focus on the two of us first, and then once we feel more comfortable, he'll start attending sessions. In the meantime, he waits in the lobby for us, only asking how it went, but never pressing for details. And he always takes us for ice cream after, stating that we deserve a treat for being brave.

Personally, I think he just wants an excuse to spoil Bridget.

Chapter Thirty-Eight

Rowan

I didn't waste a single solitary moment moving Alicia, Bridget, and yes, Lou, into my flat. Recruiting our friends and a few of my teammates, we were able to get it all boxed up and transported in record time. I wanted them there before I had to be on the road for the next week. I needed to come home to my girls. I gave them both free reign with setting up our home however they wanted, because, honest to Christ, the only things I need taking up space are them.

Bridget was very vocal about how glad she was that her room was far enough from ours that she wouldn't be able to hear us "going at it" all the time. Alicia got a wicked gleam in her eyes and threatened to make it her mission to be loud enough the whole complex would hear us. I honestly don't know if she's serious or not, but I'm game to find out.

I've one more game this week before I get to see them again, and thankfully, it's a home game at CFC. As soon as the final buzzer sounds, I'll be in my car, racing to Wilmington where the two other pieces of my heart are. *Fuck, when did I become such a sap?* I think to myself then shake my head because while my first reaction is to think myself ridiculous, that's not actually how I feel by a long shot.

I don't just have the woman I'm madly in love with, but a young lass who, for all intents and purposes, is my wee sister. She also makes me feel like a proud father, even without having known what that feels like myself. I'd move heaven and earth for Bridget, protect her with my last breath, and teach her anything she wants to know.

This match can't be over soon enough, and it hasn't even started yet. We're all in the locker room, pulling on our kits, wrapping joints, and doing whatever pre-game rituals we've come to depend on. I tried getting Alicia to engage in a round of phone sex with me since that always seems to do the trick, but she said she was driving and that I was on speaker phone. Bridget's loud gagging noises confirmed it, so I settled for listening to my pre-game playlist and visualizing a win.

Once we've been announced and run onto the field, I stand in the lineup during the beginning ceremonies, one hand clasping the wrist of the other behind my back, and let my eyes drift around the stadium. It's a full house this evening, with fans decked out in the team colors and an array of accessories. I glance up at the private box where the WAGs are watching their other halves or chatting among themselves, and an ache forms in my chest.

I have Alicia and Bridget on the list for every game, regardless of the stadium, even though I know it's usually difficult for them to get away due to Li's schedule. I don't hold it against her since her priority has always been providing for her and her sister, but I'd be lying if I said I wish that wasn't the case. Maybe it will be easier once she quits at the country club. Never did I think I'd have, or even want, to have someone up there, cheering me on, but the idea of Alicia being a part of the wives and girlfriends club isn't just a want. It's a need.

My brow furrows because I'm pretty sure my wishful thinking is making me see things that aren't there. My mind is telling me that Alicia and Bridget are at the window of the box, grinning at me, and holding up a sign.

Surprise! We love you #33!

A lump forms in my throat, and my eyes burn when I realize that they're really here. Both have jerseys with my number on them, their dark hair in matching French braids. They're so fucking adorable, I can barely stand it. I pull my arms from behind me, pressing my fingers to my lips. I send a kiss to them before placing both hands over my heart. I was already fired up for this match, but now I have no option but to own this pitch, winning the game for my girls.

"Yo, Gallagher," Marcos whispers beside me. "Is that the chick from O'Nelly's up there?"

My eyes stay trained on her face. "Yeah, mate, it is."

His elbow thumps against my arm. "She here for you? And does she have a twin sister up there with her?"

The urge to gloat is quickly overshadowed by protective irritation. "Aye, she's here for me, and *no*, that's her *teenage* sister. Keep your eyes to yourself before I tear them from their sockets."

"Jesus, man, chill out. I was just asking. From here they look identical." Marcos shakes his head, but I can see the smirk from the corner of my eye. "Paddy was right. Congrats, amigo."

I balk. "What the fuck did Paddy say?"

Marcos's shoulders shake with silent laughter. "He said, and this is a direct quote, 'Those two are going to realize soon that they belong together, mark my words.'"

Flicking my eyes back to the box, I see one of the other WAGs say something to Alicia, who then points in my direction and then back at her own chest, pride lighting up her features.

I don't get to spare another glance at the box until halftime. The first half has been brutal. We're tied one to one with Kansas City, both sides having equal possession of the ball. Their new forward, Devrim Dǒgan is from Turkey and a force to be reckoned with, but I've gone up against worse. I like a challenge on the pitch anyway.

Once we're in the locker room, Coach renews our strategy for the second half, telling us to reduce the amount of space between players. It's a shite idea. Not leaving enough room lends to crowding and fewer passing lanes, which is a recipe for injuries. I start to object, but snap my mouth shut when he glares at me. He's the coach. I'm not. I nod obediently, even though my gut is telling me this will end badly.

Turns out, I was right.

* * *

"Fuck!" I cry out when my ankle pops.

I've been going up against Dŏgan, fighting for possession, and struggling due to the lack of space, when I feel it. A cleated foot hooks between my legs and around the top of my foot, tangling us up until the only option is to hit the ground. Falling and taking hits is part of the game, no way around it really, but the angle that I go down is in a different direction than my opponent. The trajectory of the fall mixed with the way we're intertwined is the perfect storm that causes the tree to bow and snap.

Rolling to my side, I instantly pull my knee up to clutch my ankle, gritting my teeth when pain flares. I try to flex it, but the movement has me seeing stars.

"Gallagher, shit, are you okay?" I hear someone—maybe Marcos—ask.

Soon, medics are rushing me, prying my hands away, and immediately asking me what happened while stabilizing the ankle. I'm vaguely aware of a similar conversation happening next to me. I glance over briefly to see it's the other forward in a similar position. Inwardly I curse Coach for changing the play. He damn well knew it was a risk, and now two people are injured. The rage momentarily overshadows the throbbing until some arsehole bumps my foot, making me roar out in pain, a string of very colorful words pouring straight from my chest.

"Get him to PT, now!" Coach screams at the medics while sticking to my side. "Fuck, I'm sorry, Gallagher. This one's on me."

"Aye, you're damned right it's on you." I don't mince words because not only does he deserve it, but I'm in so much pain, I can't control my gob.

"I'm sorry," he starts to apologize again, but I cut him off.

"We'll discuss it later, Coach. Just get me to the doc."

I let the medics pull me to my feet and drape my arms across their shoulders. Slowly, we limp our way off the pitch to the team doc to determine how fucked I am. One thing is certain though. I won't be playing for a while.

Chapter Thirty-Nine

Rowan

"Well, Gallagher, do you want the good news or the bad news first?"

I grimace. Dr. Lawrence is a younger fella, probably a few years older than myself. Sandy blonde hair, bright smile, and easy bedside manner. He's only been with the team a couple of years now, but he's already proven to be an asset to us all.

"Just give it to me straight, Doc, will ya?"

As a professional athlete, injuries have the potential to force me into early retirement. I've only just begun my career, and I'm not interested in being benched so soon. Just rip the bandage off and tell me what's happening.

He must sense my irritation, because he nods. "It's not broken, but you do have a third degree sprain."

Fuck me. That will put me out for at least a month.

"Your x-rays show only minimal ligament tearing, which means it's possible that it's not a full third degree, but that's how we're going to treat it. I'd rather err on the side of caution."

"How long until I'm back on the pitch?" I ask anxiously.

"My guess is six to eight weeks, but I'm going to do everything I can to shorten that, as long as it's safe to do so. I'd like to get you in for an MRI just to make sure we didn't miss anything with x-rays. We'll have a clearer picture after that. For now, let's keep it wrapped, iced, and elevated."

Blowing out a breath, I rub my hands over my face. "Yeah, alright, Doc. Thanks."

"Try not to stress too much," he suggests gently, offering me a hand to help me slide off the exam table. "This isn't career ending, okay? You'll probably feel achy when it rains, but if you follow directions and don't do anything to mess up the healing, it won't interfere with your game."

Dr. Lawrence hands me a set of crutches, and as I adjust them, I'm filled with relief at his words. It's going to be a rough month or so, but I can follow orders. Whatever it takes to get me back on the pitch.

We exit the exam room, and leaning against the wall across from us is Alicia, worry etched all over her face. Fuck, I've missed her. She looks gorgeous in my jersey. I have half a mind to sneak her into an empty room, but then I realize that might not be possible.

"Um, say, Doc?" I ask, never taking my eyes off of my girl. "What other restrictions do I have?"

He looks from me to Alicia, whose eyes have gone wide, and her cheeks are a lovely shade of scarlet, then claps a hand on my shoulder. "Just don't put any weight on that leg, Gallagher. Keep any...*special* exercises...to a sitting position or something similar."

"Shouldn't be a problem," I say confidently. "Probably should have help in the shower, too, yeah?"

"Jesus Christ," Alicia mutters under her breath, rolling her eyes at me.

This gets a laugh out of Dr. Lawrence. "Good luck. I'll call you when we get the MRI set up."

"Thanks, Doc. Appreciate you."

He takes off down the hall, and once I'm sure he's out of earshot, I take a step back into the exam room, holding Alicia's gaze. "C'mere, lass."

I expect her to take her sweet time, but she launches herself at me, throwing her arms around my neck. The suddenness of it has me wobbling, but thankfully, the table is right behind me. I'm able to prop myself against it as the crutches clatter to the floor. I band my arms around her waist, pulling her as close to me as possible and burying my face in her neck.

"Hiya, hen."

"Are you okay?" She whispers, voice thick with emotion. "I saw you go down and—."

"Shhh. I'm okay, love," I reassure her, pulling away to cup her face in my palms. "I'm so glad you're here though. That was the best surprise."

I capture her mouth with my own before she can respond, the need to taste her overwhelming. She opens instantly, a soft moan leaving her as I caress her tongue with my own. Moving a hand to the back of her neck, I grip her firmly to keep her at this angle, while moving my other hand to her lower back. Her fingers tighten in my hair.

The only plus side to being out for injury is the fact that I'll get to see this woman more. I'm lucky to live under the same roof as her, fall asleep next to her and wake up to her every morning. Thinking about being in bed with her has my cock beginning to stiffen.

"Do we need to find a chair, baby?" Alicia mutters against my mouth as one of her hands slides down to palm me through my shorts.

My hips flex forward voluntarily as I grunt, dragging my mouth along her jaw. "I don't want a chair. I want to fuck you against the wall. Make you scream my name so loud, they'll hear it outside."

"Oh God," she moans. "I want that too."

The desire in her voice has me fumbling for the button of her jeans. Once it's loosened, I pull the zipper, then stuff my hand down her knickers to cup her pussy. She's soaked for me. The instant I slip a finger inside, her hips buck, little sounds of pleasure filling the room.

"Darlin', I think I need to clean you up."

"Yes," she pleads, rolling her body against mine.

Making to pivot, pain lances through my ankle and I start to go down. "Fuck!" I was so caught up in the moment, I actually forgot I was injured.

With some kind of super human ability, Alicia braces a leg against me and hooks her arms around my chest to prevent me from falling. We stand there, staring wide-eyed and panting before dissolving into quiet laughter. She drops her forehead to my chest, and I kiss her hair.

"Let's go home, a chéadsearc."

* * *

"So, wait," Bridget starts. "It was your coach's idea?"

We're on our way back home. Bridget is sitting up front with Alicia, while I'm in the back with my foot propped across the seat. After having doc send the order for the MRI to the Wilmington clinic and requesting a local physical therapist, we loaded up and hit the road. Bridget has been asking question after question about the injury and how it happened. When I explained that Coach changed our game plan, her brow furrowed in confusion.

"Aye, he did. He knew better, but did it anyway," I tell her.

"But why?"

"Wish I knew, mo stóirín. I should have spoken up."

The thought has been plaguing my brain all night. If I would have been a bit braver and challenged him, I might have been put on the bench, but I wouldn't be injured. Nor would the other forward.

"None of this is your fault, Ro," Alicia reminds me, glancing in her rear view mirror to catch my eye. "You're supposed to trust your coach to do what's best for not just the team as a whole, but for each of you individually. He's the asshole that made this call, so the blame rests squarely on his shoulders. Frankly, I think he should be reported."

"You're not wrong, love, but I'm hesitant to take it higher at the moment. Coach seemed off tonight more than once, so I'd like to talk to him personally before jumping to conclusions. If he's struggling with something, I don't want to add to it, yeah?"

She meets my eyes again. "You're too good, Gallagher."

"This means you're going to be home with us, right?" Bridget asks excitedly before I can respond to Li.

"Aye, I will. I'll have to come back to Charlotte periodically to meet with Doc, but he said I could do most of the PT in Wilmington. You'll probably be sick of me by the end."

"I mean, yeah, probably," she teases, sounding too much like her bratty older sister. "But I've lived with Li all my life, so it will be cool to have another person around."

"Gee, thanks, B," Alicia says dryly.

It does my heart good to see these two laughing and slagging each other. After the whole ordeal with their piece of shite father, I wasn't sure what the outcome would be, but I should have known better than to assume the worst. These two are made of stronger stuff than most.

Alicia did end up reporting him to the police. She's not hopeful he'll be caught, but the fact that he has prior felonies on his record should lend a helping hand. Losing the money she worked so hard for is quite the blow, but I think she'd rather have him put away for good than see a dime of what he took. She'll fight me on it, but I'll do my damnedest to make sure she and Bridget never have to worry about money again.

It's late by the time we make it back, and I'm ready to take some pain killers and crash for the night with Alicia tucked into my side. She unlocks the door and we all file in. Bridget flips the light on, and I'm stunned to see that my bachelor pad has been turned into something homey. The furniture has been rearranged to make space for the items the girls brought from their own place. I wasn't sure if we'd be able to make it work together, especially with such different styles, but with the added throw pillows, blankets, and rugs, it looks like the ultimate comfort den. It's cozy and welcoming.

As my eyes wander around the space, noting the artwork and framed pictures on the walls, I stop on a large photograph that's been printed onto canvas. It's a selfie of the three of us from when we were at the beach. Our heads are pressed together, cheeks pink from being in the sun. We're all grinning, but the absolute joy radiating from my lasses' faces is what steals the spotlight. Alicia's eyes are softer, giving her face a contented look, whereas Bridget's are bright and mischievous.

Arms loop around my waist from behind. "Welcome home, baby. Do you like it?"

Clumsily, I turn until I'm facing Alicia and place both hands on either side of her neck, stroking her jaw with my thumbs. "It's perfect. Thank you."

She stretches onto her toes and kisses me softly. "I love you."

I still get a jolt in my system whenever she utters those three words, because I know that Alicia doesn't say things she doesn't mean, especially when those things could make her feel vulnerable. And opening your heart to someone, entrusting its safe-keeping to someone else, is the most vulnerable position anyone could be in.

"I love you, a chéadsearc." I tell her with my full chest then kiss her again, holding her tighter when she starts to pull away.

"God, you two are the worst." Bridget quips from the kitchen. "Can't you keep it in your pants until you get to your room?" I almost forgot she was still in the room.

"She's right. We should go to our room," I growl against Alicia's mouth, squeezing her hips tightly. She nips my bottom lip before patting my chest and stepping away to join Bridget.

"Go sit down," she calls over her shoulder. "I'll get you a fresh ice pack and your pain meds."

"Thanks a million, darlin'. I'd be lost without you."

"I know."

I chuckle at her sass, but mentally praise myself for not saying what I want to about her bratty mouth and what I'd prefer she do with it. Adjusting to having a young lass under the same roof is going to be a challenge.

"Hey Ro, want something to eat?" The young lass in question asks.

Internally, I'm a puddle of sappy feelings, but on the outside, I grin mischievously and lock my fingers behind my head. "A bloke could get used to having a couple of lasses lookin' after him like this. What ya cookin', mo stóirín?"

The two look at each other, roll their eyes, and proceed to ignore me completely for a solid thirty minutes. Aye, we'll be just fine.

Chapter Forty

Alicia

Today is my last day at the country club. Hallelujah. I've never been so thrilled to leave a place. I had considered staying on until Bridget was out of school for the year, but with Ro's injury and needing to make appointments, it just made sense to quit now. My manager was less than thrilled that I wasn't able to give the standard two week notice, but I'm not worried about being rehireable.

When I get home, I'm busy reading a text as I shut the door then remove my shoes, so I don't notice Ro sitting in a kitchen chair until his lilting voice purrs. "Welcome home, hen."

I look up, a smile already plastered on my face, then freeze. He's naked. Totally and completely naked.

"What are you doing?" I ask on a laugh. "Do you need help getting dressed?"

He shakes his head. "No, love, but it looks like you need help getting undressed."

I give him a disbelieving look, but my core tenses in anticipation. Bridget is at school for another three hours, thank god. Making my way to the breakfast bar, I put my purse and phone down, then turn to face him, elbows propped on the counter behind me.

"What if I wanted to shower first?"

"No."

My eyebrows shoot to my hair line. "Did you just tell me no?"

"Aye. I'm in charge right now."

I snort. "That's rich coming from the one who can only use one of his legs and relies on me to take care of him."

He glowers at me, but his cock that was already semi-hard, is at full attention now. "You're gonna take care of me, alright." He wraps a hand around the base and strokes himself.

I'm instantly wet. I cross one leg over the other, attempting to hide the way I press my thighs together. Naturally, his eyes zero in on the movement and darken.

"Take it all off."

Angling my head to the side, I twist a strand of hair around my finger, and ask innocently, "Take what off?"

"Don't get smart. You know what I mean," Rowan growls, still stroking his dick.

"Sorry, baby. You'll have to be more specific."

"Fucking hell." He sighs heavily, running his free hand over his eyes. The movement flexes the muscles in his stomach and chest in the most delicious way. He drops his hand to his thigh, making a loud slapping noise. "Listen, brat, you either take your clothes off over there, or walk your pretty arse over here and I'll do it myself. Either way, you're going to be naked."

I push off of the counter, taking a few steps in his direction. "How about a compromise?"

He eyes me curiously. "I'm listening."

"I'll do half." Slowly, I begin to undo the buttons of my work shirt, never moving my gaze from his. When I reach the last button, I shrug the top from my shoulders, letting it drop to the floor. Next, I grip the bottom of the camisole I use in place of a bra and pull it over my head, then toss it towards Ro's face. He catches it easily, grinning at me with wicked intent. I bask in the way his eyes rove over me, taking in every inch of exposed skin, lingering at my breasts before continuing.

I close the distance, stepping between his spread legs. He tilts his head back, looking up at me. His muscles tense, like he's holding himself back from lunging. The hand not pumping his length squeezes into a fist on his leg. "Now, you can do the rest."

"Deal." He's already reaching for the waistband of my slacks before the word has been fully released into the air.

His long, nimble fingers making quick work of the button and zipper. He grips my hips, pulling me a fraction closer, then licks a path around my navel while tugging the pants down my legs, taking my underwear with them. His hands skim up the backs of my legs until he's cupping my ass. I want to bury my hands in his hair and push his mouth to my pussy, but he's in charge, so I'm going to let him call the shots.

"I can't reach your bloody socks," he murmurs against my belly.

Huffing a laugh, I lift one foot behind me to remove the offending garment, then repeat with the other, letting his hands steady me. "Better?"

He grunts in response while continuing to trail his fingers over my backside and lavishing my stomach with kisses. Goosebumps bloom all over my body.

"What now, baby?" I purr. "Or did you just want me to get naked?"

Cool air kisses the skin of my right ass cheek just before a sharp slap lands in the vacant spot. My jaw drops and I level him with a glare before playfully reprimanding him. "Rowan Gallagher!"

He leans back, still cupping my ass, and grins wide. "You love it. Now, get on your knees, darlin', so I can put that mouth to better use."

Giving in to the urge to touch him, I extend a hand and wrap it around the column of his throat and squeeze once. "What's the magic word?"

His Adam's apple bobs under my palm, and his tongue darts out to lick his lips. Mesmerized by his handsome face and the headiness of being in a dominant position, I don't register his hand moving up the inside of my thigh until he's sinking two fingers into my pussy, curling them immediately to rub that magic spot.

"Fuck!" I hiss, nearly collapsing in his lap at the sudden wave of lust.

Ro's fingers don't relent, pumping into me while his thumb presses against my clit. I'm almost embarrassed about how close I am to orgasm. When I feel him tug at one of my nipple piercings, I come so hard, I can't breathe. My knees buckle, and he removes his hand just in time for me to slide to the floor and kneel at his feet.

"Perfect." His voice is a low rumble that settles over my skin, causing my eyelids to lower and sparking a desire to please him in whatever way I can.

Trusting Ro with my body comes easily, but fully surrendering is something I never thought I'd want, let alone need. I exist only to do his bidding in this moment.

"Alicia." Ro's sharp command has my eyes jerking to his immediately. I sit up straight, laying my palms on my thighs.

"Yes, sir?" I'm practically purring as the words tumble from my mouth.

He shifts forward on the chair, pinching my chin between his thumb and index finger, raising my face to give me a soft, chaste kiss. Then he turns my head and whispers into my ear. "Now, be a good lass and suck my cock."

* * *

"The therapist will have a student with him today," Ro murmurs against my shoulder.

His alarm went off about ten minutes ago, but neither of us are inclined to move from the bed. I thought getting used to having someone sleeping next to me would be difficult, but it's the most normal I've ever felt. There's a sense of rightness to it. We share a king sized bed, but the man curls himself around me nightly and stays that way until morning.

Before Ro, my mind would race for over an hour before I fell asleep. Not now. The moment his arm drapes over my waist, palm flattening against my belly, I'm already nodding off.

"Because you're so difficult that it takes an extra person to get through the exercises?" I ask teasingly just to rile him up.

Teeth graze my neck, making me shiver.

"Didn't get your fill of my cock in your mouth last night, did you?" The hand that's been holding me close slips upward to squeeze my breast before rubbing slow circles around my nipple. My spine arches as I bite back a moan.

"No," he continues, like this is a conversation at the dinner table. "The new bloke is from out of town visiting family, but still has to finish up his clinical hours or something like that."

I'm not sure why that turns me on even more. "Did they happen to give you the name of the new guy?"

"No," Ro tells me as he switches from circling to long, slow tugs of my nipple piercing. The sensation never ceases to make my pussy throb with need. "Why do you ask, hen?"

"What?" My brain short-circuits when he pushes his hips into my ass, and I feel his erection against me.

"Why are you asking about some other bloke while you're in my bed, and my hands are on you?"

I hesitate, knowing that the last time I brought up Isaac, Rowan became slightly snarky, but if my suspicions are correct, I don't want him to feel like I was being dishonest with him.

"Well, I can't guarantee it, but I might know who it is," I explain, snuggling closer to his warm body. "And if it's who I think it is, there's a chance you may not be happy about it."

The hand on my tit freezes. "Is that right?"

"Yes. I think it's Isaac."

"Isaac?"

"Paddy's new lady's grandson. The one that helped get my father to leave me alone that night."

He flicks my nipple one last time, making a humming noise in his throat, before sliding his hand down my body to the juncture of my thighs and parting the lips of my pussy to circle my clit. I stretch an arm up to loop behind his head, burying my own fingers in his hair while my body rolls against him.

"Aye, I remember now." He nips my earlobe with his teeth, then asks darkly, "Do I need to be worried?"

I shake my head because I'm too caught up in the way he's moving his fingers to form coherent thoughts. He pinches my clit, making me suck in a sharp breath.

"Use your words, Alicia."

"N-no," I stammer.

"Does he know you're spoken for?"

"Yes."

"Good," Ro growls, sinking a finger into me. "As long as he knows who you belong to and keeps his eyes and hands to himself, we'll get along grand."

Maybe I'm trying to make him jealous or maybe I'm just stupid because I don't let it lie. "I think he'd take that as a challenge."

Ro's hand stills, and I nearly cry out in frustration. The need to come is on the cusp of painful, so my fingers join his in an attempt to get them moving again.

"Please, baby. I need more. I'm so close."

Nothing.

"Rowan?"

"I thought you said I didn't need to be worried?" There's a coldness to his voice.

"You don't," I tell him, pushing back into his dick to stir him into action again. "I'm not interested in him, baby. Just you."

He withdraws his hand, but I catch his wrist, digging my nails into his skin.

"What are you doing?"

Next thing I know, I'm face-down on the bed, with his powerful body pinning me to the mattress, and his hot breath against my neck.

"Ro, your ankle!"

He sits back on his knees, fisting my hair and wrapping it around his left hand. With his right, he thrusts it under my stomach to pull me back so that I'm on my elbows and knees.

Leaning over me, he snarls in my ear. "Maybe I need to mark you, darlin'. Put my brand where anyone can see, especially if this fucker is going to be there later. I want him to take one look at you and know beyond a shadow of a doubt who you belong to. I want him to know that there's only one man who wrings every last fucking ounce of pleasure from you, night after night."

"Baby, please," I beg. Any other time, I'd be kicking the ass of anyone who tried to stake a claim on me, but right now I'm so turned on, I can feel my arousal seeping out of me.

"Maybe I should have him do a house call so he can watch you choke on my cock."

Another sharp tug on my hair pulls my head back, stretching my neck. It's painful in the best way. The moan spilling from me is cut short when he slaps my ass hard enough that I know his handprint will be there a while. Before I take my next breath, his cock is slamming into me. He releases my hair in exchange for a bruising grip on my hips. I remember that Bridget is home in time to bury my face into the mattress, muffling my cries as he pistons in and out of me at a brutal pace.

"I wish he was standing right outside the door, listening to the way I make you scream," Ro grunts the words as he fucks me harder.

Professional athletes have incredible stamina, so while he's only now sounding slightly winded, I'm gasping for air.

"Rowan," I sob out. "Please."

His rhythm falters slightly, and I hear him suck in a breath between his teeth. Before I can ask what happened, he's pulled me up and against his chest, still thrusting into me. One hand wraps around my throat while the other slaps my clit, bringing me to teeter on the height of pleasure.

"Do that again," I pant out.

Ro grips my throat tighter, constricting my airways just tight enough to make sucking down breaths a little harder, then slaps my clit three more times in quick succession. My orgasm barrels through me. Before I can let loose the scream, he turns my face to his, sealing his mouth over mine to swallow the sound. His body jolts and he stills, filling me with his release.

When the pulsing subsides, we collapse onto the bed, covered in sweat, and gasping for air like we've just run a marathon. Ro rolls us until he's on his back and I'm draped over his chest.

Eventually, when my heart rate settles and I'm tracing the outlines of his tattoos, I ask the question. "Care to tell me what that was about?"

He's silent a moment before replying. "I should maybe apologize, but I'm not sorry, love. Even though I know in the deepest recesses of my heart that you'd never go willingly, just the idea of another man even attempting to take you has me feeling some sort of way."

I snort and meet his eyes. "You realize that you sound like some sort of Neanderthal right now, right?"

"Aye, I know," he admits, groaning.

"Well, it was pretty hot, so I'm not too mad about it," I admit, surprising even myself.

"It was. And definitely worth fucking up my ankle for."

"What?" I sit up fast, hands moving uselessly to his ankle. It's still wrapped, so I can't tell if it's swelling. "What did you do?"

Ro pulls himself to a sitting position then grabs my chin, forcing me to look at him. "I'm fine, hen. Just put weight on it when I shouldn't have. I'll ice it and elevate it for a bit and then make sure to let Isaac know exactly how I did it."

"You're an idiot."

"But I'm your idiot," he quips.

No arguments there.

Chapter Forty-One

Rowan

She was right. I'm decidedly not pleased with this Isaac fella, and we've been at the Sports Therapy Center for less than two minutes. The moment we arrived, his eyes widened and his mouth split into a blinding grin.

"Alicia, what a surprise," His voice is unnecessarily deep as he greets my lass.

When he opens his arms like he's going to embrace her, I step closer and wind an arm around her back and place my hand low on her hip, pulling her into my side. She cuts me a look implying that she knows what I'm doing, but returns the gesture, looping her arm around my waist.

"Are you going to introduce me to your friend, darlin'?"

"Ro, *sweetie,*" she coos warmly, but her eyes are raging at me. "This is Isaac. His grandmother, Sondra, is with our Paddy. Isaac, this is Rowan, your temporary patient, and—"

"The boyfriend?" Isaac guesses, inspecting me from head to toe.

"Well, it's a bit more than that, *Ivan,*" I say just to be a cunt then plant a kiss on Alicia's temple and squeeze her arse. "What we have is the forever kind of love."

Her hand slips down my back to pinch my arse. It takes more effort than I'd like to admit to keep from hollering.

"It's Isaac," he corrects, widening his stance and folding his thick arms over his equally muscular chest. I'm not a scrawny bloke, but this fucker is absolutely massive. That polo he's wearing is about to pop at the seams. And, fine. He's an attractive fella. "For a *forever* kind of thing, I haven't heard too much about you."

I bristle, a feeling I buried years ago snaking its way into my chest. I want to *fight* this wanker. The urge to knock that smirk from his face is so strong, I have to put my free hand in the pocket of my gym shorts.

"Fucks sake," Alicia mutters next to me, then addresses Isaac. "You haven't heard much about him because we only met recently and have had half a conversation. And, like I told you then, we"—she points between her body and mine—"are exclusive and I have no interest in changing that."

The finality in her voice has pride blooming until I realize that what Alicia isn't saying is that he's asked her out before. She must sense the storm brewing, because she tightens her arm around me.

"You're right. I'm not trying to mess that up, just giving you shit. Anyway," he turns back to me, clapping his hands together. "I really am honored to be helping out with your PT. I was watching the game when your injury happened, but I'd like to go over the details with you, if you don't mind."

I glower, but give him a quick nod. "Aye, appreciate that. I'll meet you and doc over there in a moment."

Isaac nods and retreats to where the therapist has set up.

"Hey," Alicia whispers as she places a hand to my cheek and angles my face down. I drag my gaze from Isaac and find the sapphire pools I love to get lost in searching my own. "You good?"

"You never said he made a move on you," I grumble.

"Ro, I'm a bartender," she smiles indulgently. "Men make moves on me every day. It's an occupational hazard, even though it shouldn't be—"

"No, it bloody well shouldn't."

"Might I remind you that *you* were one of them for many years?"

I open my mouth to object, but realize she's right. Hitting on Alicia was my favorite pastime whenever we went to Paddy's.

"Wait, does that mean you treat every other fella like you did me?"

She rolls her eyes. "No, Gallagher. I'm only a snarky bitch to you. Now, quit being a baby and go fix your ankle."

"Aye, alright, but kiss me first." Without waiting for an answer, I swoop in and claim her mouth. She kisses me back but pulls away before I can deepen it, seeming to know that I planned on making a spectacle of it.

"You're a troublemaker." She smirks at me.

"But you love me."

"Yeah, I do," she concedes with a sigh.

* * *

By the end of therapy, I'm convinced that my ankle will never be normal again. What should be a simple stretch felt more like cutting the foot off altogether.

"Christ, that was torture, Doc," I grouse, wiping the sweat from my brow with the bottom of my shirt.

"It will feel worse before it gets better. I'm sure it doesn't seem like any progress was made today, but you were able to complete more exercises than what the majority of soccer players can at this stage. That's a good sign." He hands me my crutches and waits for me to get them positioned before leading us toward the waiting area. As we near, I see Isaac is talking to Alicia.

During the last ten minutes of the session, he claimed to have received a phone call and excused himself. I didn't think anything of it, because while he was going through the exercises with me, he was focused and thorough, guiding me through each routine like he's been doing this for years as opposed to being a student. I forgot that he tried to snatch my lass. Until now.

I'm about to make a scene when I realize that he's not talking to just Alicia, but Bridget too. She was gone for school by the time I made my way out of the bedroom this morning so I missed seeing her.

"Mo stóirín!" I call out, smiling broadly at her. "What are you doing here?"

Bridget smiles back and stands to give me a hug. I soak it up, knowing that physical affection isn't something she does often.

"Li said you guys were here, so I had a friend drop me off after school," she explains, tucking a strand of her dark hair behind her ear.

She started her new school earlier this week and has had nothing but good things to say. I can already tell a difference in her demeanor just in the short time she's been there. Her eyes are brighter and the smiles come easier.

"Yeah? Look at you, already making friends."

She blushes and looks at her feet. I glance at Li, raising a brow and she winks. What the feck does that mean?

"When do you work at Paddy's next?" Isaac's deep timber grates along my nerves, especially when he's stealing Alicia's attention.

I start to open my mouth to tell him he can fuck right off and mind his own business when Bridget taps my arm. I glance down to find her green eyes flash with mischief.

"Hey, Ro?"

"Yeah, love?"

She's fighting a smile. "Guess what I discovered today."

"Hmmm." I tap a finger to my lips. "Let's see. Life on Mars?"

She rolls her eyes, and it dawns on me that I'm now living with *two* sassy lassies.

"You have a fan club at school."

My eyebrows shoot up so high they might have actually left my forehead all together. "No kidding? What kind of fan club? Is it for my roguish good looks or my skills on the pitch?"

She grimaces. "It's not for your looks."

Frowning, I huff out an exaggerated sigh. "Probably for the better. Your sister would have them by the bollocks. And I don't fancy being stalked by a group of teenyboppers."

The low rumble of Isaac's laugh has us both turning our heads in his direction.

"Fecking miserable pox," I mutter under my breath.

Bridget snorts. "I take it you don't like Isaac?"

I scoff. "I'd like him better if he'd pin his wandering eyes on someone else."

"Can you blame him?" She asks. "Li's gorgeous."

Not in her usual black leather, she looks soft and carefree in cutoff shorts and a worn O'Nelly's t-shirt, the pub's logo over her left breast. Her hair is down in loose waves, and her face is free of makeup.

"Aye, she is," I agree. "It's not that he finds her attractive. It's that he knows she's taken, yet keeps crowding her."

"There's like five feet of space between them, Ro. Are you afraid if she gets too close she's going to choose him?"

I give her a disgusted look. "Ach, no! He's not that good looking."

"Yes, he is," she sighs dreamily.

"Fecking traitor," I snarl, casting Bridget my most intimidating glare.

Her lips twitch and she covers her mouth with a hand to smother the laugh she's trying to keep at bay.

"Keep it up, young wan, and I'll teach Lou to shite in your bed instead of the litter box." I threaten her, but we both know I won't do a damn thing. "C'mon, then. Let's go rescue her and get out of here before I do something rash."

Bridget takes off toward her sister, interrupting whatever Isaac is saying. "Li, it's time to go. Ro's getting cranky."

"Oy!" I call out, putting my crutches into gear. "Bleeding hallion! I'm doing no such thing."

These two will forever keep me on my toes, never giving me a moment's peace, but if I'm being honest, I wouldn't have it any other way.

Chapter Forty-Two

Alicia

"Wait, how many people is she making you invite?" Norah's voice rises an octave in alarm.

I'm working behind the bar tonight, thankful that it's slower than it has been. The past couple of weeks have been complete chaos between Ro's physical therapy, shifts at work, and just the day in and day out grind of adulthood. By the time I get home from work most nights, I'm exhausted to the point where I'm crashing as soon as my head hits the pillow. Ro has learned that if he wants to get his hands on me, he needs to do it before I get under the covers. Most nights he waits up for me, ready to pounce the moment I walk through the door, which usually isn't an issue since Bridget is already asleep, but other nights, I come home to find him passed out on the couch, ESPN illuminating the room.

The pub hasn't had any new customers in over an hour, so I've actually been able to catch up with the Kennedys and soon to be O'Briens. Teagan finally proposed to Layla, and the two are planning a huge wedding, at her mother's command. Her family is Mexican, so there's no such thing as a small, quiet celebration. *Especially* when Layla is the first of her siblings to get married.

"Way too fucking many," Teagan answers for Layla as she downs another shot of Tequila.

"You should elope out of spite," Norah suggests after throwing back her own drink.

Layla whips her head toward our friend, onyx hair flying out behind her. "Ohmygodwetotallyshould."

She's been drinking at a rapid pace for the last hour, claiming she needed to unwind, and Norah said she's there for moral support. Eamon and Teagan have been sipping their beers, knowing they'll likely be carrying their gals out of here later.

"Lovely," Teagan begins softly, using the nickname he gave her before they even became a couple, then cups her face in his hands. "We talked about this. Even if we eloped, your ma would still make us proceed with the ceremony and then roast us on a spit and serve us to the guests. I'll confront your mother about a lot of things, but that's one area I'm afraid to tread."

"Ugh. Why are you always so reasonable?" Layla whines, letting her forehead drop to his chest. I chuckle and pour her one more shot, telling her it's the last one for the night. Teagan mouths a thank you at me over her head.

Norah slides from the bar stool and stumbles a step, but Eamon, the ever-watchful and protective husband, winds a muscled arm around her middle. She giggles then grabs the back of his neck and pulls him down for a passionate kiss. His eyes widen in shock, but soon turn heated, his hands snaking down to cup her ass. He squeezes, then pulls back. "Behave, Acushla. We're in public."

Norah looks around wildly at the empty pub. "We're literally the only ones here."

She attempts to pull his mouth back to hers, but he spins her so his chest is pressed against her back and secures both arms around her.

"Fire sprite, I think it's time to go home, yeah?"

Giggling again, she nods her head vigorously, auburn strands falling into her face.

"Aye," Teagan agrees, running a hand over Layla's hair. She's still slumped against his chest. "It's time to get this one home, too. Tell Ro we'll come by and see him this weekend."

"Will do," I reply. "He'll like having the company."

Not that he hasn't had social interaction, but apparently Isaac is not the company he wants to keep right now. No matter how many times I assure him that he has nothing to worry about, it doesn't change how possessive he becomes whenever he sees me chatting with the man. I'd be annoyed if not for the way he fucks me when we get home. After today's therapy session, he was surly over Isaac giving me a side hug before we left, so he took out his frustration by bending me over the back of the sofa and railing me until I came twice on his cock, then once more when he insisted I sit on his face. I'm considering paying Isaac to keep putting moves on me just to see what Ro comes up with next.

"Li!" Norah's drunken screech pulls me back to the present.

"Norie!" I respond with the same level of enthusiasm, earning chuckles from the guys.

"You know what we should do?"

"What's that?" I rest my elbows on the bar top and fold my hands under my chin.

She pulls away from Eamon—though he still keeps his hands on her—and mirrors my pose. "We should all do a triple date! Not here, obviously, but the three of us—"

"Six, love," Eamon corrects her gently.

"Six, right! Anyway, the six of us should all do dinner and some kind of activity!"

Grinning, I reach out to stroke her hair, like I would my cat. "Norie, I love you."

She beams. "I love you, too! So are we going on a date now?"

I look to Eamon and Teagan, who are shaking with silent laughter, then back to Norah. "Yeah, let's do it."

"Yay!" She throws her hands into the air and squeals happily. Since she's unsteady on her feet, she begins to topple to the side, but Eamon catches her quickly and scoops her into his arms. When he cradles her to his chest, she burrows his face into his neck, sighing happily.

"Get those girls home," I order, pointing back and forth between the two Irishmen. "We'll plan something when they're sober."

They nod their agreement and say their goodbyes. I watch as Layla takes a clumsy step, clutching Teag's left shoulder, and without missing a beat, he bends, swoops his right arm under her legs and hauls her into the same position Norah is with Eamon.

Wow. That was hot.

"Damn, O'Brien!" I call out before they reach the door. "Smooth!"

He turns, grinning broadly, and winks before carrying his soon to be bride over the threshold.

* * *

"Alicia, love, would ye mind comin' in here for a moment?" Paddy calls from his office.

It's not unusual for him to stop me the moment I arrive at work and talk my ear off before I'm able to actually do my job, so I don't think much of it.

"Yep, be right there," I answer as I hang my jacket on the hook by the back door and check my reflection in the mirror.

After determining that my eyeliner isn't smudged and I don't have any random strands of hair sticking out of my braid, I stroll into the office and perch on the edge of the chair across from him.

He doesn't look up from whatever paperwork is in front of him right away, so I wait a few seconds before clearing my throat. His bespectacled eyes slowly rise to meet mine and I can tell that something is...off. He looks like he's stuck somewhere between concerned and...excited?

"Pat," I start, going on high alert. "What's going on?"

Sighing heavily, he leans forward, resting his forearms on the desk and interlacing his fingers. "I have some news."

My heart jumps into my throat, blocking off my oxygen. I can feel a burning sensation behind my eyes, my brain preparing me for the worst. Fighting to swallow the lump that's keeping me from speaking, I square my shoulders.

Finally, I choke out the words. "What, uh...what kind of news?"

Paddy glances down at his hands then back up, and a slow grin spreads across his face, cheeks turning rosy and eyes sparkling.

"Sondra and I are getting married!"

I blink, then blink again. Then narrow my eyes at him. "Pat, you son of a...ugh! Why would you do that?!"

He rears back like I slapped him, and honestly, I kind of want to.

"What do you mean?" He asks dumbfounded. "I thought you'd be happy for me!"

"I am, you crazy old man," I yell. "But I thought you were going to tell me you were dying! You never start a conversation off like that! Especially when you're old enough to be my grandfather! Jesus, Pat."

There's a pause then he starts chuckling. I'm certainly not amused, but as his low laugh transforms into a full belly laugh, my lips twitch, and when he starts wiping tears from his eyes, I grin. God, I love this man.

Eventually, he gains control of himself enough to say, "I'm sorry, love. I didn't even think about how that might come across, but your reaction was priceless, so it was."

"Glad you find my suffering so entertaining." I shake my head in mock disappointment.

"You know, that's what I loved most about you from the moment you applied here?" He asks, giving me a fond smile.

"What? That I'll yell at you for doing shit like that?"

"Aye," he says, nodding. "I knew as soon as you walked through my doors that you'd not only be a hard worker, but wouldn't put up with any shenanigans from me or the patrons. This building may bear my name, but you're the one that keeps everything going strong."

I duck my head to hide the emotions swirling in my gut. "Thanks, Paddy. I appreciate you saying that. This has basically been my home, and I've loved watching it flourish over the years."

"I know. Which is why I want to give it to you," he announces confidently.

My head snaps up, and I'm positive my eyes are bugging out of my head. "Wha...what?"

"I'm retiring, Alicia. Like you implied, I'm not a young man anymore." He winks. "Sondra and I are very much in love and want to spend what's left of our lives together, enjoying each other. My Ellie and I," he says, then pauses, closing his eyes and taking a shuddering breath. When he opens his eyes, they're lined with tears. "Ellie and I spent our married lives working and taking care of our lads. We were always saying we'd explore the world and go on grand adventures when the boys were grown, but even when they were, we still worked. Don't get me wrong, now. We loved every minute of making O'Nelly's into what it was back in Ireland. We rarely argued and found many a reason to laugh. I never thought I'd love again after she left this world. Sondra took me by complete surprise, and I don't want to waste a single minute on anything other than loving her."

Tears are pouring down my cheeks, my makeup surely ruined, but I can't bring myself to care after Paddy's declaration. Not only am I moved by his love for his late wife, and now Sondra, but the idea of him not being a part of O'Nelly's guts me. He never thought of me as less than, never hassled me if I had to leave to take care of Bridget. He put up with my mood swings and snarky retorts, found ways for me to put in extra hours when I was short on money, often times giving me the tips *he* earned. I simply would not have survived without him. And now he's giving me the pub?

"Pat," I sniffle. "I don't know the first thing about owning a business."

"Ach, don't be thick, lass!" He scolds, removing the glasses from his face and setting them on the desk. "What did I just tell ya? You've kept this place in tip top shape and managed me, when I'm the one who's supposed to manage you."

"But..."

"No, listen. There's no debt on the building or the business. Every expense will be just to keep this place going, and everything leftover is profit. You already know how to do all that needs to be done as far as bills, inventory, and payroll, and anything else? I'm certain that fella of yours, who has a business degree, can help. You deserve this, Alicia. You've spent too much of your life believing you're unworthy of the good life has to offer, and it just isn't true, love. I've watched you raise your wee sister and work yourself to the bone, never once thinking about what you're missing out on. Aye, running a business comes with its share of difficulties, but compared to the storms you've faced, it will be nothing but a blip on the radar. You deserve to live a beautiful life."

Completely floored, I bury my face in my hands and sob. It's all too much. Never did I think that I'd have my own business, but it's more than that. It's more than Pat just thinking I'm capable and wanting to run off into the sunset. This is a fresh start, a new life. It doesn't erase the past or hide the scars, but it's a chance. A chance to prove to myself that I'm more than the broken and calloused woman who's never let herself dare to hope for anything better.

I hear Pat rise from his chair and move to stand beside me, his warm hand gently rubbing my back. Blindly, I stand and throw my arms around him.

"Thank you." The words come out garbled because I can't stop crying. "I love you."

"Well, now," he clears his throat as he holds me. "I love you too, lass. You're the only one I'd entrust this place to."

Chapter Forty-Three

Rowan

Today's PT went exceptionally well, if I do say so myself. Not only was I cleared to do warm ups with the team, but I was given the okay to drive again. Bridget and I grabbed dinner together, where I learned that I'm officially old and cannot speak *teenager,* but was still a good time. We ordered Alicia her favorite sushi roll and are going to surprise her at O'Nelly's.

It's a Tuesday night, so I know the pub will be slow. Sure enough, when we walk in, there's not a soul in the place, not even behind the bar. I set the take-out on the shining surface and motion for Bridget to take a seat.

"Oy!" I holler out. "What's a bloke gotta do to get some service in here?"

"Hold your horses, Gallagher!" The muffled voice of my leading lady calls from the kitchen.

Chuckling, I climb up onto the bar stool next to Bridget. It's been a while since I've been here, so I take a moment to look around. The same mahogany surfaces gleam under the light from the sconces spaced throughout the pub. The same tables, booths, and chairs are arranged just as they've always been. Not much has changed since the first time I came here. In fact, I think the only noticeable difference is the new register system. Alicia finally made Paddy replace the ancient cash register with a touch screen and tap-to-pay. The aul man grumbled about it for a while, but eventually came around to the idea. He still makes her handle the majority of card payments though.

The doors leading to the back swing open and out comes Alicia. The first thing I notice is how splotchy the skin on her face is and how red and swollen her eyes are. I'm immediately out of my seat and rounding the bar, cupping her cheeks in my hands.

"A chéadsearc, what's wrong?" My eyes dart between both of hers frantically.

Her fingers wrap around my wrists and she grins widely, joy lighting up her face. "I have something to tell you." Her eyes flicker over to where Bridget is sitting, watching us with a worried expression. "B, hi! I'm so glad you're here!"

Alicia releases my wrists and pulls from my grasp, making her way toward her sister. She crashes into Bridget, almost knocking her from the stool.

"What the...?" Bridget gasps. "Are you drunk, Li?"

"No!" She laughs, stepping back. "I just am so happy that I get to share this news with two of my favorite people."

Joining them, I lean against the bar and fold my arms over my chest. "Well don't keep us waiting, hen."

Glancing back and forth between me and her sister, she covers her mouth with both hands and her eyes fill with tears. "Paddy is giving me the pub!"

"What?!" We both blurt out.

Alicia giggles and nods her head rapidly. "He's marrying Sondra and retiring and said he's handing the pub over to me."

I stare in shock. There is so much to process in that one sentence. "Stall the ball," I say, unfolding my hands and raking my fingers through my hair. "He's retiring?"

"He's getting married?" Bridget asks, equally as shocked.

After Alicia fills us in on the entire conversation she had with Paddy, I pull her into my arms, kissing her temple. "Ah, love, that's incredible! You deserve it."

"That's what I told her," Paddy says, stepping around the bar, hands stuffed into his pockets.

"Ach, Paddy! Congrats, aul man! Sondra's a lucky lass," I tell him with a wink.

"Nah," he says, shaking his head. "'Tis I that's the lucky one."

"Aye, you're probably right about that," I tease, stepping toward him and extending a hand. When he grasps it, I pull him in for a hug. "When's the big day?"

"Sooner rather than later, I hope! I'm anxious to start this new chapter with my bride." He pulls back from the embrace. "You'll understand soon enough, lad."

Glancing over at Alicia, I see her cheeks flush. The term blushing bride flashes in my mind and I think Pat might be right.

"Happy for you," I tell him sincerely. "And as for the pub, I don't think you could have chosen a better replacement."

"Aye, I don't think so either. She'll do great things." He claps me on the shoulder. "And I'm glad she has you to support her along the way. I knew once you got your wild ways out of your system, you'd be exactly what she needed."

"It's more like she's what I needed to pull my head out of my arse," I admit.

Paddy laughs, squeezing my shoulder. "Well, you may not be too far off on that one, lad."

* * *

Sondra and Pat decided to have a small ceremony at Airlie Gardens just two short weeks after getting engaged. The crowd was small. The Kennedys, Teagan and Layla, Isaac, and Bridget, Alicia, and I. After the officiant announced them as husband and wife, Pat dipped his bride and kissed her soundly. The fellas and I made enough noise to properly embarrass him, while our lasses blotted at their eyes.

Afterwards, we convinced the newlyweds to come back to the pub, where Alicia and the girls set up a small reception. They had food catered in from the restaurant where Pat and Sondra had their first date and a miniature wedding cake from a local bakery. When the meal had been cleared, we pushed the tables and chairs out of the way to make room for a dance floor.

I've been waiting for this all day. Even though they insisted it was casual, we all dressed to the nines. When Alicia walked out of our bedroom wearing the dress she wore to Eamon and Norah's wedding, I had to pick my jaw up off the floor and remind myself that Bridget was in the room. It's been bleedin' torture keeping my hands to myself…or at least, keeping them appropriate.

But now I have an acceptable reason to put my hands on her as I pull her to the dance floor. She loops her arms around my neck as I settle my palms on her lower back, right above the curve of her arse. The back of the dress sits so low, I can slip my fingertips just underneath the fabric.

"Don't get handsy," she murmurs, pressing herself into me.

I brush a kiss to her cheek. "Can't help it. I fucking love this dress."

"I know," she sighs happily. "That's why I wore it."

"Tease."

Alicia laughs softly and lays her head against my chest.

"It looks fantastic in here," I compliment her as I take in the simple, yet elegant decorations strung about. "You did a great job putting this together, love."

Paddy hasn't officially signed the pub over to Alicia yet, but he's slowly been pulling back from running the joint so that she can get a feel for what it's like without him. As happy as we all are for him, not seeing him regularly will be different, for sure.

"Thanks, baby," she murmurs. "I'm going to miss him."

"Aye, me too."

We continue to sway to the music in silence, oblivious to everyone else around us. It feels like it's been ages since I was able to just hold her, and

I've missed it. She's been working more hours, and I've started traveling to Charlotte for training with the team. While I haven't been given the go ahead to play yet, I still need to practice with them. Getting used to this new routine has been harder than I thought it would be. Waking up with Alicia every morning and going to bed with her at night is my new favorite pastime. Seeing Bridget when she gets home from school is a close second. Even hanging out with Lou during the day has been enjoyable. He won't do it while Alicia is home, but when it's just the two of us, the wanker curls up on my chest and falls asleep. If not for the pictures and videos I've taken, my girls would never believe it.

I squeeze Alicia a little tighter, and she pulls back to look at me questioningly. Reluctantly moving a hand from her back, I tuck a strand of hair behind her ear then lay my palm on the side of her neck.

"I love you."

Her eyes soften and cheeks darken slightly. "I love you, too."

* * *

Paddy and Sondra left the party a couple of hours ago, and the rest of us are sitting around drinking and picking at the leftover food and cake. We've spent the evening reminiscing about the early days at UNCW and Paddy's, recounting the drinking contest that introduced Eamon and Norah, then the other drinking contest that led to us modeling Norah's costume designs for a drag show. She may seem meek and mild, but she earned the nickname Fire Sprite for a reason.

Teagan and Layla had a great time reminding me of the time I broke up their *almost* first kiss outside of the UNCW library. What they don't know is that I had been observing them for a while and could see the sexual tension building. Had I not intervened, they likely would have fucked against the brick wall in front of the entire student body. I did them a favor, really.

Eventually, the conversation dies down and the lasses start yawning. They all offer to help clean up, but I assure them we'll be good. Eamon and Norah offer to take Bridget home since she's basically dead on her feet. Once they've all gone, I double check that the front door is locked before turning to see Alicia placing some empty crates on the floor by the bar. She takes the top one and begins filling it with the decorations adorning the bar's facade. That fucking dress is hugging her body and I've had just about enough of that, so I step into her, pressing my chest to her back and taking the crate from her hands. I set it on the table closest to us then return, sliding my arms around her waist. She relaxes into me, folding her arms over mine as her arse rubs right up against my stiffening cock.

"Mmm, someone feeling needy?" She purrs, dropping her head back onto my chest.

"Aye," I agree as I slide one hand from her stomach, through the valley of her breasts, and lightly wrap it around her throat. "Always am when you're around, but even more so when you're wearing my favorite dress."

"Sorry, baby. I don't think it will fit you."

My hand tightens and I push my hips into her. "You've always been a brat to me, haven't you, darlin'? Do you know what I wanted to do the first time I saw you?"

"Tell me," she breathes out, hips rolling.

Dropping my mouth to her shoulder, I bite the soft spot that connects to her neck. "I wanted to bend you over this bar and turn your pretty arse red while fucking you."

Alicia shivers and shifts her weight from one foot to the other. The hand I have across her middle slips down to the bottom hem of her dress. Trailing my fingers upward, I drag the fabric with me, intending to plunge my hand down her knickers, but just like the first time she wore this dress, there's nothing on underneath.

I groan and cup her pussy, finding it nearly dripping. "Fucking hell, I love how wet you are for me."

Loosening my grip on her throat, I skate over her chest, dipping my palm under the neckline of her dress to cup her breast before pinching her nipple, knowing how much she loves the heightened sensation from the piercing.

"Rowan." Her voice is pleading as she attempts to ride my hand.

"What do you need, Li?" I switch to the other breast.

"I need..." She gasps as I sink two fingers into her pussy. "Oh, god. I need you to fuck me."

"Is that all?"

"No. Spank me. I need you to spank me." Alicia is desperately grinding, trying to get herself off, but I keep the heel of my hand far enough away that she can't find purchase.

Abruptly, I pull my hands from her body and step back, leaving her gasping. She spins and fixes me with a glare.

"What are you doing?"

I unbutton the cuffs of my dress shirt and roll the sleeves up to my elbows, loving the way her sapphire eyes track the movements. Next I unbuckle my belt, undo my trousers, and pull my cock out of my briefs, stroking from base to tip a couple of times.

"Dress off, Alicia. Then, I want you to put a knee on either of those stools," I nod to the stools in question, "and lay over the top of the bar."

Surprisingly, she complies instantly, dragging the flimsy straps of the dress over her arms and letting it fall to the ground. She leaves her heels on and climbs onto the bar stools, balancing a knee on each, just like I told her to. With a look over her shoulder, she slowly lowers herself so she's draped over the top. I have to stop pumping my cock or I'll go off just looking at her. Arse in the air and pretty pussy glistening in the dim lighting of the bar like that has me aching.

Closing the distance, I run my palms up the backs of her thighs and over the globes of her arse.

"Good lass," I praise her before dipping my head and running my tongue over her pussy.

"Oh god," Alicia cries out, hips bucking.

"Don't move," I order before slapping her arse.

Because she's Alicia, she wiggles again.

"Hen, that's going to cost you."

"Please."

After one more lick, I stand and palm her arse with both hands, then draw one back and bring it back down sharply. My handprint blooms on her porcelain skin.

"Fuck!" She hisses through her teeth.

Not able to wait any longer, I snatch a crate, flip it over, and step onto it so I'll be able to line myself up. Once I know it's secure enough to hold my weight, I lean over Alicia to place a trail of kisses along her spine. Straightening, I fist my cock, lining it up with her entrance, latch a hand to her hip, and surge forward, burying myself in her heat. We both moan loudly, the sound filling the room. Hers quickly turn to cries of pleasure as I piston into her, unrelentingly. She curls her hands around the edge of the bar, clinging to it, as I fuck her harder. Bringing my hand back, I deliver a slap to the other side of her arse and she screams. I spank her twice more in rapid succession, and she goes off like a fucking firework. Her inner walls clench around me, and I roar as I fill her with my cum, each pulse of my cock sending me into orbit.

When our breathing returns to normal, I finally pull out, and watch with satisfaction as my release trickles from her pussy. Alicia stays draped over the bar while I retrieve a clean towel to clean her up. Once that's taken care of, I help her down from the bar stools and hold her close while she tries to stand on wobbly legs. She raises her eyes to mine, then tilts her head to kiss me. When she ends it, she giggles.

"What's so funny, hen?"

She looks behind her at the bar. "That was really—"

"Fucking hot?" I offer.

"I was going to say unsanitary, but fucking hot works too."

"Come on, love." I kiss her forehead. "Let's get this place cleaned up and go home."

Home. The word is more meaningful now that I've got my girls.

Epilogue

Bridget - One Year Later

"How would you feel about us legally adopting you?"

My eyes widen at Ro's unexpected question. Honestly, I don't know how to respond. We've been living under the same roof for a year now, forming our own family. Yeah, there have been some ups and downs, adjustment periods, arguments, but overall, it's been great. Alicia doesn't work as much. We travel more, and when Ro's not on the road, we spend our evenings having movie marathons or playing board games.

Rowan has been a weird combination of older brother and father figure to me. He gives me shit all the time, but is just as protective and caring. When Li and I have issues, he's a great mediator. And when I'm being problematic, he's quick to call me out on it. Counseling has done wonders for us, too.

"What would that entail?" I finally ask. "Like, do I have to call you mom and dad?"

"No, and we don't want you to," Alicia says, stretching her hand across the dining room table to grasp my fingers. "The documents would technically make us your parents, but we'd still be Alicia and Ro. This would just be a step above guardianship. You're already family, but this would legally tie you to Ro, meaning that, no matter what happens, you belong with both of us."

"Would I have to change my name?"

"No, mo stóirín. Not unless you want to," Rowan tells me, smiling softly. "You could stay a Petersen, become a Gallagher, or do a hyphenated version. That part is entirely up to you. We'll support whatever you decide."

I stare at the man who has turned our world upside down, seeing only sincerity in his expression.

"And you…you *want* to adopt me?" I ask him, the words coming out in a whisper.

"Aye, Bridget. I do. You're just as much a part of my life as your sister. Even if you don't want to make it official, I'll still always claim you and love you as my own."

My vision blurs with tears. "What if you two break up?"

They share a look, smiling knowingly at each other, before Ro says, "That's highly unlikely to happen, love, but even if it did, that wouldn't change what you mean to me, or the fact that I want to be a part of your life. You're stuck with me forever."

A watery laugh bursts from me. No one, apart from Alicia, has ever chosen me just for me. While I absolutely do not want them to ever break up, knowing that I'd still have him in my corner fills me with so much love and gratitude that I erupt into chest-racking sobs. I pull my hand from Alicia's so I can cover my face with both of my own as I try to hide my reaction.

Chairs scrape against the floor, and then four arms are wrapping around me. A bearded kiss brushes my temple and his low voice rumbles in my ear. "I've got you, mo stóirín."

"I don't even know what that means," I choke out between sobs.

Rowan chuckles. "It means my little darling or treasure, because you are precious to me, Bridget."

He and Alicia hold me, murmuring soothing words, until my tears subside. Finally, I uncover my face and look between them. Alicia's crying, but smiling. Ro's eyes are red-rimmed and faint streaks from dried tears disappear into his beard.

"Okay," I whisper. "Let's do it."

* * *

Alicia - Ten Years Later

"I can't believe he's actually gone."

"The place doesn't seem right without him behind the bar."

"I remember the first time I ever met him. Nicest man in the world."

"Remember the stew he used to make?"

"To Paddy O'Nelly. May the road rise up to meet him..."

I roll my eyes and slam my palm onto the bar top. "He's not dead, you morons. He just moved back to Ireland."

Rowan, Eamon, Teagan, and Isaac are sitting across from me, full and empty pints of Guinness and empty shot glasses scattered around them. These idiots have been here for three hours, drinking and bullshitting like a bunch of old men.

Paddy and Sondra have been traveling to Ireland every year since they were married and finally decided they wanted to live there permanently. As neither one of them is getting any younger, the constant travel was becoming more difficult, and since all of their loved ones in the States are connected to the Green Isle in some way, they'll always have visitors.

"And he's been retired for ten years now, so you haven't even seen him behind the bar," I continue.

After the paperwork became official, and I took over ownership of O'Nelly's, I was terrified that I was going to screw it all up, but once we finally settled into the new routine, it seemed easier to navigate. We missed Ro like crazy when he was given the go-ahead to play again, but it made our reunions that much sweeter. Now, he's retired from MLS, but uses his skills to help kids with aggression issues channel that energy into something fun, rather than harmful.

"Ah, c'mon now, darlin'," Ro hiccups, extending his hand across the surface.

Rather then placing mine in his grasp like he wants, I toss a towel into it.

"Clean up your mess, *darlin'*," I say in my best Irish accent.

He groans miserably, but starts mopping up the condensation and spilled alcohol while the other guys just laugh. I've always loved giving them shit, but even more so when they're drunk.

"I'm surprised Norah and Layla let you two out tonight," I say pointedly at a Eamon and Teagan.

All of our kids are at the O'Brien's house right now for an epic sleepover. Norah, being an only child, always wanted a house full of kids, and Layla grew up in a huge family, so the chaos is normal and welcomed. I, however, can only handle large groups of kids in small doses, and preferably with other parents around. You'd think running a bar would make me more tolerable of the noise and mess, but no. It overwhelms my brain.

Don't get me wrong. I love all our friends' kids like they're my own, and would drop everything to be there for them, but all of them at once is a lot. The Kennedys have two boys and the O' Briens have two boys and two girls. Which is why, after we had our daughter, Aislin, we were content to leave it at that. She was definitely a surprise, but not entirely unwelcome. I hadn't planned on parenting anyone but Bridget, but sometimes the world does you a favor you weren't expecting. She's been the piece of our family we didn't know was missing. It's also fun to have another redhead in our house.

"Are you slagging me?" Teagan asks. "They kicked us out. Some nonsense about not needing adult children added to the mix."

"Aye, Norah told me I was only going to rile them up more," my husband tells me with a pout.

"Is she wrong?" I ask knowingly.

"S'pose not," he replies. "But Isaac is the one to worry about! He sneaks them all sorts of sugar and shite."

I turn to glare at the man in question, who holds his hands up defensively.

"Don't look at me. You know he's always had it out for me."

Isaac is still living the bachelor life, but has been a permanent fixture in our lives that I'm forever grateful for. Rowan eventually accepted him as friend rather than foe, and the two became thick as thieves. So much so that when CFC needed a new sports therapist, Ro secured him the job. Since Sondra was really his only family, and she's now living in Ireland, he spends the holidays with us and accompanies us on family outings. When Bridget is off doing her own thing and we need a babysitter, *Uncle* Isaac is the first to volunteer. Aislin adores him.

"Lies!" Eamon slurs from his spot next to Teagan. "It wasn't Ro that gave all the kids those minerals."

Raising a brow, I point at Isaac. "Soda? Really?"

He pointedly looks toward Eamon and flips him off, making them all laugh.

The front door swings open, letting a blast of warm summer air into the building along with my sister.

"Bridget!" The guys all sing out in unison, making her stop in her tracks.

Her black hair hangs loose, cascading down her back in waves. Her grey pencil skirt hugs her hips and the white bow tie sleeveless blouse shows off the soft lines of the peony tattoo descending from her shoulder to her elbow. Everyone tells her how much we look alike, but as she's aged, her face has taken on a rounder shape, unlike the sharp angles of my own. She has emerald green eyes, and while she rarely rests, having a desk job has allowed her to gain an hourglass figure. She's stunning and I'm constantly jealous of her curves.

Bridget helps me out at the pub whenever she's not working her day job as a youth specialist. She graduated high school with honors then went on to pursue her masters in Psychology. In a wild turn of events, the year she was supposed to start college, our father was found and arrested after trying to rob a grocery store. I don't know how they did it, but I got back almost all of the money he stole from us. I could have tucked it back into my safe, but decided to use it to pay for Bridget's college. Now, she's currently working towards her doctorate, and we're so unbelievably proud of her. Switching schools made a huge impact on her, socially and academically. The school counselor was a godsend, taking the time to actually learn and understand what Bridget needed to thrive. Now she's providing similar services to kids all around Wilmington.

She beams at us then saunters over to greet each one of the guys in turn. She gives Eamon and Teagan quick hugs before tossing her arms around Ro's neck, squeezing him tight before kissing his cheek. When she makes it to Isaac, he's turned all the way around on the bar stool and stands. He's a big guy, towering over her five foot five form by at about six inches.

"Little B," he greets her, opening his arms for a hug.

"Isaac," she responds, stepping into his embrace awkwardly.

Interesting. I make a note to ask her about that later.

"Hey you," I say in greeting when she untangles herself and slips behind the bar.

"Hey!" She gives me a side hug, before finding a glass, filling it with ice, then grabbing the nozzle to fill it with water. She gulps down half it, then sets it on the coasters I put down for her.

"Rough day?"

"Ugh," she groans, tilting her head from one side to the other, stretching the muscles. "You have no idea. Sometimes I wonder why I chose this field. It's brutal."

"It's because you know what it's like to not have the resources for a fulfilling life, and you want to make sure no other child experiences that," I remind her.

"Yeah," she murmurs, picking up her glass for another drink. "You're right. I'm just exhausted. Between the office, classes, and everything else, I feel like I'm going nonstop."

"Sounds like you need a vacation, Little B." Isaac's low rumble travels across the bar.

Her shoulders tense, but she smiles. "If only."

I turn to her, placing a hand on her arm. "You can take a break from here, for as long as you want, Bridge. We have enough part-time help to make it work."

She bites her bottom lip and glances at me. "Are you sure? I don't want to leave you in a lurch."

"Promise," I tell her. "And if all else fails, I can make Ro work."

"Oy! I heard that!" He hollers far too loud.

"But you won't remember it tomorrow," I tease. "You fellas need to sober up before you go home. The last thing your ladies want is to clean up your puke after having the kids all day."

It's late by the time we get home. Rowan collapses into our bed and is out cold almost immediately. I'm not quite ready to sleep yet, so I curl up on our overstuffed sofa and embrace the silence. Lou joins me, climbing into my lap and booping my nose with his.

"Hey, buddy." I scratch under his chin.

As I sit in the quiet and look around the house we bought and made a home five years ago, I'm reminded of how far I've come. My journey from a broken little girl to a strong and successful woman wasn't easy, and there were several times when I didn't think I'd make it, or even *want* to make it. I've been in therapy for eight years and on meds to help manage my depression. Both of those combined have done wonders for my mental health. I'm able to process my emotions and triggers easier, communicate what I need to my family, and even though it goes against my nature, I've made self-care a priority.

Rowan is responsible for a lot of my healing. Not because he, himself is the reason, but because he's pushed me every single day to put in the effort to find the best version of myself. He gives me the space I need to sort things out on my own, but never has a problem calling me on my bullshit. I don't think I would have pursued a better life if not for him.

The day we officially adopted Bridget will forever be a turning point for him. The joy on his face when they declared my sister as Bridget Petersen-Gallagher, was the same as the day Aislin was born. Never in my life would I have expected my wild Ro to embrace fatherhood the way he did. His upbringing was so similar to mine. He never really knew love, but that didn't stop him from creating the family we all needed and wanted.

My phone lights up beside me, pulling from me from my thoughts.

Bridget: *You get Ro home okay?*

Alicia: *Yeah, he crashed the moment he hit the bed.*

Bridget: *Not surprised. Old man needs to go easy on the booze.*

Alicia: *Don't tell him that. Why are you still up?*

Bridget: *Can't turn my brain off.*

Me: *Need to talk it out?*

Bridget: *Nah. Just wanted to check in.*

Alicia: *You sure there's nothing you want to tell me about concerning Isaac?*

Bridget: *What? Why would I have anything to say about Isaac?*

Alicia: *You guys seemed a little tense around each other earlier.*

Bridget: *I didn't notice.*

Alicia: *Okay. I'm always here if you need me.*

Bridget: *I know. I love you.*

Alicia: *Love you too, B.*

Bridget and I have become best friends over the years, our relationship morphing from child and caretaker to what we are now. Watching her flourish into the successful young woman she is today is something that never ceases to amaze me. She is proof that no matter how things begin, it doesn't determine the outcome.

The End.

Chapter One from Ro's POV

Rowan

Why did I even come out tonight? I should take a page out of Kennedy's book and stay in the night before a match, but here I am, fixing to get up to no good. I'll have one pint then find myself a random lass to warm my bed for the night.

Except I don't want some random wagon, do I? No, 'course not, because I can't seem to get my fecking mind off a surly bartender with the most beautifully tattooed skin I've ever had the pleasure of viewing. No one knows this, and I don't intend for anyone to find out, but I haven't done more than a quick shift with a lass in close to three months. The opportunity has been there, and more than one have been willing to take the full ride, but I cut it short every time. Fecking eejit.

Maybe that's my problem then? I need to get off by more than just my own hand and then I won't be so dead set on…

"Alicia."

I don't even realize I've said her name out loud until the blonde and leggy lass in front of me says, "No, Andrea. My name is Andrea."

Wasn't even fecking talking to this geebag. I was just scanning the room, seeing if there was a prime candidate for the night, when my gaze snagged on none other than the subject of all my dirty fantasies lately, Alicia Petersen. There she is, perched on a bar stool, nursing a drink and looking deadly in skin-tight black leather pants and a black tank top with the bottom cut off just above her waist, exposing the skin of her stomach and what appears to be a phoenix wing inked onto her side. Her hair's down tonight, which is rare. It's usually plaited or pulled into some wild knot atop her head. I never realized how long it is. The ends fall to the middle of her back, eliciting all sorts of images involving it wrapped around my hand.

"Want to go somewhere more private, handsome?" Andrea cocks a hip, eyeing me up and down seductively.

Any other night, I'd at least ask her to dance, but she pales in comparison to the broody lass at the bar.

"Nah. Not tonight, love," I tell her, flashing a grin, but never meeting her eyes.

"You sure?" A slender hand presses to my chest, sliding upwards. "I'll make it worth your while."

Grimacing, I gently grasp her wrist and pull her fingers from my shirt. "I said no." I stalk past her toward the one thing in this club I do want.

Alicia doesn't notice me come up behind her, and I can't resist an opportunity to mess with her, so I don my best American accent. "I'd love to see the tattoos *under* your clothes."

She tenses and I can practically feel the steam rising off of her as she downs the drink in her glass and spins on the bar stool. I clock the moment her eyes shift from rage, to shock, to annoyance when she realizes I'm the creep invading her space.

"Goddammit, Ro! You just about got throat punched!"

Bantering with Alicia is one of my favorite hobbies, and we do it so well. She pretends to hate me, and I wind her up just to watch the fire flash in her eyes. She's all hard edges and chipped shoulders, but I know that underneath all that jaded exterior is a lass that cares deeply for those in her life. I've watched her take care of her friends at O'Nelly's and pick up Paddy's slack. She doesn't share much personal information with anyone, so the things I do know about her are what I've observed over the years. I'm pretty certain she has a kid sister that she takes care of as well.

"So the accent worked?" I ask, flashing a smile at her.

"Are you saying your goal was to be throat punched?" She's looking at me like my mental state is up for questioning.

"No! 'Course not! I've been working on my American accent so I can better blend in."

She snorts indelicately, eyeing me from head to toe. "You wouldn't blend in if you were wrapped up in an American flag. Everything about you screams *Irish.*"

I do love it when she gets mouthy.

Leaning in close, I ask, "Are you stereotyping me, darlin'? Because I take offense to that."

Alicia shivers slightly, but rolls her eyes and turns away. She raises a hand to wave down the bartender. If she thinks ignoring me will make me leave her alone, she's mistaken. I move close enough that my chest is against her back my arms are braced on either side of her body, hands curled around the lip of the bar. Her perfume is floral with a touch of a spice I can't identify. Without actually touching her, I angle my head closer to inhale deeply. Goosebumps appear along her arms and her spine stiffens.

"Gallagher," she growls through her teeth.

"Petersen," I murmur against her ear, not missing the way her thighs rub together. Satisfaction jolts through me. She's turned on, and that's something I can absolutely work with.

"Move your fucking arms before I remove them from your body."

There's enough bite in her tone to let me know I'm walking a thin line. She can't decide if she wants to fight me or fuck me. I'm hoping for the latter.

"Ach. No need to get violent, love," I say, releasing her and moving to sit next to her. The bartender still hasn't delivered her beverage. "What are you drinking tonight?"

Alicia turns her head slightly and raises a dark brow at me. "Why do you want to know?"

Why the feck does she think? "So I know what to tell the bartender when I buy your next one."

"You're not buying me a drink."

"I am, actually. And," I hold up a finger to stop her from speaking. "as it's not your money, you can't tell me what to do with it."

She narrows her eyes at me, then finally seeing that I'm right, she heaves a sigh. "Fine. Buy me the damn drink."

* * *

I buy her three drinks because she's so tightly wound that a night of drinking and dancing will do her some good. I know that I'm right when her smiles and laughter comes easier and, rather than being closed off, she's turned towards me, hand resting on my forearm while she tells some story about about an arsehole she encountered at work. She's mid-sentence when the song changes from whatever techno shite was just playing to Ed Sheeran's version of "Galway Girl". Not a bad tune, but it's hard to beat the original. At least that's how I felt until Alicia links her fingers through mine and hops down from her chair.

"Ro, we have to dance to this song! It's *our* song!" She says loudly, pulling me toward the dance floor.

Who am I to object when the lady wants to dance?

She throws her arms in the air, swaying in time with the music, eyes closed, and a delirious smile lighting up her face. I'm too busy staring at her to notice some wanker moving in closer to her. She spins around, bumping into him. I'm expecting her to lash out when he puts his hands on her hips to steady her, but she melts into his touch. Only for a moment though. Which is good, because I'm about to rip the fucker's hands from his body. Her forehead creases and when she opens her eyes, they grow wider when she sees me standing a foot away from her. She glances up, realizes some stranger is grinding into her arse, and gives him a look that has him raising his hands and backing away slowly. With each step he takes backward, I take one forward and put my hands right where his were, right where they belong.

"You good, darlin'?" I all but yell over the music.

Alicia's smile returns, and she nods. The song fades from jaunty to sultry in the span of a heartbeat, shifting the mood in the whole club. The lights dim and the bass hits low. Without warning, Li pivots in my arms, presses her arse against my cock, then lifts one arm, looping it around the back of my neck. Her body undulates against me and I'm powerless to do anything but join in. I snake one hand around her middle, splaying it across her stomach, pulling her closer. Her free hand rests on top of mine and our bodies move to the rhythm of the music.

The air in the club thickens with lust as other couples find themselves in similar positions. Craning my neck, I catch a glimpse of Alicia's face. Her head is resting against my chest, eyes closed once more, and lips slightly parted. Sweat beads her skin, a drop gliding down her neck into the valley between her breasts. I've fantasized about this woman more times than I can count, and while this is innocent enough, I want more of her. Giving into temptation, I slide the hand on her stomach lower, brushing my pinky just under the waistband of her pants. Her back arches, pressing her arse more firmly against me. I bring my other hand up to where her fingers are buried in the hair at the nape of my neck and trail my knuckles down the length of her arm, skimming the side of her breast, and over her ribs before coasting just under the hem of her cropped shirt, my thumb brushing underneath the swell of one breast then moving to the next.

Dropping my mouth to her neck, I don't kiss her, just drag my lips over her skin. Her head lolls to the side, giving me better access. We dance like this for what could be seconds or hours. Everyone else in the room is just static at this point. I don't move my hands any further north or south, and I still keep myself from kissing or licking her like I want to.

When the current song ends, Alicia turns abruptly in my arms, returning her hand to my neck and pulling my face to hers, our lips an inch apart. She traps me with her azure gaze for a lifetime before stretching onto her toes to kiss me. She pulls back immediately, and we stare at each other in complete shock. The drinking, dancing, and flirting were strong indicators that something like this would have happened eventually. The attraction has been simmering for years, and this kiss feels like the strike of a match. But, unlike starting a small fire, it's like the match was thrown into a full can of petrol, and it's that moment right before it detonates.

We crash into each other, hands burying into hair, fists curling into clothing. I have no idea how we got to the jacks, but here we are. Alicia is pinned between me and the wall, and my hand is down the front of her trousers, stroking her where I've only ever dreamed of touching her.

"Fuck me, you're soaked," I growl before dragging my tongue up the side of her neck. She's riding my hand like she just can't get close enough.

"If you tell anyone about this, I'll kill you," she pants out.

"For someone so ashamed, you don't seem to be too upset about what I'm doing with my finger at the moment." I laugh against her collar bone and curl my finger, rubbing that sweet spot.

"Fuck..." Alicia hisses.

When she bites down on my shoulder, I groan loudly. The sensation of her teeth on my skin is euphoric.

"Christ, woman. You're not just all bark, are you?"

"Shut up, Gallagher." Her fingers wind into my hair, yanking my head from her neck and molding her mouth to mine, all while fumbling with my belt buckle. I have to start thinking of research papers to keep from coming the moment her fingers wrap around my cock. She gasps in surprise.

"Like what you feel, love?"

"Just surprised I found it and wondering if it can do what your fingers can do. *Oh...God.* Don't stop doing that."

Her inner walls clench around my fingers. She's close. "I'm going to give that smart mouth of yours a new job, hen, if you keep talking. Now shut up, and come on my hand like the good girl I know you can be."

The words have barely left my mouth when she yells out my name as she comes. She's stunning. The way her arms tighten around me, but her face relaxes, showing me what Alicia Petersen looks like when she lets her guard down, is hands down, the most beautiful thing I've ever laid eyes on.

"Fucking perfect," I mutter against her ear.

When her breath hitches and her shoulders tense, I realize that I've poured too much emotion into the words and ventured into uncharted waters. I've rattled her. Leaning back, she pulls my hand from her pants, bringing my fingers to her mouth. She holds my gaze as her lips close around them and she sucks the proof of her orgasm from them. As sexy as it is, she's using it as a way to deflect and bring us back to fucking.

That's when I remember that we're in some manky bathroom in a club. Aye, I want to fuck her as much as I want to play football professionally—maybe even more—but if and when I do get to have her naked and in my arms, it sure as fuck isn't going to be in a place like this. Alicia deserves better.

"Do you have a condom?" I realize she's working the zipper of my jeans as she asks the responsible question. I know I'm going to kick myself later, but if I don't stop this now, she's going to wake up tomorrow hungover and full of regret.

Gently, I take hold of her wrist. "No."

"It's fine. I'm on the pill, and I'm clean," She explains while trying to free herself from my grip. "I get checked regularly."

Christ Almighty, I can't believe I'm actually going to say no to fucking her bare.

"Alicia, stop," I say seriously, trying to make my voice stern.

Her eyes meet mine. "What's wrong?"

It takes every bit of willpower, but I grit out, "We can't do this."

She smirks. "Gallagher, I was kidding about the size of your dick. I'm confident I won't be unsatisfied."

Fucking hell. Scrubbing a hand over my face, I try to form the right words. "It's not that. I just...I don't want you..."

The look she gives me makes my bollox shrivel up inside me.

"Wow. If that," Alicia gestures to my cock, "is what you look like when you don't want me, I can't even imagine what you look like if you did want me."

What?

"No...fuck," The word drags from me as I pinch the bridge of my nose. "That's not what I was saying. You didn't let me—"

"Oh, I think I let you do enough," she snaps, making to scamper by me and out of the bathroom.

I step in front of her and block the door. She has to hear me out.

"Alicia, would you stop for one fucking minute and listen to me?"

Finally, she stops and folds her arms over her chest, waiting for me to enlighten her.

"We're drunk. And in the jacks. It's a recipe for regret, yeah? I don't want you waking up tomorrow wishing you'd never met the likes of me."

A combination of hurt and embarrassment mar her features before transforming to ice.

"Whatever, Gallagher. You and your excuses can fuck right off. Now, get out of my way and let me leave."

"Li,"I say pleadingly.

"Don't," She snarls. "Just move."

Knowing a lost battle when I see one, I sigh and step out of the way.

Alicia shoulder-checks me on her way out, and I know I've royally fucked everything up.

Acknowledgments

Properly thanking everyone that has made this series come to life is an impossible task. So, I'll do my best to highlight them here.

First, and foremost, my husband. He may not understand my obsession with romance books, but he always encourages me, or at least plays along. He lets me bounce ideas off of him and helps me when I'm stuck. He picks up my slack around the house and with our kids when I need to lock myself in the writing cave. He indulges my need to buy yet another book or coffee mug (okay, maybe not the coffee mug part, but if I like it, it's coming home with me). But most importantly, he's my rock. He's steadfast like Eamon, passionate about social injustices like Teagan, and banters with me like Rowan. I'm not sure if he realizes how much of him is woven into my books. Babe, thanks for being my best friend and love of my life.

My beautiful, courageous, and headstrong daughters, you will do incredible things in this world. E, the way you get as excited for my books as I do, and how you constantly ask to read them (the answer is still no), makes my heart so happy. You love love stories, just like me, and I hope that one day you'll get to experience your own that's worthy of a novel. I also really love watching KPDH with you and discussing how perfect Rumi and Jinu are for one another. C, you are a ball of blazing fire that tests me daily, and while I get frustrated in the moment, I know that one day your fire is going to burn so bright that it will light up the world. Your laugh is a constant source of joy for me, and I hope you always find humor in whatever life throws your way. Girls, I love you more than words can ever express. I hope I never give you a reason to doubt that.

Sister and Andi, your support and excitement for my achievements is something I'll never take for granted. I know that when I need a boost, I can always find it with you two. I hope that one day, the world will be a more welcoming place and that you never feel unsafe within your own skin. I will always have your backs and you will always have my love.

Whittney, thank you for being you. And for putting up with me for nearly thirty years. Even when life keeps us apart, I love being able to pick right back up where we left off.

Nova, my beloved author bestie and trusted editor, I literally do not know what I would do without you. The ways you have encouraged me, helped me, and kept me from losing my damn mind are endless and words fail to capture how thankful I am for you. I want to be you when I grow up.

To Eamon's Fan Club, seriously the best hype team ever. Each and every one of you has played such a huge role in this series. And you tolerate me flooding our group chat with Nick Bateman. Sorry, not sorry. That man is beautiful.

My Street Team, I think a lifetime of feeling guilty for every little thing has me feeling bad asking for your help, so I never send you any graphics, even though that is exactly why you signed up. Honestly, I really just love your virtual company and am still completely blown away by the fact that you all love my books enough to tell people about them. Why are you guys the best?

To my Alpha and Beta readers I want to smother all of you in gifts and love. You are such a huge part of the whole picture and this author would be lost without you.

Brea, Carliann, CJ, Dani, Darma, and Jenessa, and again, Nova, all beautiful, wonderful, talented indie authors that have encouraged me from day one, answered questions, and bring an extra jolt of joy to my life. I'm honored to know you all and to be a part of the "cool crowd" with you.

And last, but certainly not least, to you, the reader. There's not a day that goes by where I'm not completely humbled by the fact that you picked up my book and actually read it. For all of your love, support, and just plain awesomeness, thank you, thank you, thank you!

Author's Note

When I started this series, it was supposed to be just one book that would never see the light of day. I quickly learned that the author is never really in charge, but the characters are. Now, all three Irishmen have their HEA and I've loved every second of helping them find it. It's an emotional journey, creating a world and then suddenly realizing it's come to an end, when your time with these characters that you love so much is over.

Or is it?

Sometimes when the bartender pours you one good drink, you're inclined to say,
"Pour me another!"

Want to know what comes next? Scan here to follow along!

Made in the USA
Coppell, TX
13 February 2026

71286290R10173